More Praise for

Stay Up with Hugo Best

One of *Vogue's* Best Novels of 2019

"Ingenious . . . With Hugo Best, Somers deftly teases out the muddled and sometimes inappropriate relationship men like him have with fame, aging, and the women who get caught in their wake. . . . Somers does a great job balancing June's competing feelings. . . . Somers shines when depicting the little moments between the two, which are funny and poignant. . . . *Stay Up with Hugo Best* itself never feels unsure: Somers knows exactly when both the laugh lines and the cringes should hit."

—*Shelf Awareness*

"Somers sidesteps the predictable path the reader might expect this weekend to take, instead meandering into subtle, surprising territory. Within the strict temporal boundaries she has set herself, Somers depicts two equally lost souls unable to connect on a deep level. This is a winning debut."

—*Publishers Weekly*

"A timely comment on sex and power in the entertainment industry . . . There are some great laugh-out-loud moments and one-liners, and the pace is steady throughout."

—*Booklist*

"This timely and often very funny novel speaks to how the #MeToo movement swept Hollywood—and the comedy world in particular."

—*Lit Hub*

"Both challenging and, yes, entertaining."

—*AM New York*

"Erin Somers shows power dynamics aren't always what they seem. . . . Anything other than predictable."

—*Bustle*

T0071214

"Exceedingly clever . . . Erin Somers's debut novel is definitely worth staying up for."

—*The What*

"I was honestly surprised to find so many funny one-liners in a novel with the unlikely subject of comedy writing, which is usually a bruising, neurotic enterprise. Erin Somers is a clear-eyed and clever young talent who has mastered the special art of dissection with affection."

—Carl Hiaasen, author of *Razor Girl*

"Our whole culture desperately needs *Stay Up with Hugo Best*. A book so relevant and yet so incredibly funny."

—Gary Shteyngart, author of
Super Sad True Love Story and *Lake Success*

"Funny, sharp, and very fun. A contemporary story that follows a complex set of characters so self-aware that they become even more vibrant on the page."

—Weike Wang, author of *Chemistry*

"*Stay Up with Hugo Best* is sharp, funny, and moving. By the time I finished, I felt like I'd taken a weekend trip to comedian Hugo Best's mansion myself, taken a dip in his pool, smoked with his son. Erin Somers brilliantly and beautifully captures the life of June Bloom, an ambitious young woman at the point of her career where she feels like anything might happen, and also nothing might, and is driven by curiosity about what's to come. An extremely winning, relatable, and convincing debut."

—Annie Hartnett, author of *Rabbit Cake*

"An older man, a younger woman, show biz, nakedness—but wait! This is the hilarious version with characters so sympathetic you root for them all, even the guy."

—Patricia Marx, *New Yorker* humorist and author of
Him Her Him Again the End of Him

Stay Up
with
Hugo Best

A Novel

Erin Somers

SCRIBNER
New York London Toronto Sydney New Delhi

For Edith

Scribner
An Imprint of Simon & Schuster, Inc.
1230 Avenue of the Americas
New York, NY 10020

Copyright © 2019 by Erin Somers

First Scribner trade paperback edition April 2020

SCRIBNER and design are registered trademarks of The Gale Group, Inc., used under license by Simon & Schuster, Inc., the publisher of this work.

For information about special discounts for bulk purchases, please contact Simon & Schuster Special Sales at 1-866-506-1949 or business@simonandschuster.com.

The Simon & Schuster Speakers Bureau can bring authors to your live event. For more information or to book an event contact the Simon & Schuster Speakers Bureau at 1-866-248-3049 or visit our website at www.simonspeakers.com.

Interior design by Kyle Kabel

Manufactured in the United States of America

1   3   5   7   9   10   8   6   4   2

ISBN 978-1-9821-0235-7
ISBN 978-1-9821-0236-4 (pbk)
ISBN 978-1-9821-0237-1 (ebook)

Friday

On the last episode of the show, Hugo interviewed a veteran America's sweetheart who'd been on many times before. She sat on the stiff blue couch crossing and recrossing her flashing shins and baring her wholesome gums. Hugo wore his black pinstriped suit, his signature.

The actress said, "Hugo, I'm going to miss seeing you in my bedroom every night at 12:34 eastern standard time."

Hugo said, sly grin, laughs from audience, "We can arrange something if you'd like . . ."

At the end of the hour he stood in front of the swaying purple curtain and thanked his producers, his band, and his bandleader, Bony Suarez, for taking so many years of his jokes with such élan. He teared up when he got to his loyal fans, and Bony led the band in a sentimental version of the theme music.

The taping was over by late afternoon and there was a huge white sheet cake for the staff. *Stay Up with Hugo Best*, it read in the show's font. We all had a piece and a small plastic cup of champagne and then went to the oyster bar on the corner to do our real drinking.

I found it important to drain a lot of top-shelf liquor in situations like these, when someone else was buying and the revel was not wholly mine. I was out of a job after that day.

The new host would hire his own writers, and those writers would hire their own assistant. As the writers' assistant for under a year, I was so low totem I was subterranean. I was the part of the pole they buried underground.

Come next week it was back to the open mics. Back to standing outside of the midtown clubs passing out flyers to tourists, saying, "Comedy, comedy inside, don't you guys like to laugh?" I practiced it out loud in the corner of the oyster bar, spoke it into my rocks glass to remember how it felt in my mouth.

"Who are you talking to?" asked someone next to me. Bony Suarez had ditched his suit jacket, rolled up his cuffs. He was rubbing his bald head with one hand and holding a beer in the other.

"No one," I said. I swirled the fluid in my glass. "Just an old friend."

Bony nodded. He knew me only barely. "Drink up, because that motherfucker is paying."

I followed his gaze to the motherfucker in question. Hugo sat at the bar at the center of an eager throng. The most junior writer, a Harvard grad named Julian who was three years younger than me, was at his elbow. On his other side, a very young woman perched on a bar stool touching his hair. I had never seen her before—she wasn't on staff—and I wondered if Hugo hadn't either.

"Where did she come from?" I asked Bony.

"Who knows?" said Bony. "Eugene Lang? The ether? Where do they ever come from? He arrives and they just materialize."

Hugo sipped his whiskey and said something that made her laugh in a false, head-thrown-back way. In my experience a woman laughed like that for one of two reasons: to show off her delicate collarbone or to flatter someone who'd told a bad joke. Hugo still had on his pinstriped suit, though it must have held the funk of the studio by now—the faint burned-hair scent of the lights, the smell of his body. When the woman finished laughing, she reached out and smoothed his lapel. He looked satisfied with himself. His lapel didn't really need smoothing.

"You ever been so sick of a suit," said Bony, "that you wanted to do an act of violence to that suit?"

The young woman climbed into Hugo's lap. He looked over at us, over at Bony, and shrugged theatrically. I knew that shrug. I had grown up watching his stupid hammy gestures on TV, practicing them in front of my bedroom mirror.

I said, "He thinks it hides his paunch, I bet. He probably calls it The Paunch Hider in his mind."

Bony took a step back and assessed me. I was nothing to Bony Suarez, still less to Hugo Best. I was a shape on the periphery of their future nostalgia.

Bony said, "You're gonna be okay. You're young and pretty and sort of funny."

"Say it like you mean it," I said. "Give it some vim."

Bony just snorted and walked away.

I was alone again in my white-tiled corner. It had grown hotter, hazier, more crowded. The party would continue to thicken until someone led a mass migration to a cheaper bar. One-dollar shots, beer mud on the floor. Jukebox full of nothing you'd want to hear. The older people would all filter off then, to Metro North, to condos uptown, to wherever people went when they had somewhere compelling to go. The young people would stay late and drink too much, order pizzas to the bar, confess their true feelings, and pair off to kiss each other in the bathroom.

After a while, Julian gave up on Hugo and came over, frowning.

He'd been the writers' assistant before me, promoted to staff writer nine months ago. When he moved up, I had taken his place. Because of this we were bonded forever, members of the same wary club.

"I was pitching him a show," Julian said.

He took a drink of beer. He was sweaty, agitated, his pale upper neck scratched up from an impatient shave.

"The one I told you about. Remember? *Mates?* The sitcom where the characters all live in a house together but you can't make out what any of the relationships are. It's just completely opaque."

"I remember," I said. "They're all different ages and ethnicities."

Julian smiled, ran a hand through his hair. He only ever truly relaxed when he was laughing at his own jokes. "Yeah, and they all leave the house together every morning in a gray minivan. And it's unclear where they're going and you never find out."

"God, *Mates*," I said. "I love it. But can it sustain itself for twenty-two minutes week after week?"

"As a premise it's no thinner than any other sitcom out there."

"Is that how you pitched it to Hugo?"

"No, I pitched it as *Friends* taken to its logical conclusion. *Cheers*, but way dumber."

"And how'd that go?"

"It went great. He ordered thirteen episodes. No. Come on. You saw how it went. He wasn't listening to me. *She* was distracting him."

We looked back over. By now Hugo was barely visible, his face concealed by the woman's cascade of dark brown hair. She held her champagne flute aloft in a posture of victory. He put his hand on her thigh, just rested it there knuckle-side down, and I had to turn away.

"Careful," I said. "That's the president of the network."

A flash of real alarm passed over Julian's face. Then he said, "Oh. Ha-ha," and took his glasses off to clean them with his shirttail. We were silent, trying to negotiate the moment. It seemed to call for some small gesture of mutual comfort or commiseration, which neither of us was able to summon. To do so would acknowledge the presence of feelings—uncertainty, dashed hopes, even friendship—and once the levees were breached there was no telling what would happen.

"What will you do now?" I said.

"Another show. Another staffing job. Something will work out eventually. Something's got to. What about you?"

"Oh, I don't know. Maybe I'll go to law school. Prove everyone right."

Julian shook his head. "You? No."

"Why not?" I said. "Get to wear a nice suit, carry a briefcase. Go out for a power lunch, whatever that is. You know everyone who's a lawyer is just someone who decided to do it?"

Julian said, "Yeah, but . . ."

He seemed on the verge of a sincere remark, but a clanging began, the sound of silverware on glass. The room rotated to face the bar, where Hugo had risen to give a speech. Julian looked at me once more and shrugged. Then Hugo started talking, and whatever Julian had been about to say floated away toward the ceiling, never to be retrieved.

Hugo began, "I'm going to be brief because I know you all have more important things to do." He mimed taking a shot to appreciative laughter. "I came to this show as a young man."

A few feet away, Bony cleared his throat.

"A youngish man."

Bony cleared his throat louder.

Exaggerated grimace. "All right, I was forty."

Everyone laughed again.

"We started this thing twenty-five years ago," said Hugo. "Think about that. Twenty-five years. George H. W. Bush was president. Remember him? Old willowy guy? No, me neither. The Internet as we know it did not exist. Meaning people were just blindly stumbling into stores seeking pornography. Bony had hair. Unimaginable."

These were the contours of the show, its rhythms exactly. I got the sense someone else had written the speech for him. I could picture the head writer, Gil, yawning his way through this final bit of drudgery, his mind already elsewhere. He'd stop to glance out the window, sigh, think of the other courses his life could have taken—dissertations unwritten, chickens upstate—now all lost to him.

And while Gil worked, Hugo would have been where? Alone in his office squeezing a stress ball? Having a boozy lunch that stretched well into the afternoon? Passing time with one of the young women who materialized from nowhere and would return there just the same? I found these scenarios all equally likely.

Hugo was saying, "For twenty-five years, I came in every day and did my *best*." He paused for laughter, groans. It was his favorite pun, rarely undeployed before large audiences. "Did I get good at it? Did I learn how to host a talk show?

I'm sure you have your opinions on that. But I can say with confidence that it has been the greatest pleasure of my life, working with you." He eyed Bony. "Correction: most of you. You were the ones that made me look good night after night. The credit for everything we did over there goes to all of you." He took a long moment to make eye contact with each of us, even me. "You're all equally to blame."

Roaring laughter, whoops, applause.

He waved a hand, dismissing us. "Now go get drunk."

Chatter resumed and the crowd rearranged itself. Hugo was swept along to another part of the room by Laura Posner, his longtime manager and executive producer. His stool stood empty, as if people sensed it would be presumptuous to sit there. After a while Gil sat down, scratching self-consciously at his trim black beard with a capped pen.

Julian rattled his beer in Gil's direction. It was still half full. "Do you want another drink? I think I'll get another."

"You're going to pitch him," I said. "You're shameless."

Julian winced. "What choice do I have? I might never see him again, or any of these people. Her—" He was pointing at Laura Posner, still holding Hugo's hand. "I'll never see her again. Or him—" Dennis Pascale, a programming executive talking into his cell phone. "No chance. Will they remember who I am a month from now? Doubtful. How would I begin to describe myself? *Hi, I don't know if you remember me, I wrote for the show for a few months? In the illustrious sinking ship period?*"

His stubbled throat bobbed as he spoke. Even his Adam's apple seemed panicked. I remembered how young he was. He had just moved out of his parents' house in Short Hills, New Jersey. For years as a page and then as the writers' assistant he'd commuted every morning on the bus. At the end of the day, he went home and ate the dinner his mother left out for him on a cellophaned plate, and went to sleep under a Wayne Gretzky poster he'd had since second grade. He told me he couldn't remember ever liking hockey that much. Now he might have to go back.

"All right, I was only kidding," I said. "Go on and pitch him if you want to. Good for you. Maybe I would, too, if I had something to pitch."

"You would?" he said.

Between the two of us I was worse off. He had the better résumé, the parental fallback plan. He had his ideas, however silly, and the nerve to voice them aloud. Still, I couldn't help reassuring him. He looked at me so hopefully.

"Definitely," I said.

We watched Hugo break free of Laura and cross the room, making his way back to his young woman. The crowd parted for him and filled in again after he'd passed. When he reached her he took both her hands in his like they'd had a long separation.

Julian drained the dregs of his bottle, took a deep breath. "So I guess we'll never see each other again."

This was false and we both knew it. New York only ever got smaller. It contracted at the same rate the universe expanded. Eventually it would just be the same ten people shuttling back and forth between work and home, averting each other's gaze.

"We'll see each other in the next world," I said, "and not a moment before."

It was early evening when I left the oyster bar. I was buzzed, headachey. The sun was still out, and I had the disorienting feeling of emerging from a movie theater into daylight. That feeling could turn into despair if you let it.

I decided to go downtown and do stand-up at Birds & the Bees. Told myself it'd help me ease back into things. Birds & the Bees was a dank basement room on Bleecker that never filled up. If I arrived early enough, the manager would let me do a set for whatever semblance of a crowd happened to be there. In the past, results had been mixed. Sometimes the place was full of NYU undergrads, ten or more of them, out on a weekday afternoon bender. Other times it was just Randy, a neighborhood pot dealer, wiry and balding, with one rolled-up pant leg, nursing a club soda at the bar.

Today there was an act on when I showed up, an even more lost soul than me with a ukulele. Dressed in a bolo tie and cowboy shirt, he strummed a melancholy tune about the new president. His tone was hard to gauge. One minute he was close to tears, the next scornful. He flubbed a lyric about the Electoral College and started over, apparently from the beginning.

"How long has he been at it?" I asked the bartender.

She had thick, pale, tattooed biceps and a delicate doll's face. Her hair was braided into two long pigtails. She smiled rarely, laughed never.

"Since the dawn of man," she told me.

I asked her for a gin drink and swallowed it down in three gulps. It tasted like quinine, like a pinecone, like last-ditch medicine. It was restorative in its way. It restored my aversion to gin.

"Do you want your hot dog?" asked the bartender.

She stepped aside so I could see the cooker behind her. I had made the mistake once before of cashing in on the free hot dog that came with every drink.

"Oh. God no."

There was another figure at the bar, hunched, disheveled, and looking at me sidelong. The braided bartender looked at *him* sidelong, and I looked at both of them—sidelong, you might say. Then we all put the sidelong thing to rest and turned to watch the act in progress.

The guy on stage plunked away at his political epic. The tune sounded like "Clementine," only slower. I paid close attention to see if I could figure out what was funny about it, or what was supposed to be funny. Was it bad comedy or a parody of bad comedy? Was it a bad parody or a parody of a bad parody? I went around like this for a while before giving up. At the end, he pulled out an air horn and set it off, a raw, honking noise that echoed around the room. A couple sitting near the stage got up and walked out. I tried to take a final sip of my drink, but all that was left was ice and lime husk.

At that hour at Birds & the Bees there was no one to herald your arrival onstage. If you wanted an introduction you had to do it yourself, into a microphone set up in the hallway near the bathroom. Some people did, affecting a booming announcer's voice. I could never bring myself to do it. The indignity was too much. I preferred instead to walk on stage almost as if it was an accident. *Oh oops. Well, now that I'm here.*

By the time I went on, the audience consisted of two or three men sitting by themselves in the shadows. Even the bartender had disappeared; maybe she was changing the kegs. A pair of college girls wandered in with shopping bags and kept up a conversation at a table near the back. In the nearly empty room their voices sounded almost as loud as my own.

"It's too much to handle. I cannot handle it anymore," one was saying.

"You shouldn't have to," confirmed the other. "You should *not* have to."

I was doing the bit about men being able to suck their own dicks. Men can suck their dicks, it went. They can suck them and suck them. It was time to stop pretending they couldn't reach. Every time a man's late it's because he's been sucking his own dick. He may show up panting with some excuse about transit or the dentist, but really he's been sucking his own dick. He's been sucking it and sucking it. And so on in that vein.

The bit got a couple of laughs from out in the gloom. I told the feeble crowd I was June Bloom, thank you very much for coming, and then went backstage to throw up. It was a dry heave, mostly, an empty and painful going-through of the motions.

When I came out of the bathroom, Hugo Best was standing in the dim green hallway. I wiped my mouth with the back of my hand, tried not to show my surprise.

"Nerves?" he asked.

"Ennui," I said.

"I used to be a puker, too."

The hallway was narrow and hung with framed portraits of legendary comedians. Lined faces, flat eyes. What came next was the part where I asked Hugo what he was doing here, but I didn't know how to initiate this. Over his shoulder I could see a picture of Rodney Dangerfield. I had always liked

Rodney's face, his pop eyes and look of forthright insanity. Sometimes there was solace in things that were very ugly.

"Can we go stand outside or something?" I said at last. I motioned to the pictures on the walls. "These guys are making this weirdly heavy."

Hugo nodded. "We must avoid gravitas at all costs."

I followed him out through the bar, past the college girls and drunks, back up the six stairs to street level.

In front of the club, a breeze ruffled my dress and raised goose bumps on my bare legs. It was late May, the eve of Memorial Day weekend, that precarious presummer period in New York when the weather hasn't fully made up its mind about what it's going to be.

"You work on my show, right?" asked Hugo.

"*Worked* on the show, yeah. The writers' assistant. My name is June."

"June," he said. "Right. June. You were good in there, June."

A year ago this casual praise from Hugo would have felled me, sent me careening back to the bathroom to puke again in a paroxysm of nervous joy. All that time, my whole life, of waiting for this man's approval and here it was, too easily, too cheaply won.

"Thank you," I said, though. "It means a lot for you to say that." I paused. "So what brings you here?"

"This is where I got my start. I guess I was feeling . . ."

He trailed off and turned to study the entrance of Birds & the Bees, its yellowing marquee. His gray-blond hair lifted boyishly in the wind. It had gotten almost completely dark.

"What happened to the girl you were with at the oyster bar?"

"Girl?"

"On your lap."

"Oh. She didn't want to come. Can't imagine why."

He gestured toward the bar. The smell of stale beer and public toilet was wafting out.

"Don't you have somewhere to be?" I asked. "A party or something?"

It was last night, he told me. There'd been champagne and passed appetizers, those tiny puffed pastries with one bite of crab in them. A band had played. All on the network's tab.

"Weren't you there? I thought we invited the staff."

I shook my head. No one had told me about a party. "I guess I missed the e-vite."

"It wasn't that fun. Mostly just executives patting themselves on the back. For what, I don't know. Anyway, tonight I thought I'd let everyone celebrate without the boss. They deserve to trash me if they want to."

He put his hands into his pockets. I braced for an awkward good-bye. But he made no move to end the conversation, no head fake up the street. Was he waiting for me to make my excuses—dinner plans, a dog to walk, a complicated train ride and someone expecting me at home? If I didn't initiate, it might never end. But did I want it to end? Not exactly. Not unless he did.

"How did you come to be here?" he asked.

"N to Eighth, walked the rest of the way."

He rolled his eyes.

"I'm friendly with Susie, sort of. I took her stand-up class like a decade ago."

"Ah, Stand-Up Basics. And how would you rate your experience?"

The class had been a waste of money. The other students were nonserious: retirees trying out a hobby, office workers building their confidence. Susie herself had been bored. She'd taught it for thirty years as a way of supplementing the club's income and her enthusiasm had expired long before I got there. The only real upside had been her offer, extended on a whim, to let me perform occasionally. I think she kept letting me do it because she'd forgotten how the arrangement had come about. Or because she just didn't care.

"Two stars. Once she sent me out to get her an aloe beverage. Another time I helped fix her printer."

"Bravo," he said. "Multitalented."

"Hey, I'm no hero. It was a paper jam. I just reached in and yanked it out. Took thirty seconds. People tend to give me an easily accomplished task."

"Why do you think that is?"

"Maybe I seem competent, but just a little."

He laughed approvingly. "What did you think of the show today?"

I thought about what to tell him. The show had had the trappings of a celebration without feeling like one. There were tributes, special guests, a gag reel. Running jokes were reprised. Barbra Streisand sang a song. It was exactly the conclusion you'd expect, only the energy was off. Hugo's enthusiasm seemed faked. Even so, I was sure the audience felt lucky, as if they'd witnessed a historic moment. This was what I finally landed on.

"It was historic," I said. I sounded unconvinced.

He repeated, "Historic."

I tried again, "It was . . . it made me sad."

He nodded. "Me, too."

A burly guy in all black dragged a stool out of the club. It was late enough now for a bouncer. We watched him take a Sudoku from his back pocket and start filling it out. People began to weave around us and down the stairs into the club, the first arrivals for the early show.

"Listen, let's get a drink," said Hugo. "Somewhere other than this."

"I can't. I've got a thing. I've got to go stand around on a roof with some young people."

"Of course, a roof."

"I'm serious. I'm not blowing you off. Another time maybe."

He thought for a minute, swaying forward on the balls of his feet. He seemed a little drunk already. "This is going to sound crazy, but you should come spend the holiday weekend with me."

He had a house in Connecticut, he said, growing more excited. With a pool, tennis court, everything. I should come hang out, discuss comedy. We could leave right then. He thought I had potential. He wanted to hear me talk.

I said, "That roof thing I mentioned? I'm meeting a boy there. A man. We're at the beginning and I'm trying to figure out whether he loves me or hates me."

"Love and hate aren't mutually exclusive," said Hugo. "Especially at the beginning."

He smiled, a dashing enterprise that usurped his entire face. "Come to Connecticut. No funny business."

The breeze gusted again, blowing blossoms off a tree just up the street. They came at us in a small white cyclone. One landed on Hugo's lapel, an accidental boutonniere. It was warm and cool both, and what light was left in the sky looked purple.

"How can anyone make good decisions in this city?" I asked.

"They don't," said Hugo. "Nor anywhere in the world."

I directed Hugo's driver, miles away at the front of the SUV, farther downtown and over the Williamsburg Bridge. Now that we were together in a confined space, Hugo withdrew a little, composed himself after his earlier eagerness. He popped in a piece of spearmint gum and I could smell it over the new-car scent. He smoked for twenty years, twenty years ago, he told me. Unbelievably, he still needed the gum.

"My generation smoked," he said. "Today everyone vapes. You don't vape, do you?"

"I don't vape."

"Good. It's a weak simulacrum. If you're gonna do the thing, do the real thing. Not the PG version. Not the cantaloupe-flavored version. You know?"

"Sure."

The bridge was a string of taillights creeping forward in fits and starts. Below, the dark blue surface of the river reflected back streaky clouds and buildings and cars moving up the FDR.

"Lived out here long?"

"Sort of."

I'd started in Manhattan over a decade ago and been forced farther and farther east, changing neighborhoods ahead of gentrification. Now I lived in Bushwick with a friend and soon we'd be priced out again. Already the signs were there.

Hugo nodded. "Tapas bars. Coffee shops."

"Craft beer sold in growlers."

We lived at the neighborhood's limit, right between Ridgewood and Bed-Stuy. It wouldn't be long before we shipwrecked against the hard barrier of Brownsville. Brooklyn was finite. You could only go so far east.

"And then what?" asked Hugo.

"I don't know. Queens? Jersey City? Bangor, Maine?"

"Outer outer outer borough."

"I have a twelve-hour commute," I said. "But you wouldn't believe how much reading I get done."

"It's a tragedy what this city is doing to our creative class."

We stopped in traffic near the foot of the bridge. Bikes streamed by in the last of the dusk. Being in a chauffeured car all of a sudden was a shock to the system akin to jet lag. I felt transported across time zones. I struggled to recall the chain of events that had gotten me there. We'd crossed the street, I could remember that much. He'd held the car door open for me, grasped my elbow while I'd taken the step up. The contact had lit up my nervous system like a strand of Christmas lights.

"Where do you live," I said, "when you're not in Connecticut?"

"I keep a sleeping bag at the office, unroll it under my desk after everyone leaves. Laura came in early once and caught me. Gave me hell. Apparently there's something called sleep hygiene."

Laura was the self-appointed keeper of his health. I thought of earlier in the bar, her casual hand in his. Their relationship was a popular topic of office gossip, but no one seemed to have all the details. There was a consensus that they had been lovers when they were much younger. Opinions diverged on whether they still were.

"I've heard of it. You're only supposed to sleep in your bed and only use your bed for sleeping."

"What fun is that?" He pointed back toward Manhattan and north. "I live uptown. Stuffy neighborhood, you'd hate it."

I turned to look. Manhattan was still there. "I bet it's got a bad view, too."

"Rotten. Too much park."

"At least it's cheap, right?"

"A steal. It's a slum around there. Not like this."

We were in the land of warehouses, of plywood partitions and artists lofts. Even with gentrification being what it was, it had a bombed-out feel. All that was missing was the rubble in the streets, the holes torn from facades to reveal bathrooms and kitchens, the severed pipes still dripping water. I had considered telling him to skip it and making do without a change of clothes, picking up a toothbrush somewhere along the way. It could have marked the beginning of a life untethered. But there was the matter of clean underwear and my cell phone charger. The crude implements of modern survival.

On my block, the driver pulled up into the bus lane and punched the flashers. Scaffolding fronted most of the buildings. The bodega on the corner would sell you a hamburger or a loose cigarette. Our joking had acknowledged and dismissed the difference in our lifestyles, but I was still embarrassed to have taken him to such a place. It was a block like so many others I'd lived on: charmless and in flux.

"I'll only be a minute," I said, getting out of the car.

The street in the evening was as busy as midday. Kids flew by on Razor scooters. The pet store next door—Just

Pets—was getting a delivery. Two men hoisted terrariums full of gray mice up on their shoulders. Outside my building, Rocco sat in his striped beach chair, burning incense. His legs were bloated with disease, skin purple, shards of yellow toenail sticking out of his bare toes. He was a painter; he made portraits of neighborhood people and sat there all day trying to sell them.

He greeted me by name but I waved and kept going. Rocco spent his nights in shelters, smelled like patchouli layered over wet popcorn, loved to talk about his process. You couldn't engage him without a clear schedule and a heart full of hope. I glanced back at the car to see if Hugo was watching. The windows were tinted and gave nothing away.

Inside the vestibule, one of our neighbors, a tall guy named Lars, appeared to be waiting for me. He had his collapsible bicycle with him, mint green, so small he had to stoop to hold it steady. His round black helmet framed his sweaty forehead.

"You guys need to be better about getting your mail," he said.

I looked at our mailbox: Bloom/Newton. Corners of letters poked out. More were balanced on the narrow ledge above it.

"Okay," I said.

"First of all, couldn't some of those letters be important? Are you not paying your electric bill?"

Once Lars had knocked on our door to give my roommate, Audrey, an Anthony Bourdain book. Another time he asked her on a date. Both occasions she had laughed. Now he was mad about mail and taking his revenge.

"We do that stuff online. But I'm kind of in a hurry. Could we talk about this another time?"

He made his voice very calm and leaned down slightly to clutch the bike. "The mail piles up. The postal worker can't fit it all. He just puts it wherever. It gets on the ground. It gets kicked out the door and onto the street. You don't want it out there, do you? With all your identifying information on it? Today I got one of your letters in *my* mailbox."

He held it aloft. A credit card offer.

"You can just throw that away," I said.

"That's not my job! It's your mail!"

I took the envelope from him. I worked late, I told him, and sometimes forgot to get the mail. But as of today I was unemployed, so I could give it my full attention. I could watch for the mailman, have him personally hand me my letters. I could camp out with Rocco and preempt him halfway down the block.

"Oh," he said. He took his helmet off. His hair was pressed to his skull. "Why doesn't Audrey get the mail ever?"

I laughed. He'd managed to bring it around to Audrey. "I have to go."

He called after me, "Sorry about your job."

I was up the first flight already, the first of five, and didn't bother to respond.

Our apartment took up half a floor, each room longer than it was wide. I knocked over a bike as I entered, and the bike knocked over a broom. I lunged for the broom, but didn't catch it. It clattered as it hit the floor. On the couch, Audrey raised her eyebrows.

"Well, why was there a broom there?" I said.

"I was going to sweep," said Audrey. "One day."

We both laughed at the notion of Audrey sweeping.

"I ran into Lars downstairs."

"Oh God," she said. "The mail?"

"He wanted to know why you don't ever get it since you're here all day."

Audrey used to want to be a comedian, too. Now she worked from home freelancing articles for culture websites. Fifty bucks here, one twenty there. Occasionally she'd get a more permanent gig and go to an office for a few months. Then the company would realign, pivot to video, get bought out, disintegrate, and she'd end up back on the couch, sending out invoice reminders.

"It's too boring for me to contemplate," she said. "Did you tell him that?"

"I didn't feel up to it."

"Tell him that next time. Tell him I think they should discontinue the mail. Why are people still scribbling something down on a piece of paper and paying to have it delivered to another person? It makes no sense. Everywhere there's a post office they should build a wind turbine instead. Would that make a good essay?"

"No," I said. "Come with me for a second."

Audrey followed me down the hall to my room. I had a window that looked out on the street, and I beckoned her over to the blinds.

"That's my boss down there," I said.

She squinted. "You mean a producer or something?" She pulled back and cocked her head. "Or . . . You don't mean Hugo Best?"

"It's him," I said.

I told her about our encounter. My set on Bleecker, his invitation outside. How fast it had all happened. How looking back at Manhattan from the Williamsburg Bridge had been like glimpsing the Earth from space. I felt oddly like I was lying. I kept adding details to make it sound more true.

"The guy on before me had a ukulele," I said.

"How is that relevant?"

"Just painting a picture."

We looked through the blinds again. The car's smoky windows reflected the orange streetlight.

"What's he doing in there, reading emails?"

"Just chewing gum, I think."

I started jamming clothes at random into a canvas tote bag. I searched my drawers for what to bring. He'd mentioned a pool and a tennis court, but otherwise I was at a loss.

"What do I pack?"

Audrey let the blinds fall back into place. "How long are you going for?"

"I don't know. I forgot to ask. I guess all weekend?"

"Don't you have that thing with Logan tonight?"

Yesterday I'd been consumed by my relationship with Logan; today I felt barely able to picture him. What had I liked about him again? His modish swoop of hair and carefully considered interests? His tidy shirts buttoned all the way to the top? He thought it was funny that I worked in network television. He had gotten the idea that I was doing it ironically and I hadn't corrected him.

"It's not that important," I said. "It's just standing on a roof."

She settled onto the striped duvet my mother had gotten me when I'd come to the city for college eleven years ago. She wore sweats and a frayed T-shirt with cutoff sleeves, but crossed her wrists elegantly in her lap.

She said, "If you're doing this for the experience, fine. If you're doing it for your career . . ." She paused. "Also fine."

"It's not like that," I said.

"But if this is some hero worship thing . . ."

"It's not."

"But if you have expectations . . ."

"I don't."

She exhaled. "Remember when I met that author on the plane?"

I did, but she told me the story again anyway. She was on her way to California for a wedding and had ended up in business class seated next to the author. He was one of the lesser greats, upper-second-tier, bald and charismatic with a gold Rolex that rattled on his wrist when he motioned to the flight attendant for another round of drinks. His most recent book was being made into a movie, he explained, sipping, and he was headed to LA for a meeting. He was sure it would be a dreadful affair. They always were. The movie or the meeting, Audrey asked, and he smiled. They talked for a couple of hours. He paid for the drinks and they exchanged numbers.

"It felt promising," she said. "It had weight. Not just a chance encounter, but the beginning of something."

I was getting impatient, doing a lap around the room for anything I'd forgotten. "And then halfway through the flight he took his shoes off and watched a kids' movie."

"And socks," she said. "Shoes and socks. And not just a kids' movie. An animated princess movie for little girls."

"Is this an allegory?"

"It's a real thing that happened," said Audrey. "As well as an allegory."

"Can't men watch cartoons without some judgment on their masculinity?"

"It wasn't just about his masculinity."

Later, the author fell asleep and his breathing sounded ragged and wet. Audrey could feel his body heat radiating three inches off his skin like a clammy dome. She'd come close to grabbing her bags and heading back to coach. It was lurid, his humanity. It was a neon sign switched on in the dark. It ruined his books for her forever.

"Granted, I was drunk," she added.

"But that was that author," I said. "And this is Hugo."

"Author, television host. There's no difference."

"Sure there is."

I wasn't going to get into it, but the problem with allegories was that they worked in general but failed in the specific. Anything could happen with Hugo. Anything at all. The outcome wasn't limited to disgust. Plus, I could think of counterexamples. Our friend Priya from college had fucked Michael Jordan once and it was great. They watched *Ray* after on demand. He sent her home in a chauffeured limo.

"I think that's apocryphal," said Audrey. "Anyway, you're not going to Michael Jordan's house, are you?"

"I guess not."

"Say it did happen. Priya wasn't invested in basketball at all. Michael Jordan wasn't her idol. She wasn't employed by Michael Jordan. She wasn't in her twentieth year of a one-sided conversation with him in her head." She paused. "Isn't Hugo like seventy?"

"Not seventy. Sixty-five."

"And what about his thing with that high school girl? What's her name — Kitty Rosenthal? How old was she, sixteen?"

The episode was bound to come up. Hugo was almost more famous for that one night with Kitty Rosenthal than he was for the rest of his career combined. It wasn't that the story didn't bother me. It was that I had grown accustomed to it, or learned to ignore it. Shelved it somewhere out of reach.

"I'm twenty-nine," I said.

"So too old for him then."

"We can't both be too old for each other," I said. "How does that work?"

"I just want you to think about it, is all. Really think about why you're going."

I made a show of thinking, let several seconds elapse while I stared off into space. All I really thought about, though, was Hugo smiling at me in front of the club. How his smile had seemed full of possibility. How it had made me feel, briefly, special.

That seemed like a weak justification, even to me.

"I'm going for fun," I said. "Remember fun?"

I'd been clutching my bathing suit in one hand and stuffed it into the tote. I didn't get many chances in the city to wear it. I went to the beach at the Rockaways twice a year, lay out on our roof maybe once. A pool out in the country was an enticement all its own, almost separate from Hugo. Almost. "Did I tell you he has a pool?"

"Well," said Audrey. "A pool."

We laughed again.

———

There was nothing to see on 95 between Manhattan and southeast Connecticut. Streetlights and potholes, the dour monoliths of Co-op City. We hit traffic in Westchester and Hugo had his driver—Cal, I had learned by now—put on a Richard Pryor album.

The older white comics I knew all revered Pryor. Hugo himself always named him as his greatest influence, but it was hard to see what their comedy had in common. *Stay Up* found its jokes in misprinted headlines, man in the street silliness, the gentle mocking of starlets. In his late career, Hugo was bland and inoffensive and scandal-proof. He had become an affable idiot among affable idiots.

Richard Pryor, with his drug jokes and race jokes and sex jokes, his raunch and barely controlled rage, was something else entirely. The album we were listening to, stop-and-go through Harrison and Rye and Port Chester, was called *That Nigger's Crazy*.

"Back then you could shock people," Hugo was saying, "I mean really shock them. Pryor was raw. He talked about doing crack in a way that you could tell he had done crack. That was a big deal back then. People weren't walking around casually joking about crack. Now everywhere you go, it's crack this, crack that. You've got middle-aged white women talking about how their smartphone is a crack addiction or their Starbucks latte is like crack. Oh really? You're crawling around on your hands and knees sucking on carpet fibers 'cause you think a drop of your latte might have gotten on the floor?"

"Have you ever done crack?" I asked him.

"That is not my point at all. Just not even close." He leaned back to watch nothing scroll by for a while.

On the stereo, Pryor was doing the bit about the wino dealing with Dracula. Winos weren't afraid of anything, it went, except running out of wine. Wino bumps into Dracula on the street and he's like, what's that you're wearing, a cape? He's like, what's wrong with your teeth? Why are they hanging out like that? Go to the dentist, motherfucker. It's 1975. And so on.

Finally Hugo asked, "What about you? Do you like Richard Pryor?"

There were other comics I liked better, but Hugo seemed tired, not fully up to sparring, so I said, "Sure, he's funny. Reminds me of you a bit. Your early stuff."

Hugo's mouth twitched with a suppressed smile. "Flatterer."

"Was I not recruited for that express purpose?"

"Recruited is too strong," he said. "Enticed. Coaxed."

We listened to the Pryor a little longer, and then Hugo said, "What brought you to our show anyway? Besides fate I mean. It always interests me, the route our staffers take to find us."

"I was an audience page," I told him. "You know what that entails."

"Ah, a child of the purple windbreaker. I hope you kept it."

"No. I think it got lost in one of my moves."

It was hanging in the far left of my closet in dry cleaners' plastic. I saw it regularly, wondered all the time when I'd throw it out. I'd never wear it again, this water-resistant sack with the show's name over the heart. Its only value was sentimental, and I didn't think of those days fondly. The work was too boring, too physically demanding. I was twenty-five and everyone else was twenty-two, right out of college. The three-year difference didn't sound like much, but it humiliated me.

"What made you want to do it?" said Hugo.

I shrugged. "I barely remember."

It was almost five years earlier. I'd been working as an assistant in the voiceover department of a talent agency. It was a big corporate office, gale-force AC, business casual. I managed the schedules of actors who voiced radio promos and TV commercials. I booked them auditions. It seemed to me the least consequential job available. I spent most of my time there—most of two years—writing jokes in text documents that I hastily minimized if anyone walked past. That and applying for other gigs. When I took the job it seemed like it could be an avenue to something else. Maybe I could move over to the comedy or TV department. It hadn't worked out that way, though. Nothing that presented itself as a stepping-stone ever really was.

My page application had been an impulse. I filled it out online and clicked send. When I got a call back I was surprised. So many of my applications disappeared into the blank churn of the Internet. The pay wasn't better than what I was getting as an assistant, but it wasn't worse. My last day at the agency they gave me a card signed by everyone in my department and we had grocery-store cupcakes, stale and sticky, in the conference room. I felt sad in a remote way, even though I hated the place. Instead of saying good-bye to my boss, I snuck out an hour early and took the stairs all the way down. Eleven flights held more appeal than the bloodless well-wishes of people who didn't really care what happened to me.

The new class of pages started the last week of August. Summer was dead by then and the city flew at half-mast. It had been raining for two days while a tropical system made slow progress inland. When it stopped, the sky was still dingy gray and low as a ceiling. I was wet on arrival. Not just from sweat; puddles of unknown depth lingered at the curbs. I judged it right three times, four, but eventually I guessed wrong and drenched my shoes, my socks, the hem of my jeans. I had to do the whole day like that, squishing along.

"I remember the first time I set foot in the theater," I told Hugo. "The lobby floor was flooded and they had us sandbag it. That was my first day."

"It was a special place," he said lightly.

The Bob Hope Amphitheater. There'd been a war for him between networks in the early nineties and the promise of the theater had clinched it. It had been restored, keeping the best of its original features: crown moldings, stained glass windows, scrolled mahogany banisters. By the time I got there in 2013, it had faded again. The atrium needed paint and the tiled floor, below the rubber nonslip mats, was cracked. Poor lighting gave it a green, flickering cast. The only recent improvement was the addition of cardboard cutouts of Hugo, big smile, finger guns, available for photo-ops as the line inched past.

Still, he wasn't wrong. The building had a specialness, even flooded, even in the thick of summer. It was built in the late thirties as a music hall and cycled through decades of use and disuse, repair and disrepair. Everyone had played there—Buddy Holly, the Beatles, Nina Simone. Lenny Bruce and Andy Kaufman. Robin Williams, scaling the plush purple curtain like a gym-class rope.

I didn't believe in ghosts, but I did believe that the mind took what it knew about a place and projected a mood. Part of my job as an audience page was to give an introductory spiel about the building, and afterward I could always see the crowd looking around, newly awed. Here had walked the demigods of entertainment. Here the guitar. Here the brow. Here the halo of light. It made people reverent. It made them speak in hushed voices about the architectural features. It made them, anyway, less likely to stick their gum to the undersides of their seats.

"Did you like being a page?" Hugo said, and we both laughed.

The job was scanning tickets and putting on wristbands. Standing up through the whole performance and making sure the audience stayed put. Answering the same three to five questions over and over. Pointing out the bathroom. No one liked it. Or some did, the try-hards. Everyone else was stoic. Occasionally the pages all wallowed together at the TGI Fridays in Times Square. Fifteen dollars got you an extralarge daiquiri with floating components you had to chew. We could have chosen any bar in Manhattan, but we chose that Fridays, deep in the canyon of the neon signs, a place so lacking in character it could subsume you into its anonymity. It could dissolve your very identity.

"I didn't like it that much," I said. "If you can believe it."

"Did I ever meet you on one of my page rounds? I always tried to make a point of meeting everybody."

"For a second early on. You shook each of our hands and thanked us. You seemed sincere."

"I was. We need the pages. We need the whole staff."

He talked about the show like it was still going on. I wondered how long it would take for the past tense to kick in.

I said, "I remember you weren't wearing your suit and it was weird to me. An out-of-context thing like seeing your teacher at the grocery store. And you had on a baseball cap. The baseball cap in particular was really jarring."

"My hair must have been bad. I only ever wear the hat when my hair is bad."

"It made you seem like a regular guy. I didn't like that."

"Sorry for seeming regular," he said.

What I actually felt that day was excitement. Until then he'd been made of pixels. Then suddenly there he was, right there. I had touched him. I could smell him. He smelled like coffee—he was drinking one—and damp skin. He'd walked over from his office in the tiered skyscraper the network owned, two street blocks and half an avenue away.

We took a break from sandbagging and he gave us a sardonic pep talk.

"Welcome to the glamorous world of show business," he said, toeing the frayed corner of a sandbag with his sneaker. "I wish I could tell you it gets better."

The effect was low-key psychedelic. Encounters with celebrities always produced in me a fizzy dissonance. I had once seen Art Garfunkel at my gym and I'd been mesmerized. I could remember staring at the ruched elastic waist of his shorts. He dropped his keys and I picked them up. He had a Rite Aid loyalty card just like mine, which made me laugh. Folk legend at the register swiping for his rewards. It was the same the first time I met Hugo. I could not accept it as anything other than surreal. My brain simply would not yield.

"We must have met other times," said Hugo.

We had. After I was a page I worked as a show receptionist for three years. My face, along with the other receptionist's, was the first he saw when he got off the elevator in the morning. I passed him in the hallway regularly. Once we'd shot hoops together at a staff party at Dave & Buster's and I let him win. I mean really crush me. All told we had encountered each other hundreds of times, if not thousands.

"We've met here and there," I said.

We pulled off 95 and drove the rest of the way on the Post Road. I had been to Greenwich before, but was surprised every time by the generic nature of its charm. Here was the Upscale Anywhere, green lawns and avenues of beautiful shops unfurling like flags.

The driver stopped at a gourmet supermarket and both of us climbed out. Hugo grabbed a cart, navigated into the store. He steered awkwardly—who knew when he'd last done his own shopping? Inside, he looked back over his shoulder and grinned at me wildly, as if this was some great caper.

"Anything you want," he said, and spread his arms out expansively. There were lives out there that had strayed so far from the norm that a trip to the supermarket was high kitsch.

"The grocery store," I said to myself. "What a lark."

Hugo didn't hear me. He had already disappeared into the glare of lights and crush of people. He was already lost amid the antipasto.

———————

The house lay behind a solid gray gate on a long arm. A winding driveway carried us deeper onto the property. It sat in a clear field, a boxy structure of glass and pale concrete. Instantly I could imagine the way it would take on the color of the seasons. White in winter, green in summer. Tonight with the lights off it looked nearly invisible in places, a suggestion of angular geometry against the night. It was an esoteric design object you could live in. It belonged on a plinth.

"The architect chose everything. The furnishings, the art," Hugo was saying. "Unity being the idea. Blurring the line between indoors and outdoors. The dimensions of the recessed living room are the same as the pool. All of the materials are local. The granite. The wood. Every few years the state tries to make it a landmark."

We climbed out of the car. Hugo insisted on carrying my tote. The straps were filthy, I noticed, and his arm was touching a bottle of store-brand face wash I had crammed on top.

"Why not let them?"

"It's a house," he said. "Not a museum."

He led me through the downstairs, turning on lights as we went. Through the windows: acres of moonlit field in every direction. The kitchen was white and stainless, opening seamlessly into the living room. Beyond the sliding glass door the flat of the patio gave way to a dark, wobbly presence. The pool.

I sat down at the marble slab of island to unpack our grocery bags. I took out high-concept crackers and pricey Côtes du Rhône, while Hugo busied himself retrieving silverware. He had a whole drawer of tiny, specific knives and he looked down into it thoughtfully for a long time before giving up.

"So what's your story?" he asked.

I was struggling with a wine opener evidently from the future. "Me? Nothing. I'm just over here trying to figure out how much manchego is acceptable to eat in this scenario. We should all get together as a species and nail down some cheese protocols."

Hugo nodded. "A Geneva Convention for dairy. I like it. But what I meant was what's your story more generally. Your upbringing, et cetera. Are you from New York?"

"South Carolina," I said. "Outside of Charleston."

"You don't seem southern."

People always said this to me. I had lived in New York since college and didn't have an accent. I was never sure

how people expected southerners to act. The place I had
grown up was a lot like this place. The Upscale Anywhere.
Only the wealth was not as great and the worst of its ruthless
villains were already dead.

"The South isn't all that different. Except for the trees."

"So why leave then?"

"Hope. Ambition. Belief in myself. You know, kid stuff."

Hugo crossed his arms. He was tall and broad in an appeal-
ing way. His paunch seemed solid rather than flabby. What
wrinkles he had appeared calculated, left intact so he'd look
like a reasonable facsimile of a gently aged human being.
Leaning against the sink in his shirtsleeves, he was just this
side of too orange to be my thesis advisor, or my rumpled
editor in chief, or—I didn't want to think it but there it was—
my father.

"What fucked you up enough to want to become a
stand-up?" he asked.

"I'm a writer," I said. "Not a stand-up, not really. No stage
presence, you see."

"Then why do it?" he said.

"It's that or a Web series, right? Or improv."

"Improv. Ick."

He took the wine opener from me, negotiated its stainless
steel levers. He poured us each a glass and held his up in a
shy toast.

"Thank you for coming on short notice. I think you're
going to have fun. While you're here you can treat this place
as your own. That's it. You can drink now."

I clinked his glass and we both sipped.

"Mm," I said, "tannins," though I didn't know what that
meant.

He swirled his glass. "I like my wine like I like my women."

I groaned. "For real?"

"Humor me."

"Abundant? Great legs? Available for purchase?"

He looked pleased. "I was going to say dry."

He handed me a plate and I laid out crackers.

"Your childhood," he said.

"I wasn't abused, if that's what you're asking."

"It's not always abuse. Sometimes it's a stutter. Sometimes it's childhood obesity. Sometimes it's, I don't know, a back brace."

"I didn't have a back brace," I said.

"You're being literal. You were an outsider."

"You mean because I'm Jewish."

"There couldn't have been many."

"None. None that weren't eighty years old. So few that people didn't know. The possibility of a Jew didn't even occur to them. My brother and I more or less passed. Kids at school would ask us where we went to church."

"And what would you say?"

"Episcopalian was a safe bet. Evangelicals were too intense and Catholics could sniff you out. You had to know stuff to be a Catholic. When I got older I would tell the truth. People didn't know what to do with that."

"Well, there you go," said Hugo. "That must have been isolating."

"But everyone feels isolated as a teenager, don't they? The reason is almost beside the point."

"So nothing causes anything. That's your thesis?"

"I don't have a thesis," I said. "I've got my woes like anyone. No one's unscathed. My grandparents are dead. Three

of four, anyway. I was only intermittently popular in my small
town. Not, you know, full-on popular. Um, what else? I don't
know . . . I've had an abortion?"

"Are you asking me?"

"No, I definitely had the abortion. And I'm not trying to
be flip about it either. In case that kind of joke makes you
uncomfortable. What I'm asking is, is that enough?"

He chewed a cracker, half smiling. There was a poppy
seed stuck to his lower lip, and I thought of Gil. On Thursday afternoons Gil printed out bingo cards and the writers
all played while we watched a live feed of the taping: B-plus
ad-lib was a square. Glance at guest's tits was a square. Spittle
on lower lip was a square. Winner gets a raise, Gil always
joked. I never knew what Hugo thought about these games,
if he found them funny or insulting. If he saw them as a way
for the staff to let off steam, if he knew about them at all.

"Is that enough what?" asked Hugo.

"Enough bad stuff. To convince you that I'm miserable
or lonely or whatever it is you think qualifies me to be a
comedian."

"I never said you had to be miserable. I'm just saying that's
usually the case. I know a lot of comedians, too many, and
they're a pretty desolate bunch. It's not always something in
their past; sometimes it's clinical. Is it clinical for you?"

I took a gulp of wine to conceal my surprise. "You're
asking if I'm depressed? I thought this was supposed to be a
date. Or a datelike hang-out." I blushed. "Maybe I misread
it. Can we just eat these crackers? Damn."

I shoved a handful into my mouth and coughed. They tasted
earthy, like rosemary and dirt, and absorbed all my spit. I had
to drink a lot of wine to get it all down. Hugo refilled my glass.

"Nothing fucked me up," I said, when I could speak again. "Nothing in particular."

It was true. I hadn't had a difficult life. My father was a dentist and my mother ran the practice. We had health care, school clothes, summer camp. We had an extra room just for the computer. A Honda Civic that my brother and I took turns backing into street signs, telephone poles, other cars. I could get a twenty from my dad on the way out the door anytime if I was willing to needle him for it.

And it wasn't just money either. I hadn't been beaten up or neglected. I hadn't ever been mugged. I'd done well in school, well in college. I'd had a couple of iffy sexual experiences that I'd thankfully been able to shut down before things went too far. The worst I had suffered was nonsuccess. I was twenty-nine with an entry-level job and unable to pay my bills. I had been provided for. I hadn't been harmed or held back, I hadn't been scarred, but I had quietly failed anyway.

I said, "I don't hold with sad-clown theory. It's facile, superficial. The idea that something horrible has to happen in a comedian's past. Like all comics had shitty dads or dead mothers. Like that's the only reason you could have for wanting to be funny."

Hugo topped me off again and said, "Maybe that's what you need. Something big to hurt you. Maybe it would make you funnier."

"Is this a preamble to sexual assault?" I craned my neck and looked down the hall off the kitchen. "Does this place have a designated rape room?"

I knew my tone was nasty; he'd gotten under my skin.

Hugo shook his head. "Come on. I just mean that you probably need to have some more experiences."

I said, "Maybe I just want to be funny because the world is funny. Maybe it's the only way I can see of telling the truth."

I looked at him, daring him to laugh at this preposterous statement.

When he didn't I put down my wineglass, pushed back from the countertop. "Where's the bathroom?"

It was cleverly hidden under the staircase, a cubbyhole with a smooth, black-tiled floor. I peed looking at the copper bowl of the sink and considered leaving. I pictured walking down the long drive and waiting outside the spooky gray gate for a car service. There was nothing actually spooky about the gate. I was drunk. I wondered if Hugo would follow me out. *Come on, June. June, come on.* He would use my name a lot like that, I was sure. Possibly, it would work.

Or if it didn't I'd what? Call my own bluff? Get on the train? Ride back to the city, back to Brooklyn? Go to the roof party and drink a warm PBR? Tell Logan what happened? Pick up the mail on the floor of the vestibule?

It was too logistically difficult, I concluded. I had come this far and I was still curious. The experience hadn't even amounted to a story I could bring back to Audrey yet. I washed my hands, reapplied lipstick, studied my reflection for signs of credulity. There was no medicine cabinet to check for pills. Better that way, because I'd have looked if there was. I'd have been unable to resist confirming for myself the things I suspected: his sadness and erectile dysfunction, his growing prostate and failing heart.

The kitchen was empty when I got back. Maybe *he* left, I thought, and the house belonged to me now. I picked up the cheese knife and held it in my hand. A pleasing silver heft.

"This is mine," I said experimentally.

I got up and looked in the refrigerator. It was empty except for Diet Coke, pickles, and condiments. Even the condiments were sparse. The mustard lids looked crusted on. I opened a low cabinet and saw nothing. I opened another and saw a SodaStream still in its box. I didn't want to get caught gazing at an unopened SodaStream, so I sat back down.

He returned from a door off the kitchen, brushing the dust from a bottle of wine. He held it up so I could inspect the label.

He said, "No offense, but the wine you picked out was garbage compared to this."

"I read something awhile ago that said if wine tastes good then it *is* good."

"Hm," he said. "Not really."

"But if it tastes good . . . it is . . . good."

"You just said that. Are Hostess cupcakes good just because they taste good?"

"Yes. The theory holds."

He poured me a glass. "Here. Try this."

It tasted woody, like someone had dragged some grapes along the deck of an old boat. I told him that and he laughed. "You're not actually wrong."

We both sipped. He opened his mouth a couple of times to say something and closed it again. Finally he said, "I had the shitty father you mentioned."

He was trying to apologize, I realized. The special wine was an apology. His sudden openness about his childhood was an apology, too.

"Shitty how?" I said.

I already knew the answer. I knew all about his upbringing. Years before I'd found his memoir on the one-dollar rack outside the Strand and stood skimming it while smoke from the halal cart on the corner stung my eyes. It had a purple cover with raised silver lettering and brittle yellow pages that kept falling onto the sidewalk. Finally I fished out a single and took it home.

"You name it," he said. "Distant. Ragey. The type of person who would hit a kid with a closed fist."

"Jesus," I said.

"Yeah. He waited until I was ten, though. Double digits. That was his bizarre boundary. I probably weighed eighty pounds."

"And your mother . . ."

"Did nothing. I could never really get a handle on her. She was this soft, creative person, but she let him do what he did. Maybe she didn't like it, but she didn't stop it either. She had boundary issues of her own, my mother. She was a dancer. She'd been a Rockette for about an hour when she was young, and she used to put on her costume and perform the whole Christmas extravaganza in our living room for fun. Oil up her legs."

He fell silent. All of this, I remembered, took place in Woodside, Queens, in the crisscrossing shadow of the LIRR. They had a grim little row house, brown on beige, loose banister, silverfish in the tub. His room was divided from his sister's with a particleboard partition that wobbled when one of them rolled over in bed. The mailbox said Bechkowiak.

"Is that why you changed your name? To distance yourself from them?"

"I changed my name because you can't be Bechkowiak in Hollywood. Or you couldn't back then."

But yeah, he went on, he picked Best because it sounded good, was empty of association, and also because he was nineteen and pretty dumb. He picked Best because it said nothing except that he was the best, which made him laugh to this day.

"It wasn't all bad," he said. "My childhood. My dad was a mechanic and he taught me about cars. He had an incredible breadth of knowledge. He'd flown planes in World War II. Probably he should have been an engineer. He was smart enough. And we watched Carson together almost every night. That we did do. My father didn't really like it, but I could tell he thought it was a bonding thing. I can't remember if he ever laughed. I'm guessing not. I would have enjoyed it more on my own. But instead it was this weird solemn ritual. Glumly making popcorn, sitting down on the couch."

"But you loved your sister," I said. "Vivian."

There was a photo insert in the middle of the book that included some family pictures. Hugo with a terrifying Easter bunny; Hugo and Vivian on roller skates in front of the house; the whole family posed for a frowning department store portrait. Hugo and Vivian looked alike. Tall, fair, and miserable.

He narrowed his eyes at me. "You read my book."

"I might have. Does it have a purple cover?"

"I was against that cover. It was silly. It misrepresented the content of the book. People picked it up thinking it was this light, gossipy thing, and were surprised to find out it was really about a kid clawing his way out of an abusive home. It fell out of print."

He ate the last sliver of manchego, tossed in a jagged shard of cracker after it. "That's something you don't consider when you write a book," he said. "That one day it'll be out of print, and sooner than you'd like. Not thinking about endings doesn't stop them from happening. It only makes the endings sneak up on you."

He stood to clear the plate, tilted the crumbs into the sink. He pressed buttons on the dishwasher, trying to get it open, but it seemed to be locked.

"Eco wash in progress," he mumbled. "What does that mean? No it isn't."

He looked up at me and smiled abashedly. I went over and took the plate from him. "Let me."

I punched a few buttons and opened the dishwasher, set the plate on the empty rack. As I was closing it again he grabbed my wrist. His hands were aging faster than the rest of him. They were lean, tanned to spotting, and the tendons stood out. His grip was urgent, but not painful, and the warmth, the give of his skin, startled me.

He said, "You're not a sad clown, okay? It was wrong to assume that we're the same, you and me. That you're a mess just because I am."

We stayed like that for a moment, not speaking. I thought he'd do something else, pull me closer to him, kiss me, but he didn't. The dishwasher started to whoosh—all that water for one plate. I hadn't meant to run it. I hadn't meant to come to this beautiful house and needlessly run the dishwasher. It was the last thing I ever meant to do.

He let go and told me a joke, the classic Catskills one-liner about two old Jewish women in a restaurant. The joke went like this: Two old Jewish women are sitting in a restaurant eating their food. Waiter walks up to them and says, "Is *anything* all right?"

I didn't know exactly what he was trying to tell me, but because the joke was funny, and because he was a professional with perfect delivery, I laughed.

At midnight, we tuned in and caught the end of Hugo's lead-in. We had finished the bottle of wine and I sent Hugo down to the cellar to retrieve an even nicer bottle. He came back with one that tasted like a Hershey bar and we sat drinking it on the hard charcoal couch in the recessed living room. I kept getting distracted by the room's functional twenty-first-century objects, its flat-screen TV and sliding Jenga tower of remotes. It was as if a set dresser had let a few anachronisms slip through to see if anyone was paying attention.

On TV, a different middle-aged white man presided in a different signature suit. He had an America's sweetheart of his own on, this one newly minted. Her dress zipped all the way up the front and Hugo wondered aloud whether some part of her felt tempted to unzip it in a single deranged swoop and continue telling her anecdote in her underwear.

"They'd burn her like a witch," I said.

"She'd deserve it," said Hugo.

I expected the host to acknowledge the end of Hugo's show, pay tribute in some way. But he only said, "Don't go anywhere. *Stay Up* is next." The credits rolled and were interrupted immediately by a commercial for bleach.

Hugo's intro music began, dominated by jazzy, dated sax. When Bony's tenor boomed through the speakers announcing the night's guests, a bad feeling crept into my chest.

I said, "Hey, let's put on a movie instead."

Hugo didn't respond. His own face, his own body, had appeared on TV. He stood delivering his opening monologue.

Behind him, the purple curtain caught the light and shimmered like stardust.

"I, Hugo Best, being of sound mind and body," he said,
"declare this to be my last will and testament. I appoint my
bandleader, Bony Suarez, as my personal representative to
administer this will, and to make sure that there are no, you
know . . ." He paused, rubbing his palms together. "Shenan-
igans."

The audience laughed. Hugo said to Bony, standing off
to one side behind an old radio mike, "That cool with you?
You prepared to administer?"

Bony nodded. "On it, boss."

"To the incoming host," Hugo continued, "I devise,
bequeath, and give all my hackiest material." He paused.
"And man, there have been some turkeys over the years, am
I right?"

"Some clunkers," agreed Bony. "Some whiffs. Some real,
uh, what do you call it? Comedic misfires."

"All right, Bony," said Hugo. "We get it."

"And that's the best stuff. You guys should see what doesn't
make the show. Woof."

"All right, Bony," said Hugo again. He addressed the audience. "This guy's a media expert all of a sudden. A bold and
incisive critic of TV's new golden age."

Next to me, Hugo chuckled softly. I turned to look at
him. The real version of the man sat with one leg crossed
over the other, wineglass resting on his knee. But it was the
version on the screen that caused a clenching in my chest.

When I was ten, eleven, twelve, I lived for Hugo's show.
It had seemed like such an act of largesse on my parents' part
to allow me to watch him, even though it made me tired at

school the next day. Hugo was younger then, cool, something of an iconoclast. My crush had been a minicollision of forces, a science fair Krakatau. The double whammy of loving him and also wanting to be him. Here, for the first time, was a way of living. You could move to New York, be urbane, wry, ironic. You could be a wit and hover above the whole sad, grasping fracas.

Tonight he was up there for the last time, on the same set, in the same clothes, trying for the same vitality. His face was older. His body was heavier. He was carrying around the knowledge that it was all over. Even so he was almost pulling it off. Something was the same. His self. His Hugo-ness.

The Hugo on the couch reached over and put his hand on my knee.

The Hugo on the screen said, "I'm so happy you're here with me. We have a great show planned for you tonight."

Saturday

I woke up in a bedroom with the neutral colors and untouched feel of guest territory. I took that and my outfit—an oversized T-shirt and red mesh shorts—as a sign that no sex had occurred.

Then the nausea came crashing in, and with it the previous night's events. The second bottle of wine and beginnings of a third. The drunken déjà vu of watching the telecast we'd shot earlier that day. The chaste hug good night at the guest-bedroom door.

I plugged in my phone and it vibrated to life with texts from Logan. *Where are you? I'm two blocks away. Are you here? Hello? I guess you're not coming. Very fucking cool.* And then, hours later, at 3 a.m., *Are you okay?* I didn't know how to respond. I should have called him the previous night, he deserved at least that, but I didn't have a good explanation then and I still didn't. I left the phone on the nightstand and got out of bed.

When I stood, the room wavered uncertainly.

"I feel the exact same way," I said to the room.

Mornings in a strange house always required courage. It was the light coming at me from an unfamiliar angle. It was the dread of encounters to come. The tremulous, half-remembered route back to the kitchen. The fumbled greetings and borrowed towels.

Still, there was only so much girding one could do. I let my instincts guide me out of the room and back downstairs.

In the kitchen, a teenage boy sat at the island eating cereal and looking at his phone. He was tall and wore a black Yankees cap with a flat, unbent brim.

"A Gorgon," he said mildly, mouth full.

I touched my hair. "In a good way, though?"

He shook his head. "That's my T-shirt."

I looked down. Maroon on gray: Phillips Exeter Academy.

"Hugo lent it to me. Your . . . I guess . . . dad?"

He swallowed. "I'm Spencer."

Spencer rose to set his bowl in the sink. I didn't know what had made me assume that Hugo lived alone, that the previous night we'd been the only two souls rattling around that big house. Now that I thought about it, there had been a protracted, public divorce. A couple of them, actually. Hugo's face looking pink and bloated on the cover of the *Post* with a cheesy pun for a headline: "More Like Hugo Worst" or something. Of course there would be remaindered sons slouching around in tank tops. Of course there would be housekeepers and cooks on the premises, and a gardener, too, just now bringing a lawn mower growling to life.

I leaned into the counter, rested my brow in the cradle of my hand. My head ached so bad it was almost amusing.

"Wine?" asked Spencer.

"Goddamn tannins," I said.

Spencer nodded as if he knew from hangovers, as if his liver weren't a flawless sieve, gamely filtering out whatever substances he got into up at Phillips Exeter Academy.

"My dad isn't into leaving his bedroom before noon. But I talked to him last night. He said"—Spencer adopted a mock solicitous tone—"tell her to please enjoy the grounds, and don't mind all the people running around. They're just getting ready for the party."

"The party?"

"On Monday? He didn't tell you much, did he? For all your talking."

Teenagers could still wound me. They could still make me blush.

"We were talking big picture," I said. "Macro stuff. Not trivia like, '*Do you have a son?*' or, '*Will there be any parties here this weekend?*'"

Spencer picked the red and white acne on his chin. His age wasn't clear to me. But he'd been through puberty, that much I could tell. His arms in his stupid tank top recalled the butterfly, the tang of chlorine. Teens really had the attraction/repulsion paradox in hand.

"Listen, is there any coffee?" I said. "It's getting dire."

"Calm down," said Spencer. "I got you."

He hunted for coffee in the cabinets, pulling out cereal boxes. Finally he gave up and called for the housekeeper. Ana was a small, round Mexican woman of indeterminate age, dressed like an office factotum in fitted black pants, a button-up that gapped slightly at the chest, and a ponytail streaked blond. Instantly, she located the coffee in the freezer. She stood by with her hands on her hips while Spencer made coffee in the Chemex, before giving in to her impulse toward efficiency and frying me an egg.

"You don't have to . . ." I sputtered weakly at intervals. It was disingenuous. I wanted the egg even more than I wanted the coffee. I ate with humiliating appetite while both of them watched.

"How is school?" Ana asked Spencer.

Spencer shrugged. "What do you think? It's a triple-X fuckfest."

Ana shook her head. "Are you getting As?"

"Grades are patriarchal, Ana. I reject them as a measure of my intelligence."

"So you're getting Ds. Does your dad know?"

"Does he know that grades are patriarchal? I'm not sure. We'd have to ask him."

Ana sponged down the spotless countertop around my plate. I looked for ways to contribute to this back-and-forth, but they intimidated me. Their bantering ire was a closed system; I was just an interloper transported here to eat an egg.

"You're in tenth grade? Eleventh?" I asked.

"I'm seventeen," said Spencer, sneaking a look at me. "I'll be a senior this fall. How old are you?"

"Twenty-nine."

"I remember that age," he said.

"Oh yeah?"

"Greatest time of my life. You should cherish it."

"Strange. Doesn't feel that way."

"Maybe not now, but one day you'll look back on twenty-nine and wonder how you ever could have been so footloose and fancy-free."

I was too hungover to laugh. I was sure if I did I'd throw up. I put a hand on my stomach. "You're funny."

Ana rolled her eyes. "Don't tell him that. He needs encouragement like he needs another car."

"I have four," said Spencer. "But the thing is: *only* four."

"He doesn't care what I think," I said to Ana. "Who am I?"

Neither of them responded to this with any curiosity.

They seemed to find nothing unusual about my presence at all. They hadn't even asked my name. I knew Hugo liked younger women, the whole world did, thanks to Kitty Rosenthal, but their attitudes suggested that this was ordinary to them. Another weekend, another stranger in the kitchen.

Spencer took out his phone and commenced pecking at the screen. Ana began to replace everything he had taken out of the cabinets. I gathered I was dismissed.

"I'm going to look around," I said.

"Do you want headphones for the guided tour?" said Spencer.

He didn't bother to look up to see if I had gotten the joke.

———

The house had a sprawling layout, horizontal as well as vertical. Rooms were lofted over other rooms, blond wood staircases hovered without railings. The art was large and impersonal. Smeary ombré canvases took up whole walls, seven-figure minimalist boxes. Next to them, the scatter of framed photographs seemed small and hokey as proofs: an action shot of Spencer at a swim meet, one of Hugo on his wedding day in a tuxedo with no bride in sight. It must have been a picture from his first wedding, because Hugo was young and smiling, with a daisy stuck through his buttonhole.

A glass balcony off the guest bedroom upstairs yielded views of the property. I went out into the whip of the wind for a look. Below me, a man with a vacuum was cleaning the tiled swimming pool. He stood on its shores, raking the green, shirred surface with a hose. The water already looked clean enough to drink. Further on, I could see a steel airplane

hangar, a fenced-in clay tennis court, and at the rim of everything, a row of dense, privacy-preserving pines.

Across the hall in a room that must have been Spencer's,
a layer of T-shirts and sneakers covered the floor like an
adolescent loam. Two different styles of Exeter water bottles
sat on the desk, one aluminum, the other plastic. A model
airplane swinging near the window was the only trace of
boyhood. This side of the house had the poorer view. The
window looked out on the gravel driveway and the impassive
face of the gray gate. It struck me that Spencer might not
consider this his home so much as a place to occasionally
empty the entire contents of his backpack and throw himself,
exhausted, into bed.

The rest of the doors on the hallway were closed and I
didn't start opening them. Hugo was behind one of them,
and I was afraid of stumbling in on him sleeping or nude or
otherwise undignified. Newly awake and blowing his nose.
Stooping to climb into a pair of khakis.

I went back downstairs and poked around until I found
the door that led to the basement. A wine cellar off to one
side smelled of cardboard and cork. A dozen or so boxes sat
open, half unpacked. The urge to steal hit me softly, almost
academically. An impulse left over from youth and rarely
acted on: I wouldn't but I could.

Behind another door I found the rec room, the house's
only concession to bad taste. The space had been converted
into a '90s-style comedy club. There was a microphone set up
in front of a brick wall and three low tables with chairs. A red
leatherette banquette rimmed the room. From the doorway
I could see a framed gold record from Hugo's early career,
his sophomore effort, *Second Best*. On the cover, Hugo stood

in a circle of yellow light wearing a brown corduroy jacket with wide seventies lapels. He held a mic loosely in front of him and looked off to his right, half smiling. In his other hand was a joke shop gun, a black plastic pistol with a red flag protruding from it that said BANG in a comic book font.

I wondered what purpose that room served. Whether Hugo stood in front of his friends and family and did his act for fun. Whether captive audiences of party guests tittered politely at his jokes. The place didn't even feel real. It felt like an exhibit, like I'd turn around and find a wax statue of Hugo lurking in the shadows, life-sized and just short of realistic. I couldn't imagine it was part of the architect's vision.

Back in the kitchen, light streamed in from every direction. Hugo was there in a paisley bathrobe, what a certain type of decadent might call a dressing gown. Spencer still texted at the counter, though he'd retreated to a more remote stool. I felt the same trepidation I had earlier that morning, the same self-doubt.

I sat down at the counter. "You didn't tell me about a party."

Hugo had his hands in the pockets of his robe. The wattage of his blue eyes had just begun to dim.

"It's a Memorial Day party," he said. "We do it every year. Maybe it's a retirement party, too."

"I thought you already had a party. With the crab bites and the champagne. The band."

"That was a work party. Can't really let loose at one of those. This one is for friends. Anyway, last time I checked there wasn't an upward limit on how many parties you can have for yourself."

"There is," I said. "The limit is one."

"It'll be fun. It's an event, this party. We go large. One year we had a Dixieland jazz band. One year we did a Havana theme. Spencer had a puff of my cigar. Right, Spence? You puked." He addressed me. "Who's your favorite Beatle?"

"George," I said.

Hugo frowned. "Paul. Paul McCartney was at one. He was in this kitchen."

I looked around pointlessly, as if I might still find him holding a glass under the icemaker.

Hugo said, "It's been remodeled since then. Remember that, Spence?"

"Yeah. We got a garbage disposal."

"I meant the time we had Paul over." Hugo shook his head. "Nothing impresses this guy."

"Wings sucks," said Spencer.

I found myself defending Wings. "They have some okay songs. The thing is that you can't compare them to the Beatles."

Spencer said, "I was kidding. I've never heard Wings. I only said that to piss off my dad."

Hugo took the bait. "What do people your age know about music? No one even plays instruments anymore. No one even sings. They make sounds into a microphone and an engineer turns it into a robot baby voice that hits the right notes. What ever happened to authenticity? What ever happened to a guy onstage with a guitar? Now it's about having a provocative haircut, and, I don't know, taking selfies."

Spencer and I exchanged a look.

Hugo let out a breath. "God, I need a cup of coffee."

He started opening cabinets, taking out cereal boxes.

"The freezer," I said. "Do you guys actually live here or what?"

Hugo stood by the stove while the kettle heated up. Outside, the pool guy wound up his hose. The water cast palmsized amoebas of light on the stainless steel appliances.

"See this thing?" said Hugo. He pointed at the Chemex. "This is not an improvement on a regular coffeemaker."

"It makes better coffee," said Spencer.

"No," said Hugo. He picked it up and held it close to his face. "It's a glass jug. In an hourglass shape. You're not going to convince me a jug is better."

"It is, though," insisted Spencer. He turned to me. "Back me up."

I looked from one to the other. It was odd to see them together in the same room, odd to see Hugo's progeny at all. His genes repeated, maybe improved on, refracted through another person and pummeled by adolescence.

"Some people think it is," I said.

"But it's a pain in the ass," said Hugo. "Heating up water. Pouring it over manually."

"It's one extra step," said Spencer.

"The thing with the pods, that thing I liked."

Spencer said, "There's a whole channel in the Pacific that's full of those pods. A floating landmass of them. Fish can't get through. Birds try to eat them and choke. The dolphins are screwed. Those pods are ruining the whole ecosystem."

"Is that true?" said Hugo.

"Probably," said Spencer.

"I thought your generation was into technology." He gestured at Spencer's phone on the counter, pinging away. "Getting things done fast."

"We're into things that are good," said Spencer.

I got the feeling they could bicker this way all day. It was like the acting exercise where you did a whole argument making nonsense sounds. The topic didn't even matter.

"This party," I said. "Who's coming anyway?"

"Some old guys like me. Comedy people. Golf buddies. A few actresses maybe. Models."

"Models!" I said.

"Bony will be there, so that's one person you'll know."

I thought of what I had packed that I might want to wear in the presence of models. The only dress I'd brought was the one I'd worn the day before. It was black with small bright flowers and smelled like a bowling alley concession stand. It was a dress for doing stand-up at Birds & the Bees and going home alone.

"I don't have anything to wear to this party. All I have is the dress I came in, which I was wearing yesterday at a bar where you get a free hot dog with every drink. Drink three drinks, eat three hot dogs. Drink six drinks, eat six hot dogs. Nine drinks, nine hot dogs. You get the point." I wondered if I sounded as crazy to them as I did to myself. "So we need to do something about that. Unless I should wear this?"

We all looked at me. The red shorts reached my knees; the whole ensemble erased all sex characteristics I'd once had.

"I like that outfit," said Spencer. "You look like Scotty's little brother."

"Who is Scotty?"

"Don't worry about it. A buddy of mine."

Hugo held his hands open, as if to say solutions are all around us, solutions are there for the taking. "We'll go get a dress then."

The hangar out back was filled with cars. Hugo's collection was famous. For a while he'd hosted a second show on cable about rare and exotic cars. He traveled the country looking for them, talking to owners and experts. He had a cohost, Jazz, a feckless blonde whose role was to know nothing whatsoever about cars. They were always dressing Jazz up in coveralls, handing her a wrench. She'd voice her opinions and all the men would chuckle. This one's a pretty color. What makes this one so fast, the pistons? Convertibles should be cheaper than regular cars—they use less metal.

But Jazz, Hugo told me, was precisely the problem with *Car Hunt*. It got so it was barely even about the cars. It became all about Jazz and her adorable blunders and malapropisms.

"She was Amelia Bedelia with implants," he said as we crossed the field.

The grass was shorn and spongy, wet with dew.

"They wanted us to be this comic duo. Like Lucy and Desi, or—" He stopped walking, waved his arms around. "I can't think of a second example that applies here, but you get what I'm saying. They wanted a romcom basically. They wanted to appeal to women. That's not how I initially pitched it. That wasn't it at all."

Hugo left after a couple of seasons and Jazz stayed on as the host. It became *Car Hunt with Jazz Sherman*. She built a following as the antiauthority of the car world. She got a NASCAR tie-in, won a couple of minor Emmys, the kind they don't present at the televised ceremony. You could buy a shirt with her face on it at Walmart. People actually wanted to wear Jazz's face around like that.

It was fine, though, said Hugo. That he had parted ways
with *Car Hunt*. It was for the best. Because he didn't really see
the point of looking at a car on TV anyway. As far as he was
concerned, a car wasn't even a car until it was moving. It was
the sum of the engine and the body and the road, the people
inside, the scenery streaming past. This idea, the romance of
the machine, had nearly been ruined for him by it.

"By *it*?" I said. "By what?"

"*Car Hunt!*" said Hugo.

We arrived at the hangar and Hugo let us in through a side
door. Fluorescent lights buzzed on over polished concrete
floors. The cars were arranged into rows. Aisle after aisle
of candy colors and interesting matte finishes. A draft from
nowhere carried the oil change smell of a Jiffy Lube. I could
tell he was proud by the way he stood, farmerish, with his
hands on his hips, surveying all that was his.

"How many are there?" I said.

He wasn't sure, he told me. Hundreds. Cal kept an inventory, but he didn't check it that often. There were motorcycles,
too, a whole black and chrome patch of them, and a biplane,
cherry red with cream-colored wings.

"I'm afraid of it," he said. "The one time we took it out
it was utterly insane. Like flying a child's wagon through a
thunderstorm. You know the kind of wagon I mean. Those
rickety metal ones. A Radio Flyer?"

He had started pacing the rows.

"So you just buy a car whenever you want to?" I said.

"Pretty much."

I wondered what that might be like and couldn't really
get there. Money would have to lose its value completely
for me before I went out and bought what looked like three

identical Porsches with slightly different headlights. Hugo opened the door to one and climbed in.

"Come here," he said. "I want to show you something."

I leaned in the driver's-side window. It was a tough-guy car, black with a red interior. A too-literal interpretation of cool.

"My first: 1974." He ran his hands over the wheel. "I was twenty-two. It was summertime. I had just made some money touring colleges. Did Carson. Then the album came out and after that it started. I don't know if you know what it's like for a kid who grew up in New York City to buy his first car. It's a big deal. It's how you know you're finally on your way."

"Finally? But you were twenty-two."

He put his hand on the gearshift, adjusted the rearview mirror. I tried to picture him as he saw himself, mean and lean in 1974. He would have been out in LA then, long shaggy hair, fringed vest. Open shirt showcasing a necklace of spiritual significance. An ankh or an om or a chunk of turquoise. The hot wind blowing and the sound of sirens. A pretty girl in the front seat, his hand on her leg. One of those rare moments of kismet when the lights turn green down the whole stretch of boulevard. I could see how losing that, you might mourn for it. You might walk around the rest of your life missing it.

"I guess it always feels like finally, doesn't it?" he said. "No matter how old you are, it always feels like it was a long time coming."

He had half forgotten whom he was talking to. That's what it seemed like. He stared out through the windshield at something in the distance, something not even in the room. I didn't know anything about embittered victory or getting back at my father by purchasing a car. If those were actually the things he was talking about.

I said, "Maybe. I don't know."

"You will."

He shook off his revelry and climbed out, turned himself fully to the task of selecting a car. This involved looking at me closely, a full-body appraisal, as if it was crucial to make a good match here. I had wrangled my hair and changed into some cutoffs and a loose linen sweater. The sweater had a laddered hole in one arm that Audrey had told me made it more chic. I wore low-top sneakers with no socks and a couple of rings and a couple of earrings in each ear. I had not felt self-conscious when I got dressed, but now I did. Now that I was going to be compared to a car I wished I had at least selected a shirt with intact elbows.

I pointed at a yellow Lamborghini. "How about that one? With the mean face."

He scoffed. "That makes no sense."

He paced the aisles, bypassed a gold Bentley, bypassed an elegant old Rolls with its glinting winged hood ornament, bypassed a Ford truck, clunky but cute.

"There she is," he said at last, and led me to a cream-colored MG convertible.

"That one?" I said.

I was a little disappointed that he'd equate me with this car. There were sexy cars in that room. Cars that opened in hilarious and wildly impractical ways. Cars with soul.

Hugo laughed. "What, are you mad? It's a great car! Understated. Plus, what an interior."

It was true, the inside was nice. Soft tan leather puckered around strategic rivets. The seat belts were aircraft-style, the lacquer buckles held the angular MG logo.

"And in great shape, considering."

I glared at him. He added, "Convertibles are fun! America loves convertibles."

"Whatever," I mumbled. "Objects are meaningless."

Removing the car from the hangar proved an operation. He had to Tetris it out of its spot, and, while the engine idled, operate a control panel, walking alongside the door as it slid on its aluminum track.

"It's finicky," he shouted to me over the grinding of gears. He said it joyfully, like he was glad to own such a large, temperamental door.

Finally we were in the open air, following an access road around the curve of the property to where it met back up with the main drive. The gate swung wide and a psychological weight lifted. We could go anywhere or nowhere. Was this the romance Hugo had mentioned or just the human distaste for captivity? Either way we were free.

By day, Greenwich backcountry was all fieldstone walls and light through leaves, tall wooden fences, and mansions set way back from the road. Above, a riot of blue and white sky. The MG rode smoothly and had a certain plucky bravery on the hills.

"See?" said Hugo.

He drove fast, recklessly, and with skill. We stopped for gas at a Shell on the Post Road and I could feel people's eyes. I could feel their heads in passing cars, swiveling to look. It wasn't me they were looking at. It was Hugo, or it was the classic car, or it was both. I wondered if this made me visible or doubly invisible. If standing next to something worth looking at meant people would look at me, too.

Hugo went into the convenience store and came back out unwrapping a pack of gum. The gum craving was worse in the car, he told me. If he had known all those years ago when he started smoking that he would end up chewing gum for the rest of his life like an asshole teenager he wouldn't have started in the first place. He'd almost take the cancer instead.

Back on the road we listened to Steve Martin's *Let's Get Small*. Hugo had a rig—an adapter that plugged into the cigarette lighter—to send the album from his phone to the car radio via airwaves. It worked passably. Sometimes we lost the signal and were subjected to a staticky scramble, but mostly we were able to hear him. I thought of the album art. It was Steve, wearing every prop imaginable: nose and glasses, balloon hat, bunny ears, arrow through the head. Young and handsome, still brunette. I remembered his chest hair.

He was doing the one about being mad at his mother. She's 102 years old, the bit went. *"And the other day she wanted to borrow ten dollars for some food. I said, hey, I work for a living. So I lent her the money, I had one of my secretaries take it down. She calls me up, tells me she can't pay me back for a while. I said what is this bullshit."* And so on.

I said to Hugo, "Don't you ever listen to NPR or anything? Just for texture?"

He shook his head. "Why? To hear about politics? Famine, drought? Female genital mutilation? The public school system in the Bronx?" He made a face. "No, thanks."

As we sped downtown, Logan called. Without thinking, I picked up. Hugo leaned forward to turn down the stereo. We said hi and both waited, listening. I could tell he was in his room because I heard no other sounds. He lived in a brand-new condo in north Brooklyn with a view of the East River out one window and Newtown Creek out the other. He got both of them, Manhattan and Queens, the sacred and the profane, and he was way up on the twelfth floor, so he didn't hear a whisper of street noise. Not the whoosh of a street cleaner, or a truck rolling over a loose manhole cover, or an idiot shouting at another idiot. Nothing. His parents bought him the condo, as an investment of course, but he paid the maintenance fees.

"You're alive," he said finally.

"I am," I said.

We both waited again. "And?"

"I went out of town," I said. "I should have told you."

"You went out of town," he repeated with a note of awe. "Where?"

"To Connecticut with my boss. My former boss. Hugo, I mean. It's a long story. Actually, currently, the two of us are in a car."

"Great," said Logan. "Tell him I say hello."

I turned to Hugo. "A guy says hi."

Hugo raised his eyebrows.

"I was worried," said Logan. "Did you see my texts?"

I took a breath. "I'm sorry I didn't make it to the roof thing last night."

"There will be other roofs," said Logan. "There will always be roofs. There will be roofs, there will be roofs."

"Suppose so. Otherwise we'd die of exposure."

"Are you involved with Hugo?"

"Would it matter?"

I wanted him to say it did, to care enough to try to stop me. Even though what we had wasn't that great, even though it usually made me feel bad.

Hugo had slowed to a crawl to look for a parking spot. We'd reached the main shopping district, a wide avenue lined with stores that sloped down to the train station. A train had just arrived. Even at this distance I could hear its soft scream, and it occurred to me that I could leave now. If I wanted to, I could be on that platform in five minutes waiting for the next southbound to Grand Central. I could be sliding into a sticky seat and feeling the deep relief of a bullet dodged.

"Would it matter?" said Logan. "Not relative to world events, no."

"Okay then."

"Have you slept with him?"

Hugo had stopped on a side street and was clambering out to open my door. The car was so low that the curb was a step up.

"Not yet," I said. "I mean no. Just no."

"Good," said Logan. "Bye."

Which I took to mean good-bye.

I hung up. It had ended that fast. Had it ended? I was pretty sure it had ended. I stood there feeling dizzy until Hugo took my elbow to guide me up Greenwich Avenue.

"The young man from the roof thing?"

"Yeah."

"And how was it, up there on the roof? Precipitous, one imagines."

He was just going to continue with the witty banter and I was grateful. Banter I could do. It was his sympathy I didn't think I could face, the thought that I had come here and made him feel bad for me. If anything, I was supposed to feel bad for him. He was the one who had reached the end of something momentous. He was the one who found himself on the other side of it, in the uncharted afterward that for some reason included me.

"I don't know," I said. "Aren't they kind of all the same? Parties? You stand there talking to someone and then that person goes away and another person comes up."

"They're not all the same," said Hugo. "I used to go to Studio 54. One night there was a lynx there."

"A lynx?"

"Like the big silver cat."

"I know what a lynx is."

"It was sad, actually. It seemed really upset. It was pacing its cage. I think the lights were bothering it. And the music. Elizabeth Taylor kept trying to feed it gummy bears."

"What is this story?" I said. "Are you fucking with me?"

"I can't be sure," said Hugo. "After a while someone went and got Ian Schrager to come deal with it. He was the guy that dealt with things. Did you know he was pardoned by Barack Obama?"

"Nothing you're saying makes sense to me," I said.

"What does he do anyway?"

"Do?"

"The roof kid. Guy. Man."

"Oh," I said. "He designs apps."

"Apps." He smirked. "An app designer. And how did you meet?"

We'd met on an app five months ago. Not one that Logan had made. Another one, one that everyone used. I didn't want to bring up apps again because I knew how it sounded. It sounded like my whole life was app based, and maybe it was.

"We met at a bar," I said.

"A story for the grandkids," said Hugo. "Here we are."

We'd stopped in front of an unmarked storefront of white brick. He held the door for me and we went in. Inside, the boutique was spare. White walls, plain pine floors. Two or three racks held three or four garments. A salesgirl greeted Hugo by kissing him on both cheeks.

"Booboo," she said affectionately.

I studied his face. "Booboo?"

"This was Allison's favorite store," he explained.

"Oh, from TV. Your wife."

The salesgirl clapped her hands. "Drinks! Perrier, cappuccino, what are we having, champagne?"

Hugo said, "Let's make an occasion of it."

It was 2 p.m. and I had eaten a single fried egg. My hangover had surpassed comic and become philosophical. All was equal.

"Why not?" I said.

The salesgirl brought Moët on a silver tray and proposed a toast to world peace. I noticed for the first time that she had a slight Eastern European accent and that she was unhinged.

"Now what brings you in today?" she said when we'd drained our glasses.

Hugo pointed at me. "She's in charge."

"I need a dress," I said. "For a party."

"Ah, the party, of course. The famous party. Will there be a Ferris wheel this year?"

"It was a carousel," said Hugo. He turned to me. "We had a carousel one year. But no. No gimmicks this time around. I'm afraid I'm too old for gimmicks."

"It's true, Booboo," said the salesgirl sadly. "You're already a corpse who is dead in its grave." She poked him playfully with a long peach-lacquered fingernail. "But a handsome corpse."

She said to me, almost shouting, "And you. You'll be the first lady of this party. You need something elegant but with vuv."

"Verve?" I said.

"No, vuv."

"Verve."

"*Vuv.*"

It wasn't a word. I gave up. "Yeah okay, something with vuv. No cutouts or anything like that. That stuff makes me feel stupid."

The bell on the door tinkled and a couple entered. The man was in his sixties, about Hugo's age. He looked like Hugo, actually, the civilian version. More wrinkled, a bit flabbier. They wore the same style of sport coat.

"Hugo Best," he cried. "*Stay Up with Hugo Best!*"

Hugo smiled his late-night smile. "It's me."

"I love you with that guy. The other guy, the bald one."

"Bony," said Hugo.

"Bony!" said the man. "Bony Suarez! Great back and forth between you two."

"Thank you," said Hugo.

They shook hands and the man exhorted his wife to find something Hugo could sign. She dug through her purse, pulling out a long grocery-store receipt like a magician's trick scarf. A moment later she produced a ballpoint pen.

"Are you sure you don't need this?" said Hugo. "There's a coupon for Häagen-Dazs at the bottom here. Dollar off, not bad."

"We don't need it," the woman said seriously.

Hugo signed, H scribble B scribble, and handed it to the man. He folded it carefully and put it into his pocket.

"It's a shame what they did to you," said the man. "Pushing you out like that."

"I wasn't pushed out," said Hugo. "I retired."

"They shouldn't push fellas out," he persisted. "On account of what? Ratings? It's a goddamn shame. They shouldn't push fellas out."

"I wasn't pushed out," Hugo said again.

The salesgirl was hanging things up for me in the dressing room. I hadn't told her my size, and she'd had the discretion not to ask in front of Hugo. It occurred to me that our situation wasn't unusual, that all up and down Greenwich Avenue the robber barons of Fairfield County were out dress shopping with their young girlfriends.

"Is this your wife?" asked the wife. She looked at me, at my torn sweater and filthy sneakers. I hadn't even thought to bring my purse; I was holding my wallet in one hand. The zipper was broken and a loyalty card for a soup place near the office poked out.

"I thought you were married to that Brazilian model," she said to Hugo.

"No," said her husband. "The woman from the funny TV show. The Brazilian model was the first wife."

"I was never married to a Brazilian model," said Hugo. "My first wife was a schoolteacher."

"I'm his concubine," I said.

"It's like a prostitute," the man explained to his wife. "From olden times."

To the salesgirl I said, "I think we're ready."

She was standing by to lead us to the fitting room. Her face was completely blank. Blank of judgment, blank of sympathy. Her heels clicked as she led us away.

"I'm a big fan," the man called after us. "Don't misunderstand me!"

Back in the dressing rooms, Hugo sat down on a low white stool, rubbing his palms on his thighs.

"What an asshole," I said.

"Just a fan. Sometimes it goes like that."

He was trying for philosophical, but his posture gave him away. His knees fell apart too sloppily. His head hung too low on a neck that seemed barely up for it.

Alone in the fitting room, I heard my phone ring. Logan again. I didn't like how we'd left it—I hadn't been nice, and, somewhat justifiably, neither had he. But the reason I'd been mean was Hugo was there. I'd said those things mostly for his benefit. I couldn't see telling Logan this, not in a fitting room with Hugo three feet away on the other side of a curtain. I didn't pick up.

I tried on the dresses. I went out to show him when I had one on. I was doing what I thought I was supposed to do. Someone in this situation would present their body in the ridiculous red cocktail dress. Someone in this situation would need to be zipped up.

When he was done he spun me around and held me at arm's length. "You're frowning," he said. "The dress or the roof guy?"

I faltered, looked down at my feet. "The dress."

He took my hand and squeezed it gently. "Oh, sweetheart, don't be upset. The world's full of dresses."

He helped me unzip again. His knuckles grazed my lower back, maybe on purpose. I thought about what sex with him might be like. Would he make jokes the entire time? What would I do if he did? Probably laugh.

We landed on something more simple. Cream-colored silk with a plunging back. I chose the dress out of partial loyalty to the car. When I emerged from the fitting room he took the hanger from me.

"I'll get it," he said.

"I can't let you do that."

"Are you kidding?"

I couldn't afford the dress, not now when I was unemployed, not ever, really. It would take me months of painfully small installments to pay off my credit card.

But I made myself say, "Not at all."

"I'm not bragging here, I'm just stating a fact, but I'm incredibly rich."

We were standing at the counter now. The older couple had gone and it was just us in the store. He glanced at the salesgirl to corroborate.

"He is," she said. "Grotesquely so. He owns half of Vail."

"She means Aspen," said Hugo. "And she's exaggerating."

I said, "I know you're rich. I saw the garage. I know about residuals."

"So why not?"

I was afraid I'd like it too much, was why not. I was afraid that it was for me, this life of nice cars, and nice dresses, and nice houses paid for by an older man.

"I just can't. It's against my principles."

Hugo looked hurt. He put away his wallet. "You fourth wavers."

The salesgirl wrapped the dress in tissue, slid it into a white bag with silver satin handles. She and Hugo exchanged an air kiss.

"You take care of our Booboo," she said to me, slipping the bag over my arm.

We were driving again. We listened to Nichols and May, the telephone sketch, where Mike Nichols is the caller, down to his last dime, and Elaine May the recalcitrant operator. The adapter wasn't working well and fragments of rap music kept jangling in, breaking up the chatter. Between that and the engine noise, I could barely make out what they were saying.

Hugo shook his head. "Gadgets," he said, and switched it off.

We rode in silence. I tried to think of what to say and I could see him thinking, too. I wanted to ask him if the guy in the store was right, if he'd been fired. The version the writing staff had been told was that it was mutual all around. The ratings had gotten bad, sure, but Hugo had wanted out for a while.

"It's no one's fault," Gil told us when he broke the news. It was the first week back after New Year's. His face looked puffy from whatever he'd done over the holiday, strained from the careful containment of his misery. He had a new plum sweater on that seemed like a Christmas gift. His beard had been freshly trimmed. "This is part of it. Shows end, shows begin. Shows begin, shows end. Turn, turn, turn. We all knew it was coming anyway, right? It was just a matter of when."

But we hadn't. I hadn't. Or I had, in the remote part of my mind where I stored sensible, unappealing information. So I was surprised, and I wasn't the only one. We were in the conference room, some standing, some in chairs. We'd been gathered informally. Julian stood up abruptly and left the room. Layla, another writer I was friendly with, put her head down on the table. Others were joking about it already, revving up the irony machine for the long haul. We'd finish at the end of May, Gil told us. He hoped we'd all stay and see it through, but he understood if we didn't want to.

"Do what you have to do," he said. "Take care of yourselves. And don't hold it against Hugo. Hold it against the network or hold it against nobody or, I don't care, hold it against me. We can put names in a hat later and all choose someone to hold it against. Just don't hold it against Hugo. None of us would even be in this room if it wasn't for him."

I didn't hold it against Hugo, but I did wonder. What if he had been funnier? What if he had gotten better ratings? What if he'd tried, really tried, to improve the show in its last months? A good faith effort, that's what had been missing. Probably it wouldn't have changed anything and the show would have ended just the same. But it would have been heartening to see him fighting, even futilely, instead of how he'd gone out: irritable and tired, exasperated but mostly acquiescent.

We came to our turnoff, and Hugo kept going.

"I have an idea," he said. "Let's drop in on Roman. He's got a house in Westport. Big place, right on the water. You'll like it."

Roman Doyle was a shock jock who sometimes came on the show. That he hadn't been at the wrap party the day before was unusual. He had a talent for sniffing out show-related activities, attaching himself to the staff, staying too long. If he hadn't been invited to the party, it was probably deliberate, someone doing all of us a favor. Personally, I'd looked forward to never seeing him again. I told Hugo so.

"Roman's great," he said. "What do you have against Roman?"

It wasn't just me. The whole staff dreaded his appearances. He wasn't funny, not in the way we valued. He wasn't clever or goofy or dry. He had no finesse, no mastery beyond provocation. He would do one thing in rehearsal and a completely different thing during taping. He'd even managed to offend Gil once. Gil, who was consummately laid-back, who made an effort to be that way. Something Roman said about all female tennis players having penises. *All of them?* Gil had gone around shouting. *All of them?*

"He's unpredictable," I said. "And he's . . ."

"What?"

We got on the highway. Everything in this area, all the green-and-white townships and fine brick schools, existed in relation to the highway. It laid out two stark options: back to the city or far away.

"Nothing," I said. "Let's go see Roman."

———

Roman lived in a groomed and gabled house on the water. Hugo buzzed and the gate slid open on a manicured lawn with mulch around every tree. I was disappointed by the gray restraint of the place. Where were the garish classical touches, the marble nymphs and cherubs in repose? Even shock jocks had taste these days. You had to go to Los Angeles to see anything truly vulgar anymore.

A handful of cars were parked in the driveway. A BMW, a pickup truck so big and round it looked inflated. Roman was waiting for us on his front steps, drinking a Budweiser out of a bottle. He was stocky with reddish brown hair and a waxed handlebar mustache that curled up at the ends. He wore a Knicks jersey, tux pants, and soccer sandals. To my knowledge he always dressed like this, even to go on television. He liked to sit on the blue couch wagging his hairy toes at the audience, while the cameramen rolled their eyes.

"Great car," he said as we climbed out, and Hugo looked at me pointedly.

They shook hands. Roman shook my hand, too, saying, "I remember you. You're the girl writer who sits there judging."

Days he came on the show, Roman hung out with the writers. Gil tolerated it because he was a friend of Hugo's and because he got the show good ratings. Somewhere out in America, whole towns split their sides over Roman Doyle. Where those towns were was a mystery to me. Once, he'd horned in on our staff lunch, taking a seat at the conference table to eat his falafel and listen to people punch up monologue jokes. I shrank from this kind of working lunch. I couldn't bear the pell-mell of it, the giddy, crumb-spraying laughter. Roman must have noticed.

I shrugged. "I don't participate. I'm the writers' assistant. I help out. Take notes. Sort out releases. Go where I'm needed. Was, I guess. *Was* the writers' assistant."

"Can I give you some advice?" he said.

I knew what his advice would be. That I should speak up and make myself heard. That this business was no place for the circumspect. I had the kind of face that invited advice: youthful, impressed, faintly humiliated. I'd heard the lecture before.

"If you have to."

Hugo pointed at Roman's beer. "Can we have one of those before you start dispensing wisdom?"

Roman led us inside. The living room was wide open,

with exposed beams and a second-floor landing that wrapped around three sides. The centerpiece was a grandly rugged stone fireplace. Someone had decorated the house like a ski lodge. Navajo textiles were mounted on the walls, antlers above the mantel. It was another grown-up theme park. Impeccable, sterile, and well staffed.

In the kitchen, a housekeeper got us drinks.

"Do you want something other than a beer?" Roman asked me. "You seem like the fancy type."

"Do I?" I said.

"Actually, you seem like you fancy yourself the fancy type, but really aren't," said Roman.

I looked at Hugo. He smiled like I was receiving a light-hearted ribbing. I couldn't tell, maybe I was.

"We've never spoken before," I said.

"I'm perceptive," said Roman. "You have an expensive education, don't you?"

I wondered what about my appearance or my bearing made him think that. In reality the class divide swung far the other way. The housekeeper had poured my beer into a tall tapered glass and handed me a coaster cut from a geode.

"I went to college," I said. "It cost the usual amount."

"I knew it. Gender studies?"

I had been an English major, which embarrassed me. Telling people only ever elicited a snide remark about Jane Austen. That or they'd lecture me about liberal arts as a waste of money. How I should have learned a trade instead, or skipped college altogether. The founder of Facebook didn't finish college, they liked to say. As if I should go back and do that.

"You're right," I said. "Gender's a construct. How'd you know?"

"I can spot a castrating bitch a mile away."

It was all so hackneyed, so tired. I wondered if Roman was smarter than he seemed, if he was doing some kind of knowing self-parody. How could he be serious? He couldn't be serious. I glanced at Hugo again to see if he planned to do anything. He leaned back against the countertop, enjoying himself.

"Is he joking?" I said finally. "I honestly can't tell."

"He is and he isn't," said Hugo.

Roman rattled his mostly empty bottle. "This guy gets it."

I found the bathroom and stared at six mounted arrowheads as I peed. The bathroom was always where I asked myself what I was doing there. Maybe because I had to look at myself in the mirror. My hair was wild from the convertible ride and my eyes tired. This time I did look in the medicine cabinet and found a huge translucent container of generic-brand Tums. That cheered me up a little.

Hugo and Roman had gone out to the deck and joined a small gathering. Hugo sat on a rattan couch with maybe ten people clustered around him. They held foam koozies that said *I'm the Asshole*, the name of Roman's Sirius Radio show. I noticed a lot of them were wearing hats. Trucker hats or camouflage hats or those straw cowboy hats that curl up at the sides.

A woman about my age with long dyed black hair and a sleeve of tattoos came over and introduced herself. Her leather leggings made her walk stiff and squeaky.

"Gypsy," she said. "Roman's wife."

She shifted the toddler on her hip, a little girl with pretty copper curls, and we shook hands. I hadn't known Roman was married, or that he had a kid. The thought that someone could stand him intrigued me.

"You have a nice house," I said, and she said thanks, it was a bitch to keep clean.

The people around Hugo found seats and it turned into a Q and A.

A woman in a straw cowboy hat asked, "I've always wondered: Where do you get your jokes?"

Hugo caught my eye and gave the same hammy shrug he had given Bony in the bar the day before. Only now it was for me.

"Well, they begin as ideas," he said. "Notions, I guess."

The woman in the hat shook her head impatiently. "But what I mean is, where do you get the notions?"

"I'm confused by the word *notions*," said another woman. "How are they different than ideas?"

"Forget notions," said Hugo. "Notions isn't right. I mean you just have impressions, perceptions. And you train your brain over a number of years to process them a certain way. To structure them as jokes. Or filter them through your outlook."

I went to the railing and looked out on the yard. Dense blue-green sod unrolled to the water's edge. There was a weeping willow kneeling so its skirts touched the water, and a dark wooden swing set with a yellow slide. A motorboat rocked gently against a floating dock. Far across the Sound, too far to see, Long Island stuck out like a finger. Good views were wasted on the rich.

"So how is he doing?"

Roman had appeared, passing me a joint. I took a drag and coughed for a long time, until he thumped me on the back with his palm.

"He's fine," I said finally. "Why?"

"He doesn't seem down?"

I tried to think. So far we'd eaten crackers and watched his TV show, ridden in a car and bought a dress. All of it fell within the scope of normal behavior. I thought of him on the street in front of Birds & the Bees, listing on his heels, inviting me out to his house after a ten-minute set in a hostile room.

"Maybe he seemed a little wistful yesterday, back in the city."

"Wistful?"

"Yeah, sweetly regretful. With twinges of longing. Like a Frenchman or something." I became aware of how high I was. "Missing a woman he lost, a lover, but he was the one to drive her away in the first place."

Roman frowned at me doubtfully. "But has he said anything to indicate that he's taking it hard? The show ending?"

"We watched it together last night and he seemed okay. Calm."

"Regular calm or eerie calm?"

I didn't know. In person, I could barely read his true feelings better than when I had watched him on TV. He was basically the same slick product as always. A cereal box, a MacBook Air. His fame stood between us and I couldn't see around it. It occluded him from view. I felt proud of myself for locating the word *occluded*.

"You know we're the only species that has fame," I said. "Think about it. Dogs don't have it. Rabbits don't have it. Even dolphins don't have it, and they're supposed to be really smart. You won't find dolphins idolizing one specific dolphin. Going around imitating one dolphin who can swim in a particularly compelling way. So why does fame even exist? It must serve an evolutionary purpose. Some advantage it gives us as a species. It helps us self-select or something. I think about that a lot."

Roman took a drag of the joint. His cheeks collapsed inward as he sucked. I saw lines on his face, the slight sag of jawline that would one day become jowl. I pictured him old, sitting on one of the rattan couches with a blanket over his legs, hooked up to an IV, unable to stand without the help of a nurse. Maybe he's not so bad, I thought.

"Is he putting it in your ass?" he asked me, his voice pinched from the weed.

There was the Roman I recognized. My dad listened to his show sometimes in the car, never remembering the station, spinning the dial until he found it. It was always the same brand of bigotry lite. Roman and his sidekicks snickering about a woman athlete, a woman politician, a woman pop star. Every three years or so he said something to cause a mainstream controversy, but mostly he failed to astonish. You couldn't shock the American populace anymore. Not in the perpetual eleventh hour. Too much had already happened.

I took another hit and coughed mightily. Everyone there, the whole cluster of hat people, swiveled to watch.

"Is she okay?" asked a man near Hugo wearing shorts made to look like the American flag. One leg stars, one leg stripes.

"She's just being dramatic," said Roman.

They all turned back around. "So what's next?" a woman asked Hugo. A streaky, bright orange tan made her age impossible to guess. "Now that you can do absolutely anything you want?"

"A nice long vacation," said Hugo. "Maybe Florence. Or Macau."

"But there must be something you wanted to do that you never got to."

Hugo shook his head. "I truly haven't thought about it. There was nothing else I wanted to do. Ever. *Stay Up* was it."

"You know what you should do," said the guy in the flag shorts. "One of those shows where you're you but a bunch of actors play your friends. And a more beautiful woman plays your wife." He glanced over at me. "More beautiful than your real wife I mean. I love those shows."

Everyone murmured in agreement. Those shows were good.

Roman tried to pass me the joint again but I shook my head.

"Do you want that advice I was going to give you before?" he asked.

"Not really."

"Go home," said Roman. "Don't get involved. Find another way to get what you want. Whatever it is you want."

"I don't want anything," I said.

"What are you doing then?"

That question again. I thought about it, looking out on the Sound. There was Hugo's magnetism, his charisma. But it wasn't just that. I'd spent my childhood yearning for him, the last however many years working for him. I needed to find out what all that time meant, and what it meant now that it was over. I thought Hugo might reveal it to me, or the weekend might. Because surely it hadn't meant nothing.

This wasn't a sentiment I could express to Roman Doyle. What had Roman ever yearned for? Floor seats for the NBA play-offs? A pair of real-life hot twins to make out in front of him? An endless supply of Monster Energy drink?

"You know how all your life you've wanted a whole lot of Monster Energy drink?" I said.

"What?" said Roman.

I gave up and told him basically the same thing I'd told Audrey: I was spending the weekend at someone's country house. I was enjoying the use of a swimming pool. Or at least the proximity of a swimming pool. I didn't have any motives. I just wanted to see what would happen next.

"And what do you think will happen?" he said.

"Probably nothing. Nothing is what usually happens."

"Nothing is not going to happen," he said quietly. "Not with Hugo."

We stared at each other while I tried to sort out the negatives. Even high I could tell that this time he wasn't joking. I thanked him for the warning, but really I was annoyed. He was what? Concerned about my safety? He licked his fingers and used them to extinguish the joint, then turned back to face the party.

"Who wants to go in the hot tub?" he said.

———

It was not strictly true that there was nothing else Hugo wanted to do. He'd wanted his show to move up an hour to 11:30, the *Tonight Show* slot. He had almost gotten it, too. Ten years earlier, the host who was on at 11:30 announced he was retiring early, after a coronary. He'd had his chest sawed open, he told the audience, and he'd glimpsed the saw. Well if not the saw, the towel covering the saw. Well if not the towel, *a* towel.

Either way, it had scared him. It had made him reassess the direction of his life. He wanted to spend more time with his family, he said. He wanted to spend so much time with them that they came to loathe him for his foibles. At the moment they liked him, which indicated they didn't know him very well. He was confident the network would be able to fill his shoes. There were tons of great comedians out there, some of them on this very network, and they weren't such big shoes after all, were they? A predictable pan down revealed he was wearing giant red clown shoes.

"Oh right," he said as the audience laughed.

Negotiations began for his replacement. Jockeying. It was in the news, impossible not to follow. Later there was a book about it, an oral history, and I read that, too. The network made up a short list and Hugo was at the top. He was the natural choice. He'd been doing *Stay Up* for fifteen years, and had often guest hosted at 11:30. He had carved out an audience of college students, stoners, insomniacs, weirdos, young marrieds, lonely people. Their desirability to advertisers had increased over the years with their spending power. They would make the jump to the new slot, some of them at least. And as for new viewers, they'd find in Hugo a variation on the familiar: a big, handsome white guy, medium funny, with a good head of hair.

There was one other serious contender. He was Hugo's opposite in every way: a Christian, a family man so wholesome he didn't even curse, a veteran of the improv scene not above donning a wig. You could tell by looking at him that he liked camping and he'd be the one to set up the tent. His following skewed to conservative middle-aged moms. He sold out stadiums full of them. He had the irksome name of Jeremiah McCabe. Somehow, he was also really funny.

Still, Hugo was poised to win. They made him an offer. Thirty million, plus his dream job. He could stay in the theater if he wanted, have the set overhauled, rethink the

space, or upgrade to a new one. Whatever he wanted. All he
had to do was sign the paperwork.

Instead, he took his Mercedes out of the garage on Seven-
tieth and Amsterdam and crashed it into a guardrail on the
Henry Hudson. They found a bag of coke in his pocket and
a Chapin junior in his front seat. This was Kitty Rosenthal.
She was locally famous already for being the daughter of the
New York County DA and for getting caught shoplifting from
the Ricky's on Sixth Avenue in her field hockey uniform.
She'd taken some self-tanner and a couple of exfoliating face
masks, then, at the police station, laughed and claimed it
was all performance art. The incident lived on as a citywide
in-joke. It was a popular Halloween costume that year, a
field hockey uniform and handcuffs, and for a period there,
maybe four to six months, mentioning it to anyone would
earn you a quick, cheap laugh.

Kitty Rosenthal was not wearing her field hockey uniform
that night with Hugo. She was wearing a rose-gold Herve Leger
bandage dress that retailed for $1,090 at Saks Fifth Avenue.
Hugo could not really be blamed for thinking she was older,
or at least that's what he told the press. They'd met at a club in
the Meatpacking District and she'd said she was twenty-two, a
classics major at Barnard named Francesca. All of this was in
the tabloids, including Hugo's mug shot. In it he looked raw and
red, pupils dilated, chapped lips parted as if to explain himself.

"I had no idea she was sixteen. I'm not insane," he told a
reporter before his lawyer made him stop giving interviews.

The DA, Rosenthal, wanted to get Hugo on intent to sell,
but the bag of drugs was laughably tiny and Hugo had no
priors. Contributing to the delinquency of a minor was the
best they could do, plus a DWI.

Hugo got probation, community service, a fine. He did his community service up in Harlem. Mentored an at-risk teen, played pickup hoops and took the kid out for soul food afterward. The pictures from that time — Hugo in a T-shirt and baseball cap; Hugo with his arm around his Little Brother; Hugo digging into a yellow mound of mac and cheese — did a lot for his image.

He went to rehab and that helped, too. It helped him look contrite, anyway. But of course he lost the 11:30 slot. There was an old-fashioned idea in late night that you had to be a certain type to sit in Johnny's chair. That type didn't do drugs or haunt the Meatpacking District or get behind the wheel under the influence. That type definitely didn't mix with teenagers.

Jeremiah McCabe went ahead and grew his hair out long and Jesusy. Wavy tendrils framed his face. His suits were custom-made to accommodate his wide shoulders and trim torso. In the promos you could see his pecs through his shirt. And he did things his way, not at all how Hugo would have. He started each show with a list of puns he liked. He had an a cappella group instead of a band. He invited a different precocious kid on every week to demonstrate a talent, and this was presented without irony, as something you were really supposed to enjoy.

The biggest surprise was that they let Hugo keep doing Stay Up. They didn't have to: His contract almost certainly included a morality clause. But money persuaded and so did lawyers. And audiences liked their celebrities squeaky clean first, but failing that, redemption could play, too. Redemption could always play.

It all mostly blew over, except that it ended his marriage to Spencer's mother. Except that it dogged him forever. Came up in profiles, served as a constant footnote to his work. Hung in the air over every interview he gave. What had he done with that girl in the mid-2000s or what was he about to do? Made people question, once again, if you could like the art but not the artist. If you could like the artist but not the man. If you could like the man but not the way he treated women. Not the way he comported himself in New York City between the hours of midnight and 3 a.m. on a weeknight in November.

The network's gamble paid off. Hugo's first show back was his highest rated in years. Viewers tuned in for a mea culpa and he gave them one. The network higher-ups were worried he'd do it sarcastically, make a joke of it. But he did it straight, and straight into the camera. I'd watched it from the common room of my college dorm. Sophomore year, scratchy furniture. *"Mistakes,"* he said. *"I've made a few."* I found I half believed him.

Now he sat in a deck chair indulging Roman's friends. I could see the gray-blond top of his head from the window of the master bedroom, where Gypsy had taken me to lend me a bathing suit. The toddler had followed us there, bumping up the stairs backward on her butt.

"I probably have something that will fit you," said Gypsy, rummaging in a drawer.

I couldn't see how. She was maybe five-five, four inches shorter than me, with breast implants hovering in the vicinity of her collarbone. She started pulling out tiny swatches of neon fabric and holding them up to the light. Her nails were black and each contained a tiny golden arrow, the star sign for Sagittarius.

Hugo got up and went into the house. I waited for him to reappear in the yard on his way out to the dock. I wanted to watch him crossing the green lawn. Gazing out on the water and searching the horizon. I thought it would tell me about his state of mind. But he returned to the deck a moment later holding a ramekin of olives and a fresh beer.

I sat down on the edge of the bed. The room was as devoid of Roman's personality as the rest of the house. Its color scheme was navy and white.

"What's that?" I said, indicating a minifridge next to the bed.

"It's a refrigerator," said Gypsy.

I crouched down to look. It had a clear glass door and I could see bottled drinks lined up neatly. Coconut water, kombucha. The bottom shelf held an assortment of yogurt cups in chia, flax, and cacao nib.

"You guys eat yogurt up here?"

She laughed. "Sometimes. You want one?"

"No, thanks."

"We put that here when I gave birth to Heaven so the doula wouldn't have to keep going downstairs to get drinks." She shrugged. "Kinda genius. And then we liked it so we kept it."

I looked around the room. The path to eccentricity was winding. One day you were making practical adjustments to facilitate a home birth, the next you'd adopted bedside yogurt as a permanent lifestyle.

"You gave birth here?"

"Right there," she said, pointing at where my bare feet sank into the patterned area rug. Theirs was a shoes-off household.

"We put down a tarp," she added quickly.

"I'm surprised Roman went for a home birth. It seems like the kind of thing he would find . . ."

"What?"

In the silence, Heaven hopped a stuffed pig around the perimeter of the room, making oinking sounds. It changed the room somehow, knowing a person had been born there.

"I don't know. Crunchy. Hippieish. Progressive."

Gypsy regarded me coolly. "It wasn't Roman's choice. In the end, he got into it. He was the one to catch her as she came out."

It was so hard to picture I thought she might be joking. Incense haze and primal, feminine smells. Roman kneeling on the ground while a midwife in hemp pants uncapped essential oils. The baby in his hands, a screaming ball of blood. An honest-to-God miracle delivered into the hands of a boor in a Knicks jersey.

"He's different in real life than he is on TV, you know."

"I know," I said. "I can see that."

But I couldn't, not really. To me he seemed the same.

"It's a persona," she said. "The obnoxious thing. Just like with Hugo."

In theory, it made sense that there would be some separation between the two. That the real guy would have depths the TV persona didn't. But I felt sure there were people out there who were exactly what they seemed to be, people you could pin down immediately. For instance, the moment they grabbed your ass in the workplace, which was something Roman had done to me.

I had been on my way to the snack machine to buy some peanut butter crackers, a task so mundane I'd forgotten the existence of my body. When he touched me, I froze. Over my shoulder I glimpsed his face, expressionless, like he was the one getting the crackers. After the grab was mostly over, he let his thumb linger on the underside of my ass cheek. Then he walked away without saying anything.

I wanted to know how Gypsy accounted for that. How did real-life ass grabbing fit in with her idea of personas and hidden complexities? I was high enough to ask.

"He was already in character?" she suggested.

I laughed at the idea of Roman as a method actor, committed by his art to the worst possible version of himself. Gypsy laughed, too. Her indifference to her husband's actions seemed genuine.

I glanced again at the window to see if Hugo had gone down to the dock yet. He was still there, drinking beer and listening politely to the tan woman.

"How did you guys meet anyway?" I asked.

She had worked in radio, too, she said. She'd been in sales. Her job had sent her to a trade conference in Cabo, where Roman was the keynote speaker.

"We met in the lobby of the hotel. He was sitting there alone. I just walked up to him."

She wasn't normally like that, she said. Brash or aggressive. But she had gotten a feeling that something was meant to happen. She came from a long line of women who were a little bit psychic, so when she got those feelings she tended to trust them. If you thought about it, what reason was there for a girl from Texas to have chosen radio of all things to get interested in? What made her go out and get a communications degree unless it was all leading to something bigger? What made her boss send her to that particular conference? What made her walk into the hotel lobby instead of going out for tacos with her colleagues?

"The universe tells you when to pay attention," she said. "Maybe it's stupid, but I believe it."

She made a credible witch, the way she looked. Her long

black hair and razor talons. The glitter on her eyelids that made her blink heavily. One of her tattoos was a spider, another a moon with a purple aura. A thorny stem climbed her arm and bloomed into a dark yellow rose at her shoulder.

I said, "If you're psychic, can you read my palm?"

"I stopped doing that. You wouldn't like what I'd see."

I looked down at my palms. They were medium-sized and ordinary. The three creases in the center made an M. They gave nothing away. "I might."

She shook her head. "You wouldn't. People are always offended by what I see. It makes them mad. In general, people are unprepared for honesty."

It echoed one of Roman's favorite ideas, that critics didn't like the things he said—the racism, the sexism, the baseline cruelty—because all of it rang true. I had forgotten for a second that she was married to him.

"Tell me something that will make me get it," I said. "About Roman."

"He's a Pisces with Leo rising; that should tell you everything." She paused. "If the fridge didn't do it, I don't know what will."

She held up a one-piece bathing suit with a tiger on it, orange on a black background with an obscene reaching tongue. She turned it around so I could see the deep U of its back. It was a confusion of predators: the whole thing shimmered like snakeskin.

"I think it's you," she said.

I laughed again, then realized she was serious, then wondered if she could be right. Was it really me somehow? Was my essence captured by the yawning jaws and yellow fangs of a dead-eyed tiger? Everywhere I caught glimpses of the person I could be if only I were a completely different person.

As expected, the suit hung a little too loose in the chest and came up a little too high on the leg. I went back downstairs, the tiger's mouth half-covered by my cutoffs. I had reservations about wearing that suit in front of Hugo. I didn't want to lose whatever slim margin of mystique I had. I didn't want to seem ridiculous. But when he saw me, Hugo laughed.

"This is what I'm like," I said, relieved. "A lewd bathing suit person."

The hot tub was a sunken octagon laid into the smooth boards of the deck. Roman had already peeled back the thick vinyl cover. Four people sat in its rumbling depths with their hats still on. They held their koozies out of the froth. Hugo was back on the couch, doing a bit for everybody, the one about the depraved troop of acrobats. It was a shaggy dog story, all in the telling, different every time. The punch line was that it was upper-class people acting this way. Pissing in each other's mouths, shoving their genitals into USB ports, and so on.

I slipped into the hot tub between a woman in a pink bikini and the guy in the flag shorts. They were trunks, it turned out, or else shorts he had decided to get wet. Roman, across from me, watched my descent. With his jersey off he was annoyingly buff. He even had abs. He held his beer deliberately, so his biceps popped.

"Hey, tiger," he said.

I remembered that I hated hot tubs. Especially hot tubs with this many people in them. With five of us in there it was about at capacity, everyone trying not to bump slippery knees. I felt a foot slither against mine, and looked up to see Roman smiling. Someone had turned on a radio. An ad played, a woman's voice listing items you might want to buy at the grocery store for your summer kickoff party. Charcoal and beer and shitloads of beef. She didn't really say shitloads.

Gypsy came out on the deck carrying Heaven. The toddler wore a bathing suit, skirted and frilled at the shoulders, red fish against teal water. It made her eyes look bluer, her hair more red.

Roman set his beer down on the deck behind him before reaching for her with wet arms. "Give her here."

Gypsy passed her into the hot tub and onto Roman's lap. She smacked at the surface of the water with her tiny palms. Roman kissed her cheek, cooed in her ear. It wasn't a good idea to put a baby in a hot tub, but I knew better than to say so.

"It's good for her," said Roman, as if he'd read my mind. "She likes it."

My high had ceased to move through my veins, settling into my jaw, making it inert. The other people in the hot tub carried on a conversation, but I found it impossible to participate. I had nothing to add about the latest superhero movie. I had nothing to add about the best clubs in the Hamptons. I had nothing to add about the New York Yankees, except that they were a bunch of millionaire mercenaries and that the abstraction of baseball, how far apart everyone stood from each other and the arcane, lopsided rules—three strikes but *four* balls?—made it all about as comprehensible to me as particle physics. I didn't say any of that, but I did think it, and I must have smiled, because Roman jabbed my shin with his foot and said, "What?"

"Huh? Nothing," I said. "I was thinking about something funny."

"Care to share?"

Everyone shut up and looked at me. Hugo smiled over the lip of his beer. I thought of the beautiful cream MG sitting in the driveway like a child we'd let down. Someone would have to drive it home.

"Definitely not," I said.

"You were judging again," said Roman.

"No, I was . . ." I took a breath. "I was thinking about the rules of baseball. How dumb they are. Three strikes but *four* balls? It's about as comprehensible as particle physics."

They all stared at me, and then away. At the speckled rim of the hot tub, the streaky white clouds overhead, the fine blue expanse of the Sound. I should have left it there, it wasn't going to translate, but for some reason I pressed on.

"It all seems so improvised. Like someone was making it up as they went along." I heard myself doing a voice, a sort of blue-collar Brooklyn accent. How it applied to what I was saying was not clear to me. "And there'll be, uh, nine innings. Not ten, but nine. And the guys will stand one here, one here, one here. The one with the stick will stand there. No girls. If girls want to play they have to use a different ball."

We all sat in silence, contemplating the low thrum of the hot tub jets until the guy in the flag shorts cleared his throat. "You're a comedian?"

"No," I said.

"What he's getting at is that you're not very funny," said Roman.

This people laughed at, shifting nervously in the foam.

"I agree with you," I said.

I hoisted myself out of the tub as gracefully as I could. The suit streamed water. It had grown even looser and hung limply off my front. A new fold had appeared in the tiger's face, dragging its mouth downward.

"That fucking baby shouldn't be in a hot tub," I said. "Anyone could tell you that."

I passed Hugo on the way back inside and he looked away. My wet feet slapped the boards of the deck.

———————

Hugo tried to convince me to drive back, but I said no. My brain still felt stepped on from the weed. Like a giant was toeing the frontal lobe.

"Oh come on," said Roman.

We all stood in the driveway. Gypsy laughed into her phone on the front lawn while Heaven ran around, peeking under bushes. I had changed back into my normal clothes. The tiger suit I'd left dripping from a hook on the back of the bathroom door. I hoped to never think about it again.

"It's actually really easy," said Hugo.

He was talking about driving stick. They both thought it was a good time for me to learn.

"It tells you what to do," said Roman.

"It?"

"The car. The vibrations, the noises." He turned to Hugo. "Maybe she shouldn't drive."

"Are you not okay to drive?" I said to Hugo. "Is that what's going on? We could call a car."

"We are not calling a car," said Hugo. "There is absolutely no need. I had one-point-five beers. Two-point-five at most. I just think you should learn to drive stick. It's a good life skill. What if there's an emergency someday?"

"An emergency I have to drive out of in a stick shift?"

"You never know," said Hugo.

"Have you ever heard of state-dependent learning?" I said. They looked at me blankly.

"If I learn to drive stick shift high, I might only ever know how to do it high. I might have to smoke pot every time I want to drive stick. Or, you know, eat an edible. I think we can all agree that's absurd."

"This is a waste of time," said Roman.

I didn't want to wreck Hugo's car, was the real issue. I felt it had been entrusted to me in some way. I didn't want to wreck the car, and I didn't want to hurt him. I didn't want to create a situation where we were standing by a smoldering ruin, blowing for sobriety, while people slowed down to gawk. I didn't want to immediately ram into Roman's BMW parked behind the MG because I had it in the wrong gear. And I didn't want to hit the oversized pickup truck that I assumed belonged to one of the people in the hot tub. I didn't want those people to get out of the hot tub. Ever. I wanted them to die in there.

"I don't feel comfortable," was how I put it.

"There it is," said Roman. "The comfort card."

Gypsy held her hand over her phone and shouted, "Leave her alone."

This settled it, though I didn't know why. We got in and buckled up. Hugo would drive.

"I'm fine," he said to me again. "Anyway, I'm sorry to tell you this, but at any given moment most people on the road are drunk."

"Is that true?" I said.

"Let's hope not."

He started the car.

"Thanks for having me," I said to Roman.

Roman said, "You're welcome."

It was the most civil exchange we'd ever had.

Hugo started the car and made a careful K-turn. "You okay?" he said.

"Sure," I said. "It's a short drive, right? It'll probably be fine."

"No, because of the hot tub."

I shrugged. "Oh that. I don't care what those people think. I don't care if they think I'm funny."

Actually, it was the opposite. I did care. I preferred that everyone found me funny. It was the only thing that felt good. I suspected Hugo knew this and was the same way. I suspected that his need exceeded even my own, that it was dense and lightless as a black hole, more dire for having been fed.

"Good," said Hugo. "You know you were right about one thing. That baby should not have been in the hot tub. She was being cooked like veal."

"Do they boil veal?"

"An imperfect analogy."

As we drove away I could see Roman in the rearview mirror standing on his front steps. He looked like one of the bobbleheads we used to keep on the reception desk at work. Big head, small body. When he held up a hand to wave, there was a toylike solemnity to it. Hugo and I both raised our hands without looking back.

———

Back at the house, teenagers had commandeered the pool. Hugo and I stood in the kitchen watching them. A teak table held smudged glasses, an ashtray overflowing with butts, a bottle of Crown Royal and its empty purple bag. There were four of them: Spencer, another boy, and two girls. The boys were goofing around, splashing, holding each other underwater. The girls wore bikinis. The blonde lay smoking on the diving board. The brunette was draped across a swan-shaped pool float, one arm thrown around the swan's neck and the other dragging in the water. Spencer was still fully dressed in the same outfit I had seen him in that morning. His soaked tank top stuck to his chest and the brim of his black baseball cap dripped water.

"I guess you want me to discipline him," said Hugo.

He'd concentrated intensely the whole way home, gripping the wheel with both hands, chewing gum two pieces at a time. He hadn't put on a comedy album. He hadn't even spoken. Now he looked drained, like someone had slowly poured the life-giving goo out of him, left a trail of it along 95.

"Me?" I said.

"It's not as simple as it looks. I go out there in front of Spencer's friends and I, what?"

"Ground him?" I suggested.

"I've tried. It doesn't take. Spencer doesn't respect me. You think he asks my permission to do things?"

"So get his mom to ground him then. Allison."

"Allison's shooting a movie in Thailand. A street-racing movie. Can you imagine? What time is it there?" He looked at his watch. "Five in the morning. Even if I could get through, what would I say? *Hi, it's me, I can't control our son. He hates me just like you do.*"

"I don't think he hates you. I think he . . ."

I caught myself before I said pities you.

"What?"

"He's seventeen," I said. "I think he's seventeen."

Spencer had gotten out to retrieve the liquor bottle. The girl on the diving board sat up and flicked her cigarette at him. It arced high and landed in the deep end.

"They just cleaned it this morning," said Hugo.

"Why don't you go out there and ask him to wrap it up. Be chill about it. Hey, it's me, your fun-filled, easygoing dad. How about putting away the bong for the night . . ."

"Bong?" said Hugo.

I pointed to the far end of the pool where a red, blown-glass bong sat on the rim of a concrete planter. "Sorry."

Hugo sank back onto a stool. His shirt pooched out stiffly over his belly. One sleeve had come half unrolled. He looked older to me than he ever had, less outside of time. Shaped by the fourth dimension like the rest of us. I thought of his doppelgänger in the store, Hugo's show of not being bothered by him. Maybe he believed he wasn't, but years of dealing with fans must have taken their toll.

"He gets bad grades," said Hugo. "He's on scholastic probation. We're giving him the best education in the world and he doesn't even care. He's not stupid, he just thinks it doesn't matter. And he's right, actually. He'll get into college based on who we are and how much money we donate and he'll get bad grades there, too. When he's sick of it he'll drop out and we'll help him do the next thing. So on, ad infinitum."

Spencer was eating now from a bag of Doritos, alternating drafts from the whiskey bottle. Whiskey, chip, whiskey, chip.

"Will you go out there and do it?" he said. "I just don't have it in me."

I didn't know anything about parenting a teenager. My life in New York was child-free. I saw kids as a part of the urban terroir, interesting landscape features in bright sneakers and jean jackets, but mostly I didn't think about them. Other than Spencer that morning, I couldn't think of the last one I had even spoken to. We lived downstairs from a baby and occasionally I cooed at her in the hallway, but that hardly counted. Did the same threats still work on today's kids that had worked on me? Revoking privileges, taking away screen time? Or were they as cynical as everyone else these days, weary heirs to an unimpressed age?

"All right," I said. "No big deal. I'll take care of it."

I crossed to the sliding glass door and let myself out. Spencer sat on the diving board now, legs swinging. The blonde had joined the brunette on the float and the other boy was pulling them around by the swan's orange beak.

"June," Spencer called. "Have a drink."

I put my hands on my hips, felt silly, let them fall to my sides. "You have to wrap this up."

Spencer laughed.

The blond girl raised her head from the float. "Spencer, is that your *mom*?"

"Yeah," said Spencer. "That's her all right."

I said, "I'm not his mom. How old do I look to you?"

She said, "I can never tell old people's ages."

She sat up further, pressing down on the other girl's stomach for leverage. The float bucked and the swan nodded its head. Small waves lapped at the side of the pool.

"If you're not his mom, why are you telling him what to do?" she said.

"I'm a friend of his dad's. It doesn't matter. The point is, you guys need to clean up and go home. Not you." I pointed at Spencer. "You need to stay."

"Why should we listen to you?" said the blonde. Her hair was in a sloppy topknot and she wore mirrored aviator sunglasses, though the sun had dipped behind the trees.

"Spencer . . ." I said.

Spencer stopped swinging his legs. "No, I want to hear your reason. For why we should listen to you."

They'd made me nervous until then, especially the blond girl who was pretty, mean, and mostly nude. But all at once I stopped caring. We were acting our ages and it struck me as theatrical and a little corny. I was an adult because I had aged into it. That was all. The same thing would happen to them.

"There's no real reason. Your dad asked me to say something is why."

The sliding glass door opened and closed behind me. Hugo said, "Everything okay out here?"

He'd retucked his shirt and freshly rolled the cuffs.

"Hey, Scotty," he called to Spencer's friend. "What's good?"

Scotty looked amused. "Hey, Mr. Best."

"Been watching our Yankees?"

Spencer climbed off the diving board. Scotty did a circuit around the deck, picking up empties. I realized I'd been manipulated.

"Am I the bad cop?" I said to Hugo.

Hugo shrugged. "It worked, didn't it?"

Spencer came over, wringing out his tank top. "Is Noam coming to cook dinner?"

"I don't think so," said Hugo. "Wouldn't he be here by now?"

They both looked at me.

"I don't know who Noam is," I said.

"He's Israeli," said Spencer, as if that helped. "Well, what are we gonna eat?"

"I hadn't really thought about it," said Hugo. "Any ideas?"

The other kids walked up, wrapped in towels or stepping into shorts. They looked at me hopefully like I was going to solve this problem. Oddly, it made me want to.

"Let's just order a pizza," I said.

I thought maybe I was an adult after all, if being an adult meant having the fortitude to reach for the most obvious solution. Hugo smiled at me like I'd passed a test.

"There you go," he said.

———

After Spencer and his friends went back inside, after Ana materialized to sweep cigarette butts into a garbage bag and sponge down the teak tables, after the pizza place we'd chosen had been relitigated three times, I walked out front to call in our order. The sprinklers came on while I was on the phone, black plastic heads that rose out of the ground. They ticked and whirled, casting low jets of water over the grass.

There was no reason to water that lawn. We'd had a wet spring. Many consecutive days of rain as the show wound down. The theater flooded and the pages were sent out in their windbreakers to sandbag the atrium. Upstairs in the office, we felt like people must have felt not before or after the flood, but during. The people of the deluge. The ones who Noah left for dead. Everyone made ark jokes until it became insufferable and Gil wrote on the whiteboard: No Ark Jokes.

We didn't go outside during that period. Not for coffee, not for lunch. The network had turned on us, then the elements. Gil developed circles under his eyes. He kept leaving meetings to take calls from his wife. Hugo came in late and holed up in his office. His assistants were afraid to knock on the door. We started drinking early, usually during the taping. Our last ever, special edition game of Thursday bingo, no one even played. We poured bourbon into Dixie cups and stared down at our cards. Phoned-in interview was a square. Gallows humor was a square. Affected nostalgia was a square.

One day it stopped raining and within half an hour the sky was clear. A rainbow stretched over Lower Manhattan. The city sparkled as it dried, a moment of grace. We were annoyed, betrayed. Our suffering was undermined. There were days left yet until the final show. It had seemed that we were projecting the bad weather, beaming it out, or at least that our suffering was universal. But it took only five minutes for people in shorts to start emerging from buildings, five minutes for the sandals and shades, the sundresses in floral prints. We knew our shiva had ended and we'd have to start feeling different. Resigned or angry, fatalistic or cheerful. Anything but crushed, which couldn't be maintained in the long term.

I didn't know why people watered their lawns at dusk. It reminded me of my childhood, of summertime, of dads out there still in work clothes hosing down the grass. Hitching up their khakis as they crouched to adjust sprinklers. My brother and I used to ride our bikes down our street at that time of night and it would be an avenue of spray. The mist coated our faces as we pedaled.

I looked it up after I got off the phone with the pizza place: Why dusk? In the middle of the day, the water evaporated too

quickly. And too late at night it didn't evaporate fast enough.
It clung to the blades and caused lawn disease. That was the
first Google result anyway. Lawn disease. It sounded to me
like a euphemism for something else, like the name a polite
person might use for what ailed the very rich.

The pizza took forty minutes to arrive. An electronic chime
told us the delivery guy was at the gate. His car was visible in
black and white on the screen next to the door. I watched his
blurry approach, watched him take the steps in one leap and
mash the doorbell. He seemed surprised when I opened. He
had a skinny neck and wore the polo shirt of the restaurant.
He couldn't have been more than nineteen.

"You called in an order for Hugo Best?"

"Is that not plausible?"

"No offense."

"You work at a pizza place."

"Hey, it's fancy pizzas," he said. "Anyway, this is just my
day job."

We looked at each other. I knew what was coming. He
waited another beat to say it.

"Really, I'm a comedian. Actually . . ."

He handed me the pizzas and reached into his back pocket
for a flyer.

"Here. Maybe you could give this to Hugo?"

I balanced the pizzas on one arm and took it from him.
It was for a comedy night at a bar in town, the same kind of
glossy, cheaply produced flyer they handed out everywhere. I
myself had handed them out more times than I could count.
It was part of the deal when you were low on the bill or part
of a showcase. No-names had to help scare up an audience.
I had spent some of the worst afternoons of my life that way,

standing on street corners, thrusting unwanted literature into the hands of passersby shaking their heads.

"Tomorrow," he said. "Five minutes down the road. Frogger's, you know the place?"

"I don't know it," I said.

"It's not bad there," he said. "Ladies drink for free on Tuesdays."

"Tomorrow's Sunday."

"The drinks are cheap every night. Tell Hugo I promise he won't be disappointed. No, wait. Tell him something funnier. Tell him . . . hm." He leaned against the doorjamb, thinking. "Okay, tell him—maybe you want to go get a pen to write this down?"

"I'm not getting a pen."

"All right, just tell him to come. Will you tell him?"

His persistence was sweet and stupid. It reminded me of Julian. The pizza boxes had started to burn my forearm. I set them down on the floor of the foyer and told him he should do something else with his life while there was still time. If it was at all possible, if there was another career he was considering, another thing he had aptitude for, he should do that instead. The entertainment business was a bad life. Unstable, low odds, unimaginably degrading. It was beneath him. I didn't know anything about him, but I could tell for sure that it was beneath him because it was beneath everyone.

He was silent for a second. Then he pointed at the pizza boxes. "You shouldn't put food on the ground like that."

"No, you're right," I said. I picked them back up.

"There's something very, very wrong about it. Plenty of people don't have food and you go and put it on the ground."

"I said you're right."

"So will you give it to him?"

I had to laugh. He was back on the flyer. He'd probably hyped himself up on the way over, expecting Hugo to come to the door. Instead he'd gotten me, an obvious poor person who would put food on the ground.

"Okay," I said. "I'll give it to him."

———

The kids took their plates down to the basement and Hugo opened a bottle of wine. I tore into a veggie slice, relieved. I hadn't eaten since Ana's egg and I was shaky with hunger.

In between bites, I told Hugo about the pizza guy.

"He was really tenacious." I studied the flyer. "It's got an eight-bit frog on it. Maybe they have arcade games. Have you been there?"

Hugo wiped his mouth with a napkin. "I have not been," he said slowly, "to a place called Frogger's."

When all that was left of the pizza was errant mushrooms and cheese hardening in the bottom of the box, I said to Hugo, "Now what?"

He said, "What would you do if this was your place?"

I glanced around, trying to picture it. I imagined a broom leaning perilously close to the door next to a crummy old Schwinn, and that made me laugh.

"Enslave my enemies in the comedy club you've got down there," I said. "Brick them in to die."

"What enemies could you possibly have? Julian?"

"No, Julian's my friend. We were pages together. He helped me get my job. But he'd be thrilled to hear you know his name."

"Of course I know Julian's name. Julian makes sure people know his name. He broadcasts desperation like the radio tower in the RKO logo."

"He's not so bad," I said. "He's sort of endearing once you get used to him."

"Sure."

"No, he is. Let me see what I can tell you about him to make you see that he's okay. I had to drop something off at his place one time on the weekend and he lives in just one room in the West Village. This tiny studio. How stupid is that? He could have a bigger place in Brooklyn, but he told me he likes it. It makes him feel like a woodland creature. He insisted I stay for tea and he gave me a book about Lyndon Johnson. Not lent. Gave. I'll read it one day, too, when I have exhausted every other entertainment option. He was wearing this vintage Communist Party lapel pin on his blazer. I forgot to mention he was wearing a blazer. In his own house."

Hugo seemed bored. "Sounds obnoxious."

"No, because it's totally sincere. Okay, how about this: He's got a car, an old maroon Volvo. He parks it on the street, and he told me the thing he likes best about it is having to move it all the time. He actually looks forward to getting out of bed in the morning three days a week, moving it across the street, sitting there while the street cleaner goes by, and then moving it back again. He eats a bagel and reads the newspaper. The print newspaper. He's got this idea that being a real New Yorker means suffering for every convenience anyone else would take for granted."

"Are you in love with him? You sound like you're in love with him."

"Well yeah, but just the normal amount," I said. "Nothing serious."

"It seems like he's not cut out for the writers' room," said Hugo.

He was probably right. Writers' contracts were renewed every thirteen weeks. Every thirteen weeks you had to worry about whether or not you'd be fired. Some people were able to take this in stride. Others were not. Julian was destroyed by it. His contract came up twice during his time as a staff writer. Both times he'd been pushed to the brink of a nervous breakdown.

The first time it happened, he started campaigning for himself four weeks out. Pitching more than usual, becoming manically participatory. He stopped by the offices of the senior writers and got them to weigh in on the odds of his renewal. He showed up with obscure confections for the staff. Montreal-style bagels, macaroons. He made sure everyone knew who had brought them. The more he worried, the worse his joke writing got.

A week out his hands were shaking.

His office mate, Layla, came in one morning and found him asleep under his desk. He'd spent the night there, she told me. He'd been too keyed up to go home. Or else he'd gone home and been too keyed up to stay. She couldn't really get a straight story. But the anxiety prevented him from being anywhere but work. That was the gist. He smelled terrible.

The next time it was even worse. He ran himself down so thoroughly he got pneumonia. He left work in the middle of the day for a chest X-ray and had the audacity to come back. Gil found him in his office, flushed and coughing, brainstorming a list of games for Alec Baldwin. Don't be an idiot, Gil told him. People die of pneumonia all the time.

Hugo probably didn't know any of this. He was insulated from office happenings by a trio of assistants who orbited him like satellites. Communication with him went through Gil, or through Gil and Laura, or through Gil, Laura, and the assistants. A game of telephone that inevitably distorted the message. But I guess he'd had enough interactions with Julian to pin him down. Julian was that openly neurotic. That known and that knowable. I envied it.

I said, "What do you want to do? What do you do when you're alone here?"

Hugo shrugged. "Drink. Watch bad TV or an old movie. Google myself. Same as anybody."

"That's kind of funny," I said. "As something to do. I'll look you up and you look me up."

We took out our phones, tapped at the screens.

"First five results," said Hugo. He looked down and let out a low whistle. "Are you sure you want to hear these?"

"Give me the worst."

"One: 'June Bloom, Bloom and Associates Realtors. A fifty-five-year-old resident of Boca Raton with twenty-three years of full-time experience in real estate.' Two: 'Vancouver teacher June Bloom diagnosed with Ehlers-Danlos syndrome, an underrecognized tissue disorder.' Three: It's Boca June again. She also coaches a local girls' basketball team. Busy lady. Four: Your IMDB page, thank God. You got a writing credit for the roast. Five: A humor piece about food you wrote for—I'm clicking through—some dated-looking website. No pictures or anything. Just text."

"It's not dated. It's an antiaesthetic."

"Looks low paying."

"No paying, thank you very much."

Hugo set his phone down on the counter. "Which joke was yours at the roast?"

Back in fall, the network had pressured Hugo to sit for a cable channel roast. He'd been fourth in the ratings for two years in a row, fourth of four, and they were trying anything to raise his profile. Nearly everyone on staff had been against the roast, including Hugo. In the writers' room, Gil had remarked on how grotesque and unfunny these things had become. Except for Bony, none of Hugo's real friends even wanted to participate. But the network prevailed in the end, and the writers were asked to contribute jokes. Hugo sat in the seat of honor in a tux. He was a good sport, too. He smiled the whole time, though his smile looked false to me. Like he held a piece of chalk on his tongue, like he'd been forced to hide it there, and it would be awhile before he could spit it out.

"The one about your pinstriped suit," I said. "About it being hoisted battle torn above Fort McHenry."

I'd given it to Julian and Julian had given it to Gil. It had been delivered by a pop star who'd just left his boy band to go solo. He seemed confused, as if he'd wandered into the wrong studio. His emphasis had been odd and he'd stumbled over *battle torn*. He'd pronounced it "battletron," like the name of a nonexistent video game.

"Not bad," said Hugo.

I shrugged. It was only the crowning achievement of my career.

"Do me," said Hugo, nodding at my phone.

Hugo had the expected Internet presence. No Boca Realtors shared his name. I could go twenty pages deep and still not run out of think pieces, news items, video clips, all about him.

"One: your Wikipedia page. Two: your IMDB page. Three: network website. Four: Twenty-five years of *Stay Up with Hugo Best* in pictures. Five . . ." I hesitated.

"Go ahead," said Hugo.

"'Anatomy of a Downward Spiral: How Hugo Best Tanked His Career.'"

"Click through. I want to hear what it says."

"Aren't you supposed to not look at these things?"

Hugo raised an eyebrow. "You think I can't take it?"

"I don't know. That guy in the boutique today seemed to bug you."

"Him? He didn't bug me."

"He did a little."

"I've been doing this my entire life. You think I give a shit about some old-timer in a dress shop?"

I knew I wasn't wrong. He'd minded. But I clicked through anyway. The site took a second to load. Spencer and Scotty trooped back into the kitchen without the girls. Scotty opened the freezer and retrieved a pint of ice cream.

"What are you doing?" Spencer said to me.

"I'm about to read this hit piece out loud to your dad."

Spencer came around and peered at my screen, resting his hands on my shoulders. "Definitely don't read that one."

Scotty jammed a spoon into the mint chip. "Is that the downward spiral one from yesterday?"

"Even Scotty's read it," said Hugo.

"What do you mean, even Scotty?" said Spencer. "Scotty's well informed. Scotty wants to be a journalism major." He began to knead my trapezius muscle.

Hugo looked at Scotty. "Is that true?"

"Hell yeah, dude. Fourth estate," said Scotty around a mouthful of ice cream. His eyes were bloodshot and he seemed on the verge of laughter.

"Bravo," said Hugo. I thought he might turn to his son and remark on Scotty's ambition. Instead he said to me, "Read it."

"It's like four thousand words long," I muttered, scrolling down. "All right, here we go. 'Anatomy of a Downward Spiral: How Hugo Best Tanked His Career. Late-night stalwart *Stay Up with Hugo Best* exits the airwaves this week with the conclusion of its twenty-fifth season. Once a ratings juggernaut, *Stay Up* struggled in recent years to maintain its audience. Was it the fractured TV landscape that finished off Best, or was it, as incoming *Stay Up* host Eric Marshall implied earlier this week, his inability to take advantage of the current zeitgeist—" I stopped. "This is mean."

Spencer moved on to my neck and Hugo frowned at me. I wriggled forward in my seat until Spencer dropped his hands.

"Play the video," said Hugo.

"How do you know there's video?" I said.

We looked at each other. Over his shoulder I could see the pool and the backyard lit up by the pool lights. It would have been a good time for something distracting and magical to happen—a dryad emerging from the woods, a fawn bending her supple neck to drink from the pool—but all was still. Hugo had read the piece. Of course he had.

I played the clip. Eric Marshall was giving an interview in a suit and skinny tie. I always felt I knew Eric, though he was five or six years older than me and we had never met. He had grown up in South Carolina, too, in a place called Batesburg-Leesville, tracker and dip country, a cracker crumb on the state's broad shirtfront. My own town on the coast was metropolitan by comparison. It had a couple of movie theaters, a sushi place. In his stand-up, Eric talked about growing up in central South Carolina, how everyone assumed that it was hell for him, a brainy biracial kid with two Yankee parents. But in fact, the town had treated him with the same sense of ownership and reverence that they would a local attraction. For instance, a quarry. Hey, been out to see the quarry? Damnedest thing, the quarry. We don't know how it got here or exactly what it's for, but it's ours, by God. It's ours.

Eric sat with his hands resting on his knees. He was answering a question about being a black guy hosting a network talk show.

"You're the first," said the interviewer.

"Come on," said Eric. "Arsenio Hall? Okay, technically you're right for a very obscure reason, which has to do with Paramount not being a network and the affiliates wanting to effectively—I can't believe I'm being this boring on TV—program over Pat Sajak, who had a talk show on at the time."

"Who could blame them?"

"Pat Sajak is *Wheel of Fortune*. Taking him out of that context and giving him a talk show was a bizarre idea. No disrespect to *Wheel*. *Wheel*'s an American institution. It's like the Liberty Bell. In a hundred years, schoolchildren will be singing songs about it."

"I want to switch gears for a minute and ask you about Hugo Best," said the interviewer.

"Obviously I'm a huge admirer. There would be no *Stay Up* without Hugo. He invented it. I loved his self-awareness, the way he made fun of his playboy image. How he'd fix a martini for his guest and fill the glass with ten or fifteen olives, until it was overflowing. Or wear a smoking jacket onstage and take it off halfway through the show to reveal a second smoking jacket underneath. Those are classic bits. At the same time, I think viewers today may be looking for something a little different. I think they want someone to engage with the political moment a bit more."

"He's not critical enough, is that what you're saying?"

"I'll put it this way: The world has changed. I don't think anyone would deny that. The medium has to continue to evolve to meet it. Otherwise why would anyone keep watching?"

The video ended, and the only sound was Scotty scraping away at the sides of the ice cream carton. Female laughter drifted upstairs from the basement rec room.

"It wasn't all bad," I said finally.

"It was backhanded," said Spencer.

"There were some compliments in there, too," I said. "He's a decent guy, Eric Marshall. A funny guy. He's trying to get people to watch the show. I'm sure he didn't mean anything by it."

"What are you, in love with him?" said Spencer.

Hugo smiled meanly. "Just the normal amount. Anyway, it's perfectly natural for young men to want to kill their fathers." He glanced at Spencer. "So to speak."

"And fuck their mothers," added Scotty, accidentally spitting a hardened lump of ice cream onto the floor. He scooped it up with his hand and popped it back in his mouth.

"Is it about time for Scotty to head home?" asked Hugo.

"Nah," said Spencer.

I thought that Hugo had made his point and we could move on to other things. I started to slip my phone into my pocket.

"We're not done. Read on," said Hugo.

"For real? I get it. Whatever you're trying to prove. I get it. You can take criticism. You don't care what people think. Fine. Why are we doing this? I could tell you what it says without even reading it."

"Oh?" said Hugo. He made a gesture like I should continue. "By all means."

I shifted in my seat. The right thing to do was demur. If I backed down I looked cowardly. If I didn't back down, offense was almost guaranteed. I thought of how Julian would react if I told him what I was about to do. How he'd yank his glasses off his face, clean them irritably. *Never tell people what you really think of them. Never. Even if they say they want you to. Even if they beg.* Then again, Hugo hated Julian.

"It's a breakdown of every mistake you've ever made in your career," I said. "Probably with special emphasis on your personal indiscretions. Your arrest, et cetera."

"He got community service," said Spencer. "It was really not a big deal."

I shrugged. "I'm guessing it also maps the decline of the quality of the show. How it had gotten stale. Lost its edge. How it hadn't really been funny in ten years. How you seemed to give up after you lost eleven thirty, to not want to try anything, to not want to offend. Or lists all the ways you sold out. For instance, the time George W. Bush came on the show after he'd started a war under false pretenses. Just completely lied about WMDs. And everyone watching thought you were going to let him have it, but you didn't, did you? You sat for him while he sketched you. You got him to sign it. You asked him what Dick Cheney's favorite movie was and he said he didn't know, but maybe it was *Rudy*. He sure did like *Rudy* himself. You did everything short of tousling his hair."

I paused for a minute, remembering. I was omitting that the George W. Bush episode had been oddly charming. The president's innocence had been irresistible. The twinkling eyes, the lipless, simian grin. Hugo was indulgent with him, even gentle. He'd held the drawing up to the camera and it, too, was sweet. He'd captured something about Hugo, a downturn of the mouth, a worried crease at the bridge of his nose. The drawing wasn't good, but Bush's perception of him was. He'd seen Hugo's longing and low-grade despair and he'd been able to render it, if crudely, on the page.

I went on. "Probably it finishes with a dissection of why the show ended. It seems thorough, so maybe there's a chart of the ratings. A zigzag trending downward, flatlining over the last two years. Maybe they got an anonymous source to say that retirement wasn't your idea. That it wasn't voluntary, per se. These aren't my opinions, of course."

"Of course."

"It's just a dumb article on the Internet. Some quote-unquote content. They have to put up something so they can have ads there."

"Much like television."

"Much like television. The ads on this one are"—I looked back down at my screen—"a memory foam pillow and one of those meal-delivery services for lazy people."

"They've got you pegged," said Hugo.

I sat back in my chair and Hugo sat back in his.

"How'd I do? Could I write for the Internet?"

"You're not cruel enough and you know your topic too well."

"You missed the thing about Laura," said Scotty. He opened the freezer to replace the pint.

"Just throw it out," Hugo said to him. "It's completely freezer burned."

"I might want it the next time I'm here," said Scotty.

"What thing about Laura?" I said.

"We'll get more," said Hugo. "We'll get you any flavor you want. Just tell Ana."

Scotty put the pint in the freezer and shut the door. "It doesn't hurt to have a backup. In case it falls through with Ana."

Hugo turned to Spencer. "You should be more like Scotty. He's a new breed of ultraperson."

We all looked at Scotty. He was skinny with a mop of floppy brown hair and a geeky, limb-swinging confidence. One second ago we had witnessed him spit food onto the floor and shovel it back into his mouth.

"Please," said Spencer. "Scotty's as normal as it gets. He had a bear named Bear when he was little. He's on the soccer team. He loves his parents so much."

"They're good people," confirmed Scotty.

"I bet he requests some completely unpredictable flavor of ice cream," said Hugo.

"Red bean," said Scotty.

Hugo threw his hands in the air. "Red bean! Outstanding!"

The girls emerged from the basement. The blonde had put on a huge gray sweatshirt. The hood was up and the drawstrings cinched so only a small circle of her face showed.

"How could you leave us downstairs for so long?" the brunette whined.

"There's no Wi-Fi down there," said the blonde. "It's like Guantanamo."

"Ladies, I'll be honest. We totally forgot about you," said Spencer.

"I didn't think of you once," added Scotty. He pointed at the brunette. "Especially you."

The blonde scowled. "You guys are hilarious."

"What thing about Laura?" I muttered under my breath.

The blonde gave me a bored look through the aperture of her sweatshirt. "Can we have a ride home?"

"Sure," said Hugo. "Go get Cal."

He stood to stack plates in the sink. As he passed me he said, "You can read it later if you're so interested. The Internet belongs to everyone, as I'm sure you know. Information wants to be free."

———————

Later, Hugo and I climbed the stairs to go to sleep. For the second time he left me at the threshold of the guest room. I thought of what Roman had said earlier. Nothing is not going to happen. He'd misunderstood his friend, I thought. Or the power of inertia.

Logan had texted again while we were eating pizza, twice. *I can't believe you*, said the first. *Call me*, said the second. I held my phone in my hand, deciding whether or not to respond. Likely it would be the last time he tried. If I had anything to say to him, if there was anything to salvage, I would have to do it now.

Instead I put on Spencer's Exeter shirt and sprawled on the taupe bedding reading the full article on my phone. The tone was strident but all the facts lined up. When I finished, I got up and made my way down the darkened hall to Hugo's room. My feet felt cold on the hardwood. Outside his door, I awaited the courage to go in. The best I could manage was a meek knock.

"Yes?" he said.

I cracked the door and stuck my head in. Hugo was sitting up in bed in a pair of readers and a worn navy blue T-shirt. The glasses made him look feminine and scholarly, the T-shirt, charmingly ordinary. He dog-eared his book and set it on the nightstand next to a glass of water and an uncapped bottle of Advil. I couldn't see the title, but it was a mass market paperback, with raised lettering and yellowing pages.

"I was just—" I said.

"Come in."

The room was the biggest in the house. One wall made of glass looked out over the yard. Spencer had left the pool light on and the swan float had run aground on the staircase. It lay tipped over on its side with its head on the deck.

Hugo patted the place next to him in bed. Tentatively, I slipped under the covers. Opposite the bed hung a huge painting I recognized as a Frank Stella. The neons of its interlocking fan shapes—the peaches, limes, and lavenders— warmed the room like an indoor sun.

I pointed at the painting. "I like that. Can I have it?"

"Does your place have a big enough wall?"

The largest stretch of wall in my apartment was in the living room. Currently it held a tattered periodic table of the elements, the pull-down kind from a classroom, that had moved with us four or five times. It had a long gash from *magnesium* to *radium* that had been mended with Scotch tape.

"I could make room," I said.

"In that case, I'll bag it up for you."

There was a silence while we both considered the painting. I wondered at what point you got sick of a Stella, at what point it became just another thing that oppressed you. Sitting up in bed, both staring in the same direction, it felt like we were watching TV. I tried to think of a joke to make about it, but everything I came up with sounded lame in my head.

"I read the article," I said at last.

"I don't want to talk about it right now."

"So it's Laura's fault?"

"Of course not. It's complex."

"But she pulled the plug. After all those years you guys spent together."

"It's the business, it's . . ."

"Not personal, I know. Turn, turn, turn. But she decided."

"We decided together."

"But she strongly influenced the decision."

"Hey, you can continue to oversimplify this in the morning, if you want. But right now can we go to bed?"

We had turned away from the painting to face each other. I thought we might finally kiss. I'd been mentally preparing myself for the possibility of sex since he'd zipped me up in the dressing room. Reminding myself that I wanted it, or sort of wanted it, or had sort of wanted it once, not that long ago.

But the more time that passed, the more far-fetched it grew that we'd touch. Every moment compounded it. Hugo seemed to sense this, too. He laughed softly. Shaking his head, he reached over to switch off the light. In the dark, the Stella was a grayscale rainbow.

"Good night, I guess," I said.

"Night," he murmured.

I lay there as quietly as I could until he started to snore. His body was so warm that I had to kick off the covers. I couldn't sleep. After a while I gave up trying. I asked myself whether I was repulsed yet and found I wasn't. I thought about texting Audrey to tell her that. I only didn't because it seemed too feeble, the kind of brag that betrays itself right away as something else.

I sat up on one elbow so I could see out the window. The night was clear and the stars stood out. More stars than the eye could take in. You couldn't see them where I lived due to light pollution. New York in toto. A classic example. Gain the city but lose the whole visible universe. I readjusted so I could just make out the curved lash of a moon on the wane. Tonight it was barely there, tomorrow it would be gone altogether.

Sunday

The house's windows were screens stuck on a single, serene channel. The field channel. Sunday morning brought more of the same. Crew cut grass barely moving in the wind, needles blowing off the pines. Small birds pecked at the ground in twos and threes then lit out for the woods, brown streaks against the sky. Midmorning was overcast, outside and in. I roused to the dull scrape of a branch on glass. Hugo was gone. He'd made the bed on his side, smoothed down the blanket that was the same depthless gray as the clouds. I thought again of the architect's vision, to pull everything together under a single umbrella of muted opulence. This time I could remember that Hugo and I hadn't slept together.

I went downstairs, expecting to see Spencer bent over his phone, Ana tapping her fingers on the countertop. Instead I found Laura Posner. She sat on the floor of the sunken living room with the Sunday *Times* spread out all around her. The magazine had slipped under the coffee table and I could make out half of its cover image, a woman frowning deeply over the latest systemic collapse.

Hugo was there, too, shaven and seated behind Laura on the couch. He was not wearing yesterday's robe, but a white collared shirt and jeans. Spencer sat in one of the Danish armchairs, laughing at something Laura had said. There

was a plate of pastries laid out on the coffee table. Someone
had put orange juice in a crystal pitcher next to a bowl of
fruit salad. They looked forged from sunlight, like a family
from an ad. Except if you got closer, those were pot leaves
on Spencer's shirt.

Hugo noticed me first. "June!" He sprang to his feet.
"Come in, come in. Laura brought pan au chocolat."

Laura rose to greet me. "How are you, June?"

I was wearing the Exeter shirt again, and Spencer's red
shorts. Laura wore a white silk top, black bottoms that seemed
neither skirt nor pants, and a necklace made from an asym-
metric slash of metal. She wasn't beautiful—her nose was too
beaky, her jaw too square—but she had a mystery about her.
Dark eyes and platinum hair that fell in a thick, luminous
sheaf. She gripped my shoulders in a stiff hug and I felt like
Scotty's little brother, far from home.

"We're going to lunch," said Laura. "At the country club."

"Once a year Laura consents to eating a club sandwich,"
said Hugo.

"My annual dose of nitrates," said Laura.

She paused as if I was supposed to respond to this. I looked
around, at a potted cactus, at the placid outdoors.

"I like how they cut those into quarters," I said. They
stared at me. "Club sandwiches."

Hugo pressed on. "Laura despises the club."

"I do," said Laura. "It's stuffy in there. It smells like a vacuum cleaner and they have those bad floral drapes. Plus, it's
awfully dated, isn't it? All the rich people in town belonging
to a club together. All the rich white people."

She was pandering but I had no idea why.

"*You're* white," I said.

She cocked her head. "Well, yeah."

"What does a vacuum cleaner smell like?" asked Spencer.

"Oh you know," said Laura. "Ozone. Carpet fibers. Vacuum cleaner smell."

"It's not just white people," said Hugo. "Dan Swan's a member."

"Dan Swan is white," said Spencer.

"But he's got an Asian wife," said Hugo.

"All white people and one Asian wife, then," said Laura. "I hate how you don't even pay there. You just sign your name to a slip of paper and wink at the waiter."

Hugo turned to me. "She's joking. You don't really have to wink at the waiter."

"I know that," I said. "I just need half an hour to get ready."

"Oh, it's not . . ." said Hugo. He glanced at Laura.

"It's a just-the-two-of-us thing," she said.

"Ah," I said.

"You can come if you want," she said. "But it's going to be businessy. You'll be bored. Wouldn't you rather stay here with Spencer? You two could"—she looked around the room for some diversion Spencer and I could enjoy together—"watch TV. Play cards? Or, I don't know, go for a swim? Have you been to the bunker yet?"

"The bunker?"

"I'll show you," said Spencer.

Laura smiled. "Great. And when we get back we'll all play tennis. Do you play tennis, June?"

"I took lessons as a kid."

"It'll come right back, I'm sure," said Laura.

"We'll do mixed doubles. You can be on my team," said Hugo.

"If you want." I pointed to the pastries. "Is anyone going to eat those or are they just for show?"

"Oh, of course!" said Laura.

We filed back around the coffee table. This time Laura took the other armchair and Hugo and I sat together on the couch. I didn't actually want a pastry. The idea of it was sickening, the too-sweet slick of chocolate in the middle. But I thought some stage business might help, something to occupy our hands. It was the whole reason people smoked.

I picked one up and took a bite. Phyllo dough flaked down onto my lap and the couch. Everyone looked at it, all four of us. I wondered if I was going to brush it onto the floor. Finally, I cupped one hand and nudged the crumbs into it with the other. Some of the pieces deteriorated, leaving floury grease spots on the couch.

"You'll have to excuse me, it's my first time eating," I said.

No one laughed. I didn't know what to do with the crumbs so I closed my fist around them.

Laura poured orange juice and passed around the glasses.

"How is your family?" she asked me. "Your parents?"

My parents had come to a taping the previous fall, and I was embarrassed that she remembered. They had made a special trip of it, booking a room at the Midtown Marriott without even complaining about the price. They had been trying to come for years—they would have come my second week as a page—but I held them off. Each piece of my life compared badly to the other. My job could never live up to my parents' expectations of big-city glamour; my parents, in the historic theater, in the sleek, bustling office building, in the streets of Manhattan, could never be anything but small and middle class.

Before the show they insisted on seeing where I worked, so I took them up. My father was determined to shake my boss's hand, but I never found out exactly whom he meant. Gil? Hugo? The head of the media conglomerate?

Up in the office they looked just as I expected. They looked like each other and like the dog they left back in South Carolina. Their three faces were all becoming one: the face of a graying labradoodle with bladder trouble and an otherwise easy life. My mother wore hot-blue Mizuno running shoes for all the walking. She kept taking hand sanitizer out of her purse and dousing her palms, though I didn't see her touch anything. My father had a halting gait, the product of a small stroke a few years prior. His herringbone sport coat, one he'd had my whole life, was now huge on him, and luffed like a sail every time we passed a vent.

They were shrinking. I knew that this was what happened— the bones lost their mass—but it was awful to see. You grew bigger and stronger until you stopped and then the parabola began its descent back to the x-axis. It was unfair, unasked for. When I was a teenager, I used to say to my mom I didn't ask to be born. As if this was an original thought and not the oldest retort there was. Yeah, she'd say, but if you had to ask, wouldn't you? We'd stand there until I had weighed the hassles of the imaginary application process against the qualified splendor of this world and decided that, yes, I guess I would, okay? I probably would ask to be born.

On the way out of the office we encountered Laura waiting for the elevator. She was dressed in one of her minimalist outfits, high priestess of a future religion.

"It takes thousands of years," she said to us, jiggling the already illuminated down button. "Better get comfortable."

None of us could ever get comfortable, my father informed her, jacket sleeves flapping. Not in this situation or in general. Laura laughed.

After that, I had to introduce them: Jon and Susan Bloom. I had never spoken to Laura before, but not to do so would have been, to my parents, an egregious betrayal of my upbringing. We'd spend the next ten years going over what I possibly could have been thinking.

"You must be so proud of June," Laura said. "Working her way up from the bottom like she has."

"We are," said my mother.

"Well, cautiously optimistic," said my father. "If not proud."

Laura chuckled again. "I see where you get your sense of humor," she said to me.

"Don't give him too much credit," said my mother. "June was born funny."

Laura said to me, "Is that true? Were you born funny?"

"Definitely not," I said.

The elevator came and I prayed for it to deliver us straight to hell. At street level my parents shook Laura's hand again. They even thanked her, though I didn't know for what. All the way into the theater, they chattered about what a nice woman she was. Totally kind and pleasant, not at all what you'd expect.

I had reserved us good seats, a ways back from the stage. I didn't want either of them to interface with the warm-up comic, a guy named Gary Scary who did the same lame crowd work every single day. *Where are you people from? Cool it, lady, I'll tell the jokes. Oh wow, fraternity brothers, huh? Out on the town in the big city. Sucks you're all gonna get arrested tonight.* And so on.

They were unprepared for how freezing the theater was. Nordic, I had told them. Oslovian. But they still suffered from it, my father especially. He huddled under his jacket the whole time, even drew his knees up under it. Since his stroke, unfamiliar situations made him childlike. His hands were blanched white and gnarled around a wrapped granola bar he was not allowed to eat during the show. It crossed my mind that it might kill him, that he might become the first person to ever die of exposure in the Bob Hope Amphitheater. They'd have to stop the show to call an ambulance, load him on a stretcher. Pull a sheet up over his head to spare the tourists in the back, in from Wisconsin and just trying to have a good time.

The act that day was bad. Springsteen had canceled and instead we got a troop of puppeteers from Queens and their life-sized animal puppets. The climax was the lurching entrance of a canvas elephant that took four people to operate. It was supposed to be impressive, but I cringed. It was all so chintzy. I had built my life around a second-rate variety show. I had brought people hundreds of miles to see it.

Afterward, we went to St. Patrick's Cathedral and had a fight under the canopy of arches. My father hadn't enjoyed himself and told me so.

"It would have been better," he said, "if Hugo was even remotely funny."

His voice was strained. We had stopped in front of the tall, shiny pipes of the organ. All around us people were praying or taking pictures.

"He just riffs on pop culture. I didn't know what he was talking about half the time."

"Yeah, that's what jokes are about. What do you want them to be about?"

He motioned around. "You know, things that happen to you. An experience everyone's had. The bags of peanuts on an airplane. Why are they so small? That kind of stuff."

"Got it," I said. "Observational bullshit."

There was a cluster of three nuns lighting candles near us. One of them looked up at me.

"June," said my mother.

"Comedy is meant to challenge the culture," I said. "That's what it's for."

"No it's not," he said. "It's for making people laugh."

I would never admit it to him, but he was right that it hadn't been a particularly funny show. Hugo's face looked bloated, swollen around the eyes. The audience had laughed as much as usual, applauded as much as usual, but the jokes had been stale. Even the monologue lacked energy. The entire time, Hugo seemed to desperately want to sit down.

Plus, the puppets. I could barely bring myself to think about the puppets.

"Can we just look at the stained glass?" said my mother. "It's really quite impressive."

"Susan, Jesus," said my father. "Stop trying to experience awe right now. It's pathetic."

I laughed and instantly felt bad. My mother looked wounded.

"So you're just the authority on everything and the rest of us are stupid, is that it?" my father said to me.

No, that was not it. I was a quasi authority in this one narrow, highly specific arena. Or not even a quasi authority. Just a person who knew more about it than a sixty-five-year-old retired dentist from South Carolina. I had worked at learning about it, thought about it, tried to understand what went into

it. Even if he was somewhat witty for a retired dentist, which
he was, I still knew more about comedy than him. It was
important to me and I was trying to share it with him and
he was ungrateful. Also, he needed a smaller jacket because
he looked like a twelve-year-old playing Willy Loman in a
middle school production of *Death of a Salesman*.

"What?" he said.

"Arthur Miller!" I shouted.

All three nuns were watching now. I hated myself
immensely.

I turned to my mother. "Get him a smaller jacket."

"Okay," she said.

My father's face splotched red and his mouth twisted into a
faint smile. "I think we should go back to our hotel. I'm tired."

My mother had forgotten to take a picture of me under the
marquee, so I walked them back that way. It began to drizzle
but none of us, not even our lady of the sensible shoes, had
thought to bring an umbrella. Back in front of the theater we
ran into Laura, taking shelter under the overhang.

"Hello again, you Blooms. Did you enjoy the show?"

"Sure. Absolutely," said my father. "You all are doing
wonderful work."

"It was very special," added my mother. "Once in a lifetime."

"We aim to please," said Laura. "Weren't those puppets
something?"

"Oh, they were," said my mother. "That elephant. It moved
so realistically."

"I'm thrilled you enjoyed it."

She insisted on taking a picture of the three of us, tiny and
smudged, far below the marquee. My mother posted it on

Facebook twenty minutes later. She was smiling determinedly, I was squinting with a slash of wet hair across my forehead, and my father was standing a little bit away from us like a stranger who had wandered into the frame. The sign was so large that only part of it was visible: ITH HUGO BE, it read, which was not a phrase anyone would recognize.

I didn't know if Laura had any concept of how unhappy we were that day. None of us had ever been that good at hiding it. My father, for one, had been frowning so deeply through the whole encounter that it looked like the skin of his face was sliding off.

"Everyone's great," I told Laura. "Everyone's the same."

"I loved meeting them," she said. "It really was a treat."

"I loved it, too," I managed to say.

Hugo and Laura left when they'd finished their orange juice, backing out of the room apologetically, almost bowing. They told us to stay out of trouble, which made Spencer and me grimace in unison. Then we were alone.

I still clutched a handful of crumbs and I wiped it into a napkin. "What was that?"

"Couldn't you tell? It's a bad news lunch."

"The show already ended. Laura pulled the plug. What other bad news could there be?"

"I don't know. But that's how they act when they have to go have a difficult conversation. Nice work on the couch, by the way. You really put everyone at ease."

It wasn't my job to put everyone at ease. It was someone else's—Hugo's maybe—but I didn't bother pointing this out.

"Why are they eating breakfast and lunch so close together?" I said. "They just had breakfast, now they're going to go have lunch? That's not what people do."

Spencer laughed. "It must be really bad news."

"He didn't tell me she was coming. I would have gotten dressed."

"I'm sure it's nothing personal. He probably just didn't think about you."

"That's nice, thanks."

"But as a rule, just go ahead and get dressed."

"Their relationship," I said.

"I know," said Spencer. "Believe me."

"What does your mother think of the two of them?"

I expected him to bristle at the mention of her, but he said, "It drives her nuts. Or used to. Now she doesn't have to deal with it. She's got a new boyfriend. He's like, royalty? In Europe. Minor Europe. Luxembourg or somewhere. At official functions he has to wear this outfit where he carries a sword." He thought for a minute. "Actually, it probably does still bother her. My dad and Laura. She can't really let things go. She could win twelve Oscars and still be pissed about the one time Laura ruined Thanksgiving."

"Has she won an Oscar?" I asked him.

He shook his head. "Not yet. Four Emmys. And a People's Choice Award."

He made a face.

"Ruined Thanksgiving how?"

"Not even ruined. She just showed up when my dad invited her. I guess, according to my mom, she shouldn't have accepted. She didn't even do anything specific. She brought this loaf of bread she made herself. To my mom that was too much. Because my mom doesn't cook and had the whole thing catered and she saw the bread as an insult or something."

I thought of the pastries she had brought that morning, their subtle superiority. "Maybe it was."

"It definitely wasn't. It was just bread. Laura likes to bake."

"And then what happened?"

"Then nothing. It was tense and my mom and my dad had one of their signature fights after."

"What do those entail?"

"Just normal shouting. But really unpleasant."

"That's not a signature thing," I said. "You can't trademark shouting."

"You can if you're famous."

He kicked at the leg of the coffee table. Swooshed the *Times Magazine* around with the toe of his sneaker. "So," he said. "Do you want to go fool around in the pool?" He sat there gauging before he clarified, "You know, go for a swim."

He was wearing his Yankees cap again. The pot-leaf shirt was short sleeved and snug across his chest. The pool was visible from where I sat, a shade of mint so crisp it could whiten your teeth. It'd have been easy enough to say no. I didn't even really owe him an excuse. The one word would have sufficed.

"You go on," I said. "I'll meet you."

I went upstairs and pulled my bathing suit from the scramble of clothes in my tote. It was a black two-piece. I put it on and stood in front of the mirror. Turned to the side, sucked in. I had no idea what teenagers expected from adult bodies. The men who came into contact with mine seemed to like it. Or they didn't bother to comment. Logan effused, in his way. It was one thing I had over him, my main sphere of power. He liked the obvious things—my ass, my smooth olive-tinged skin—and he liked small, weird things, too. The way my pinkies bent all the way back. The knobs of my hips, there if you looked.

I felt vaguely guilty again, thinking of him. But it was too late to call him now, wasn't it? Getting to be too late, anyway. And I could see Spencer down by the pool, kicking off his shoes and leaving them there on the deck as if he cared not at all for the objects of this world, what happened to them, or where they ended up.

He was crouched by the edge of the pool when I got there, testing the water. He'd turned the heat on and a layer of steam floated on top.

"You gotta make it toasty," he explained.

He rose and took off his hat, rubbing his forehead where it left a band of red. His hair was dark and glossy, chin length. I thought of his mother, a sitcom star whose hair got better reviews than her show. I was still thinking of her, of that sitcom's twanging theme song, and her comic timing, which had been above the material, when I heard the abrupt bend and release of the diving board and looked up in time to see Spencer coming out of a lazy jackknife and entering the pool. He surfaced to tread water in the deep end. With his hat off and hair slicked out of his face he was more man than kid.

I dipped in a toe. The water felt silky, warm as a bath. He watched as I eased down the wedge of staircase and underwater. When I opened my eyes I could see his legs, tan and muscled, moving like eggbeaters in a swirl of red-orange trunks.

"He was stabbed, you know," said Spencer when I surfaced.

I wrung out a handful of hair. "Huh?"

"Someone stabbed him. A fan."

"I've never heard about this. When?"

"In the seventies. Seventy-six, I think."

"Who was it?"

"Just some crazy person, outside a club after one of his shows. A woman. He was signing his picture for her. Out of nowhere she pulled out a knife." He swam toward me and laid three fingers on my sternum. "She got him there." He moved his hand to my side. "And there." He moved his hand again, right below my breast. "And there. That one was the worst. Pretty deep between the ribs. After the third time Laura and Robert pulled her off him."

"Robert?"

"The bouncer at the club. They're still friends. My dad sends him a Christmas present every year. Sports equipment, mostly. Golf clubs, skis."

He hadn't let go of my rib cage. His knuckles grazed the bottom of my bathing suit top. He was squeezing my side faintly. Squeezing and releasing.

"I have a boyfriend," I said.

"No you don't," said Spencer.

"I do."

"What's his name?"

"Logan."

Spencer laughed. "Okay."

"For real," I said. "It's really Logan. He does tech stuff. He works at a company that makes apps for brands. Like Oscar Mayer needs a baloney app and he helps design it."

I thought he'd find it more respectable than his father had, that it would read more to him as a real profession. But he said, "What's a baloney app?"

"It was an example."

I sank lower in the water until he let go of me. His hair was drying in lank pieces around his face. Now that I had seen his mother there, I couldn't shake her. There she was, Allison. Choice of the people, patron of local boutiques. I wondered what kind of mother she was, what the three of them had been like when they were all together. Did they have fun, or were they, like my family, unable to relax in each other's company? Did they have the same petty argument over and over with no beginning and no end? Did they leave it unfinished every time, remembering their spot exactly, like a Monopoly board saved out overnight?

"Anyway, you have a girlfriend."

"No, I don't."

"That blond girl from yesterday isn't your girlfriend?"

He laughed. "Colby? Are you serious? Both of her parents are chiropractors."

"Why should that matter?"

I started swimming away and he grabbed my foot, held it out of the water, tossed it idly from hand to hand.

"It just does. It matters. I mean, both parents?"

"Does she talk about backs a lot? Or, you know, spines?"

"No."

"Does she comment on your posture?"

"No."

"Does she want to be a chiropractor herself?"

"I don't know. No. She wants to be a vet or an actress."

"So what's the big deal? You're seventeen years old."

He let my foot splash back into the water. "And?"

"And you can date someone with kooky parents. It doesn't matter. Nothing matters at your age. It's a period without consequences. A gimme."

I swam away from him, out toward the field and the dark green woods. The sky was still gray and the air felt cool on my face. I wanted to hear more about the stabbing. In all my years of following Hugo's career, I had never read about it.

"Where was the club?"

"LA. On Sunset. He bled all over the sidewalk. Laura said the most shocking part was how much. She found a taxi and they went to the hospital. The seat was drenched."

I tried to picture it. Nighttime LA, street-lit and temperate. The crowd spilling out of the club, Hugo pausing to greet them. The woman in his arms—maybe he thought she was hugging him. The fat lag in comprehension before anyone acted. Then shouting and running, Laura cradling Hugo's head in the back of a taxi. The blood pooling along the seams of the seat.

"Let me guess: Your dad buys the cabby a Christmas present every year?"

"He helped put his kid through college."

"And the lady who stabbed him?"

I imagined her, for some reason, in a ratty blond wig and giant, pink-tinted sunglasses. She'd have hatched the plan in an airless yellow and brown bedroom, a cigarette burning between her lips. Maybe she was a bank teller, respectable by day, running twenties through a bill counter. Waiting for night to indulge her bizarre, violent fandom.

"Robert held her down until the cops came."

"What happened to her?"

"She went to jail," said Spencer. "She's out now, I think. For a while she sent letters. My dad never let me read them. He threw them away. Then they stopped." He shrugged. "Maybe she got her meds adjusted."

"Or died," I said.

We were quiet and I could hear the soft chuff of tree branches rubbing against each other in the distance. There was a possibility that he had made the story up. Maybe this was how he hazed the women who showed up here. Maybe it was his way of flirting with me. I walked backward until I hit the wall of the pool and found a tiled ledge to sit on.

"Why isn't any of this online? Or in his memoir?"

"You read that? I don't think *he* even read that."

"It seems like it would be a famous incident. A Valerie Solanas thing. People love that stuff."

"You've seen the scars. Haven't you?"

I tilted my head back until the rough concrete edge of the deck bit into my neck. From where I sat I could see into the empty kitchen and living room. The lights on the second floor were off, the windows reflecting the sky. I thought of Hugo propped up in bed the night before, working his way through his cheesy paperback. Spencer was asking if I'd slept with his father and I didn't feel like telling him no. Briefly, I considered telling him yes.

"Why'd she do it? Did she ever say?"

"Who knows?" said Spencer. "She was nuts."

He dunked his head and reemerged, seal-like. "We don't trust fans."

It didn't make sense. That Hugo invited me to his house on a whim suggested the opposite. He hadn't been reluctant. He'd even had to convince me. And what about Kitty Rosenthal? What was she if not a fan? A business associate? A sixteen-year-old friend of his?

"I'm not a fan," I said.

"Oh, you're not?"

"I was his employee. It's not the same. We're colleagues, almost."

"Okay, sure. You're not a fan. You don't still own any of his albums on compact disc. You didn't buy the re-release of *Second Best* in 2001. You didn't save the free poster that came with it. You don't still listen to it sometimes just to feel a certain way."

I had owned that album. I could remember getting a ride to Sam Goody to buy it. I had listened to it on my Discman that skipped every time I moved. I could remember the poster, too. It was Hugo, pinstriped and serious, standing in the middle of an empty Times Square. It said across the top: Hugo Best, Comedian. I hadn't saved the poster. Spencer was wrong about that. By then I had recognized that it was weird for a thirteen-year-old girl to be too obsessed with a middle-aged talk show host, and modulated accordingly.

I laughed. "I'm not going to stab your father."

"If you laugh while you say it, it makes it sound like you are."

I made my face as humorless as possible and repeated without inflection, "I'm not going to stab your father."

"That was way worse," said Spencer. "Now I'm sure that you are."

"I guess we'll have to wait and see," I said.

We got out and draped ourselves in plush striped towels and Spencer led me back into the house. In the basement, beyond the wine cellar and comedy club, a hatch in the floor opened up to reveal a second flight of stairs. The subbasement was colder, unfinished. Spencer took the stairs at a trot and paused in front of a door at the bottom.

"The bunker," he said, letting us in.

There was an octagonal room inside with metal utilitarian shelves, and a dry, carefully ventilated atmosphere. It was as bunkerlike as a room could be without containing canned goods or a chemical toilet. Instead the shelves were lined with cases, their spines stickered and dated. It was Hugo's archive, every show he'd ever made going all the way back to the premier, preserved on clunky, degradable VHS.

"Don't they digitize these?"

"They do now," said Spencer. "Or they have been for a few years. Someone will have to go back and do the old ones someday. He likes them like this, though. Instead of just on a drive, or"—he motioned all around us, at thin air—"wherever things are stored."

"But how do they get here?"

"Huh?"

"How do they physically get here? He doesn't take them home with him from work. He doesn't walk out of the building in Midtown carrying them."

"He might. I don't actually know."

"No way," I said.

Someone boxed them up at the office, was my best guess, one of his assistants, and shipped them there. Ana intercepted and unpacked. When Hugo came down to look—how often? Once a month? Twice? Weekly?—they'd have magically appeared for his perusal. It happened seamlessly and below his notice, the same way someone else catalogued his cars.

"Yeah, maybe," said Spencer. "Why?"

I walked halfway down the aisle, pulled out a tape, and listened to the rattle of plastic inside. I felt in danger of uttering something about Marx's theory of alienation. "What if there's a fire?"

"People always ask that."

"And?"

"There are sprinklers. But like I said, these aren't the only copies. It's mostly just for whatever."

"For whatever?"

Spencer shifted uncomfortably. "For his hobby. His collection. Whatever you want to call it."

I held up the tape. "Let's watch this. Is there a TV down here?"

There was, and a small blue couch with passing resemblance to the one on the studio set. I found it hard not to question where everything had come from and how it had gotten there. Spencer put the tape into a VCR and we sat down on opposite ends. My bathing suit had not fully dried. I felt aware suddenly of my bare midriff. I tented my towel over my knees and wrapped my arms around my waist.

The episode started and Bony's voice rang out flat and close in the low-ceilinged room: "Stay up, America." I had chosen the tape at random, but it turned out to be the Christmas special from 1998. I remembered it well, even after all this time. There was a big cut-crystal bowl of eggnog on Hugo's desk. He entered with a Santa sack of objects he'd taken from the office and handed them out to people in the first row. A stapler, a bag of Utz pretzels, a three-hole punch.

The tension that existed between Spencer and me in the pool hadn't dissipated. He inched closer until he was sitting right next to me. He let his arm graze mine and goose bumps prickled my skin. I considered my options. I was mad at Hugo. He was off with Laura at the country club, basking in white guilt, deploying old jokes even as they talked over bad news. Drinking Arnold Palmer. He'd brought me here for a fun weekend and absconded. Left me in his house to entertain myself.

Now his son wanted to kiss me. I could tell. I sensed from him the full-body tension of acute interest. He wasn't looking at me, but he was alert to me. He breathed rapidly, laughed nervously. I should have walked out already, but I hadn't. The old physical versus mental divide. It was a shame your body contained your mind and not the other way around. Your mind would walk out of the room every time, if it was able, dragging your body along with it.

A flurry of fake snow began to fall on screen. Hugo ladled himself a viscous cup of eggnog and sat drinking it in his chair. Spencer had his arm up on the back of the couch behind me. I felt his fingers in my hair, on the nape of my neck. He pulled the string of my bikini top, untying it in one swift motion. I caught it before it fell, and held it to me as I stood up, the towel sliding off my legs.

He made a round-eyed, innocent face. "What?"

Bony and the band played "Little Drummer Boy." I looked at the screen and back at Spencer. The dissonance made me light-headed.

"Is there any popcorn?" I said.

"You can go check."

I left the bunker and climbed two flights of stairs to the kitchen. We both knew I was not going to hunt for Pop Secret. I was not going to stand in front of the microwave for three minutes while it popped. I was not going to pour it into a bowl and, still in my bathing suit, carry it back underground to the bomb shelter screening room. We were not going to eat it side-by-side on the blue couch while a studio audience from twenty years ago heeded the applause sign.

I sat down at the counter. I could feel Spencer directly below me. I pictured his arms, how they'd been shaved for swimming and the hair was growing back in bristly, transparent filaments. I pictured his face, two celebrities mashed into one with good results. Nothing was not going to happen, I thought. Whatever it was would pull me along in its wake. I stood there some more and watched the pool darken as a scrim of clouds covered the sun. Then I went upstairs and got dressed.

———————

When Hugo and Laura came home at two, they found us at the island, eating grilled cheese sandwiches like siblings. The pool cleaner had returned to suck up the remnants of Spencer's party—the leaves and waterlogged Doritos, the floating cigarette butts—and we watched him as we chewed. He had dreads and wore expensive cherry-red headphones. He wielded the hose with what seemed like style but may have just been experience.

Laura put her bag down on the counter, smiling. Hugo looked grim and unwell, his mouth pressed into a bloodless line.

"How were the nitrates?" I asked. "Get your fill?"

"I'm good for twelve months," she said.

Spencer beckoned Laura over to his phone. He was high. After I'd left him in the basement he'd made his way out to the patio and packed a moody bowl, gazing out at the pool like it was open ocean.

"Check this out," he said.

It was a video of a mountain goat climbing vertically

up a cliff, licking at a seam of salt. One of its curled horns pressed up against the rock face. Its darting tongue looked obscene.

"That's you," said Spencer. "You crave that mineral."

"Who? Me?" said Laura.

"Yeah. With the nitrates."

"But I don't like the nitrates. The nitrates are bad. I don't understand."

She looked at me for help. I shook my head.

"You crave that mineral," Spencer said again, and cracked up.

Hugo took a Diet Coke out of the refrigerator and popped it open.

"Diet soda is full of toxins," Laura told him. "The aspartame accumulates in your joints."

"That sounds made up," I said.

Hugo ignored her. "Are we playing tennis or not?"

Laura turned to Spencer and me. "What do you think, guys?"

Spencer looked at me and I looked away. I had decided that going forward there would be no covert glances, no loaded dialogue or physical contact. In fact, him on the other side of a net, separated by yards of clay, sounded great to me.

"Let's play," I said. "Why not?"

We made a sorry foursome. I had refused any more borrowed garments and played in cutoffs, the flat soles of my sneakers slapping the clay. Everyone else had changed clothes, Hugo and Laura into pristine whites, and Spencer into a neon-green tank top and a pair of mesh basketball shorts from his bottomless collection.

As promised, Hugo and I were on one side against Laura and Spencer. Spencer fixed himself a gin and tonic before we started. He played holding it in his off hand, splashing all over the court when he attempted to hit a ball. He'd made me one, too, but I knew better than to drink it. Hugo narrowed his eyes when he'd handed it to me, sweating and overfull, garnished with a lime.

I set it in the slatted shade of a bench and picked up a racket. I'd taken tennis lessons for years at the run-down yacht club in my hometown. The court there was fissured and dusted with pine straw from the trees overhead. It was hot all the time, too hot for tennis. No one cared that I never got better, not me and not my instructor. She was getting paid either way and I was just trying to please my parents, who thought children should learn tennis for social reasons. To get an advantage in some vague, upper-middle-class future.

In a way they had been right. The day had finally come when knowing how to play tennis would have been useful. But my skills did not, as Laura had suggested, come right back. When it was my turn to serve I waited for muscle memory to kick in, but the racket felt like a prop. On my second try I managed to hit the white tape at the top of the net and the ball trickled over. It struck the ground, rolled four inches, and stopped.

Hugo said, "I thought you took lessons."

"When I was twelve."

Already his face was red from exertion. He was the only one of us playing in earnest. Spencer was louche and giggly, Laura subdued. Hugo was beating them easily. Even I had scored, almost by accident, a volley so soft it floated, which Spencer nevertheless missed.

"Nice one, Spence," Laura said every time he managed to hit the ball.

It seemed to vindicate Hugo to be winning and also to make him mad. Every time he got one past Laura he sniffed righteously and said nothing. Whatever had gone on between them at lunch, this was an odd coda. The addition of a stoned teenager and a puzzled guest, the addition of sport, only muddled things further.

The afternoon was gray, but a bright gray with the intensity of a light box. The fluorescent ball through the strange atmosphere was captivating. Soon Spencer and I, and finally even Laura, stopped trying to hit it, and just watched as Hugo gave it one last grunting whack and it cleared the net and bounced off toward the fence.

"None of you are trying," he shouted as he spiked down his racket.

The three of us stood there with our arms limp at our sides. Laura picked up the racket from where it had landed. Her white-blond ponytail made her look younger and older at the same time. Her forehead was lined and age spotted in places. I thought of what her life had been: decades of managing the kind of man who raged at her via tennis.

Why did she continue to do it? There was no way she needed the money anymore. Was it that she'd helped save his life? That was the kind of trauma that bonded people forever. Or was it that she'd molded him, a kid from Queens? Taught him what shoes to wear, how to credibly sample wine while the waiter stood by tapping his foot? Discouraged him from letting aspartame build up in his elbows?

She and Hugo were a codependent couple but celibate. If they actually were celibate. Laura's appearance gave away nothing about her sexuality. She seemed hyperevolved, like she got mineral injections instead of fucking. But those were the people you could never tell about. The ones who turned out to be the most inventive, the most depraved. It was no wonder Hugo's actual wives didn't stick around. Laura filled every role—colleague, lover, confidant—with irksome competence.

"This was supposed to be a family activity," Hugo said. He wasn't shouting anymore.

I said, "Family?"

We all looked at each other. Spencer laughed. Laura opened her mouth to say something, but then closed it again. Hugo snatched his racket from her and stalked off toward the house.

I walked back with Laura across the field, Spencer ambling behind us. The grass was dry and minutely longer than the day before. Itchy on the ankles. I sensed that with infinite resources I could easily lose my mind about the grass. I, too, could get a lawn disease. It would take no time at all. Poverty was sanity's best enforcer, it turned out. A crazed billionaire lurked in all of us, ready to have the lawn mowed on the hour.

Laura strode along in my periphery. Sweat had plastered a curl of hair to her cheek. I suspected she would not let things go without comment, and I was right.

She motioned behind us with her tennis racket. "Sorry you had to witness that back there."

"No," I said. "It was fine."

"You have to understand how upset he is. He doesn't handle things like this well."

"Things like what?"

"Change. Getting older. Recognizing endings."

"Mixed doubles," I offered.

She laughed softly. "Exactly. Anything, anything."

I admitted it had been a little weird that I had been there at all, witnessing what seemed like a personal conflict between the two of them. I spoke carefully. She had an easy authority that inspired respect without demanding it. I wondered when she had last been condescended to, and what had become of the person who'd done it.

Laura smirked. "Actually, that part wasn't weird. It's not the first time he's brought around someone . . . from the staff before. I've gotten used to it. I'm sure Spencer has, too."

She pronounced *from the staff* so that its meaning was unmistakable. I laughed, surprised. Of course, everyone's behavior so far had indicated that he brought young women here often. Ana and Spencer had integrated my presence instantly. But I had thought, or anyway wanted to think, that they liked me.

"I meant for me," I said. "It was weird for me."

"Oh," she said. "Right. For you. Well, sure."

We had reached the pool. We stopped in front of the deep end. Spencer overtook us, and, shucking off his shirt, jumped in. He stayed down there awhile, hovering near the bottom. He had an impressive lung capacity. His dark, slick hair floated kelplike above his head. I imagined how our voices must have sounded to him down there: distant, stripped of malice. Harmless and melodic as wind chimes.

Laura and I stood regarding each other. She was tan and stylish, in her sixties, but looked a decade younger. Her appearance was without fault. I wanted badly to land an insult like she had, to prove that I, too, was complex enough to possess a cruel streak.

"You guys are too old for all this, don't you think?" I said. "Huh?"

"This 'will they/won't they.' It's a little adolescent."

She made a dismissive gesture, a brush of her hand. "You don't know what you're talking about."

"Yes I do," I said. "It's not so hard to tell what's going on."

Spencer came up and went back down again. He swam the short length of the pool, flipped deftly underwater, swam back to the other wall. He continued back and forth like a metronome, without coming up for breath.

"No you don't," she said. "You strike me as a person who doesn't know very much about the world."

Hugo flashed by the kitchen windows in his whites. A chorus of cicadas rose from the grass like applause. I waited until it died back down to respond.

I did know something about the world, I told her. Everyone did. Except maybe those dudes Plato talked about, turned around backward, looking at the shadows. But even they weren't actually wrong.

She stared at me. "Are you talking about the allegory of the cave?"

"Yeah. That."

"They *were* wrong, the prisoners. That was the whole point. That they were wrong. Their perceptions were limited. They thought the shadows were everything. All of life. They didn't have the rest of the information."

"I thought the whole point was who's to say? Who's to say whose perceptions are right?"

"No." She was getting frustrated. "An objective reality exists. The world isn't made up of just shadows on the wall of a cave."

"Maybe it is," I said.

She said, "Look around. Are we in a cave right now?"

I looked left and right. We were very obviously not in a cave. We were standing next to a swimming pool in high spring. I was staring at a hydrangea bush, its conical blooms a saturated blue.

"There might be one nearby," I said.

Spencer splashed to the surface. His wet head bobbed near our feet. He blew his nose into his palm. Twice, three times.

"What are you guys talking about?"

She said, "Nothing," at the same time I said, "Spelunking."

Laura shook her head. "Listen, it's fine that you're here. It's good. He needs a distraction this weekend, God knows. So enjoy yourself. Post photos, text your friends. It'll be a nice memory for you when you're my age. But don't get confused about what it means. Because it doesn't mean anything. Not to him anyway. So it's better if you don't have any illusions about that. He's not going to do anything for you. He's not going to change your life. Trust me, it hasn't even occurred to him."

There were a lot of reasons to suck up to Laura. She'd been my boss until two days ago. She could give me a job if she wanted to, somewhere down the line. But people kept telling me how to feel around Hugo, and it made me want to do the opposite.

"You're wrong," I said to Laura.

"What?"

"You're wrong about him. He's not as shallow as you think he is."

She laughed. "He's exactly as shallow as I think he is. I've known him for forty years. You've hung out with him for two days. Part of the time you were sleeping. Presumably."

Spencer lifted himself out of the pool. I thought he was

going to intervene, but he only shook the water out of his ears and kept going. He walked into the house, shorts slicked to his legs. I saw him open the refrigerator and take out a jar of pickles.

"Look at that," she said. "We made Spencer uncomfortable."

"He'll be fine," I said. "I think he's just hungry."

She laughed and her posture relaxed a little.

"Women should not fight like this," she said. "We should support each other. Build each other up. We have enough working against us as it is."

Laura wasn't exactly a gold-star feminist. She'd had a great career, sure, made a name for herself in one of the most hostile, male-dominated industries in the world. But in the mid-2000s, during the Kitty Rosenthal controversy, she'd stood by Hugo, refusing to drop him as a client. She'd raised questions about Kitty Rosenthal's past. Her shoplifting arrest, her bad grades.

She'd even defended him, in *People* magazine. I remembered reading it. Hugo had done so much, she said. He was the source of a lot of joy. Banning someone forever for one incident, ruining his career, closing the gates to him and never letting him back in, was about as hypocritical as it got. If we, as a culture, didn't believe in rehabilitation, in the ability of people to change, what basis did we have for a justice system? Why were we bothering to incarcerate people instead of just executing them outright?

Growth was possible, she said. For Hugo personally and the industry at large. Hugo was going to rehab for his substance abuse issues and sex addiction. After that he'd go to therapy, and she believed he'd learn from it. She believed he'd emerge a better person.

"Okay, sure," I said to Laura. "Let's get along."

She surprised me by leaning in for a hug. Our second wooden hug of the day. Her attempts at warmth seemed like first-generation AI. Uncanny valley territory, still some kinks to work out.

"I'm only thinking of you," she said. "Your best interest."

Nothing could have been more false. I was secondary to whatever was going on between her and Hugo. I was a footnote, wrought in tiny font, superfluous and soon forgotten.

"I know," I said. "Thank you."

"You should email me when you're back in the city. Maybe I can help you find your next job. I know a few people."

She smiled. Her phoniness was a leash, leading me along.

"That's nice of you," I said. "I will."

I knew I'd email her, eventually. But I'd wait until I'd exhausted every possible option. Only when I was desperate, without pride, down to mining my most tenuous contacts, only at the witching hour in the long, dark night of unemployment, would I finally email her. I could already see the subject line: *Hi!* And she'd help me, too. I believed she would. She'd connect me with whoever, her dear friend who was staffing a show, a producer she knew from way back in need of an assistant. I would be grateful and she would be gracious and we'd treat each other like this weekend never happened.

Laura walked away toward the house, letting her racket spin loosely in her hand. There was a slight brag in her step. I was tempted by a tennis metaphor. The word *ace* crossed my mind. But it wasn't quite right, because I had gotten a piece of it, hadn't I? I had tried for it anyway.

————

I texted Julian afterward for everything he knew about Laura. She came from old California money, he told me, Sacramento. The kind of people who called their house the ranch, their father Father, their maid the girl. She'd gone to USC, never married. She and Hugo had met in the seventies at one of the comedy clubs. She wasn't a groupie exactly. She was too smart for that. She saw there was money to be made and started managing comedians. They were a couple for a while. Hugo was her main client and then her only client. In the early days of the show she'd been famously ruthless. She'd alienated people that way. The network had attempted a coup at one point, but she survived because Hugo backed her up. The two of them were a package deal; he wouldn't do the show without her. Oh, and she had a loft in Tribeca that had been featured in *Architectural Digest*. There was a Warhol in her dining room, a big aqua-lipped Mao. Two cute rescue dogs. She rode a bike to work.

A moment passed. Pulsing ellipses. He was thinking.

Why? he wrote at last.

I told him I was at Hugo's house, long story, I'd just had a run-in with her. Immediately, he called me.

"For real?" he said.

"Yes."

"It's so unfair. Girls get opportunities that guys just don't."

"You're not serious."

"What's the house like?"

"Big, bright, a little sterile. Green-tiled pool. It's got this weird basement. And there's a son here."

"A son?"

"His son."

"Oh, Spencer Best. No shit. You know, you could be

describing this better. I'm having trouble seeing it. Can I ask you a favor?"

"Is it *Mates*-related?"

"Okay, fine. Forget it."

"I'm not mentioning *Mates*."

"I said forget it."

I was sitting on a lounger next to the pool. Inside, Spencer had finished with the pickles and was fixing himself another drink. I didn't know where Laura and Hugo had gone. Up to Hugo's room, maybe, to have sex or kill each other.

I had an idea. "There's a party here tomorrow. Do you want to come?"

"You're allowed to invite people?"

No one had told me I wasn't. "Probably?"

"Are people gonna be like, 'Who's this twerp? What's he doing here?'"

"It's supposed to be big. I don't think anyone will notice you."

"Well, perfect."

"Will you promise me you won't bring up *Mates*, though?"

"I won't bring it up. But if it *comes up* organically . . ."

"Julian," I said.

My voice sounded plaintive. Even I could hear it.

"Wait, is something wrong?"

"Not really," I said. "It's just," I thought a moment. "You know how things aren't fun?"

I didn't know why I kept coming back to that.

"What do you mean?"

"You know. How everything that seems like it's going to be fun ends up being tense and sort of terrible. How nothing really lives up to its promise."

"Come on," he said. "Some things are fun."

"Name one fun thing."

He considered it. "I don't know. For me, Groucho Marx. Willie Mays, the second movement of the Jupiter Symphony, Louis Armstrong's recording of 'Potato Head Blues.' Swedish movies, naturally." He was quoting from *Manhattan*. "The crabs at Sam Wo's. Tracy's face."

"Gross," I said.

"Sorry. What about memes? Memes are fun."

"All right," I said. "Memes and nothing else."

We were quiet and I listened to the background noise, trying to figure out where he was. In his burrow in the West Village or his parents' house in New Jersey or outside a restaurant while a friend waited inside. I couldn't figure it out. I couldn't hear much over his breathing. I listened to that until it started to seem too intimate.

Julian and I didn't hang out outside of work. I'd been to his place only the once, to bring him his laptop when he forgot it at the office, and he'd never been to mine. It was a tacit rule we had. I didn't know why or how it originated, but it served us. Sometimes we texted, but otherwise we didn't exist to each other once we left the office. The single context, Monday through Friday, work clothes only, created a curious type of freedom. It limited your personality to a handful of easily managed traits. To Julian I was hardworking and reserved, serious and trustworthy, receptive to jokes. That was about as much as he knew. His coming here would break our rule. Talking on the phone was already breaking it.

"So you'll come tomorrow?" I said.

He hesitated. "I don't know, man. You ever get the feeling he doesn't like me?"

"Hugo?" I said. "No way. He likes you. He definitely likes you."

"Wow, you're a bad liar."

"He likes you," I repeated. "Why does it matter anyway? It'll be a party. He'll be distracted. He'll be drunk. He'll barely look at us. There will be women there. You know how he is with women."

This last statement went too far. Silence swelled between us again. I could tell he wanted to ask what exactly I was doing there. How it had happened, what it was all leading up to. Maybe he wanted to ask about my safety. If he had I would have insisted I was fine. It was a reflex, the *I'm fine*, honed over years of being one of the only women in the office.

"Can you just come?" I said. I sounded plaintive again.

"Okay," he said at last. "I'll come. But only because I'm a brazen careerist."

I told him what time to show up, guessing. He agonized for another minute about whether he should bring something.

"Wine?" he said. "Is it a wine kind of party? Beer?"

"You don't have to bring something," I said.

"June," he said. "Really." And we hung up.

———————

Laura left after she had another fight with Hugo, in the driveway this time. I watched them through Spencer's bedroom window. It was still bright out and the wind had risen. It wrapped Laura's ponytail around her neck like a platinum scarf. She had put on sunglasses, giant tortoiseshell cat eyes that covered most of her face. He was drinking a Diet Coke again, maybe to annoy her, and the can shone as he gestured with it. I couldn't hear what they were saying.

I stood in a hole I'd cleared in the debris on the floor. I'd released a rich, skunky smell carving it out. I felt angry. This wasn't exactly the romp I'd envisioned. Though what had I envisioned? Something glamorous, intimate. Something exciting, at least. For sure it hadn't involved kicking a damp UConn sweatshirt and history textbook out of the way the better to spy on two old people fighting.

Laura sat in the car now. It was an Audi. Tiny and low to the ground. Hugo bent way over to lean into the open window, tennis shirt sticking to the meaty hemispheres of his lower back.

I sat down on the bed, tired. It hadn't been made since the night before and the sheets were rumpled. I lay back and smelled Spencer even more strongly. His deodorant, his shampoo. I thought of him lying in the same spot. Sweating faintly, or touching himself, or just thinking. What did Spencer think about when he lay there thinking? I felt turned on and weary, a new combination, and closed my eyes against the feeling.

I woke up to Hugo rubbing the place where my jaw met my ear. It took me a minute to locate myself in Spencer's room. The model airplane finally tipped me off.

"You fell asleep," said Hugo. "In the creature's lair."

He had changed out of his tennis clothes into a thin cashmere sweater. His hair was wet from the shower. I'd thought I might dream about Spencer but I hadn't. I'd dreamed about

Hugo and Laura. White-clothed figures on a dark gray drive-way. In the dream they were my parents, arguing over who was going to take me. Take me where? I didn't know. Neither of them wanted to.

"Would you like to eat something?" said Hugo. "Noam cooked."

Noam again. He'd been there, braised some lamb, and gone. I couldn't help but picture an actual gnome. A tiny bearded guy sneaking in to perform magic while the mortals slept, then departing without a trace.

"Does he have a beard?" I asked.

"What?" said Hugo.

He was touching my hair now. Holding a curl between his forefinger and thumb. Pulling it straight and watching it spring back.

"Noam. Like a gnome? Never mind."

"I'm sorry about before," said Hugo.

He could have been referring to a lot of things. Laura's sur-prise arrival, the tennis match, the argument in the driveway. Leaving me stranded for hours with his seventeen-year-old son.

"We have a history, Laura and me. We've known each other longer than you've been alive. It makes things com-plicated."

I watched the underside of his chin. The skin was smooth and red. It looked manually tightened. He was only ever clean-shaven—he kept an electric razor in his office, paced around shaving while he talked to Gil—and I wondered how he'd look if he wasn't. Older, crazier, kinder.

"Okay," I said.

"You're angry."

"You left me here with Spencer for most of the day."

"It couldn't be helped."

"Should I even ask what that lunch was about?"

"Probably not."

"Why didn't you tell me Laura was coming over? You made me look stupid."

He looked away, out the window, up at the model airplane. I expected him to launch into a story about the plane. How he and Spencer had built it and Spencer had been texting the whole time. How he had built it for Spencer and Spencer had shrugged. How they'd built it together as a part of some scouting experience and it had been their last best bonding moment before everything fell apart. But he didn't.

He said, "You're right. I should have told you."

"Were you drunk when you drove us back from Roman's yesterday?"

"Now you're reaching." He paused. "You're going to feel better after Noam's lamb. Do you like sauces? There's a creamy yogurt sauce that goes with it. Of course you do. Everyone likes sauces."

"I don't think that's true. I think some people have a textural issue with them."

He blinked at me.

"Were you stabbed?" I said.

I reached for his side, where Spencer had touched me, and felt for the raised ridge of a scar. He shifted away before I could feel anything under the soft fabric of his sweater.

"I shouldn't have left you two alone," he said.

"But it happened, right? A lady stabbed you. A fan. On Sunset? The bouncer pulled her off you. You took a cab to the hospital, blood sloshing all over the place."

"Spencer's got an active imagination."

"But some version of that happened."

He rose and opened the window. Cool air reached in like an arm and the airplane twisted in the breeze. He peeked down at the driveway like Laura might still be out there, glaring up at him, waiting for him to come down for another round.

"I have one more thing to tell you, in the spirit of openness. I've got a tiny obligation tomorrow before the party. An interview."

"Oh no," I said. "TV?"

"Casey Caruso from E! News."

I pictured a crew trampling in with boom mics and gaff tape. The host in a jewel-toned dress. Her huge white veneers that made no pretense of looking like real teeth. The B-roll they'd shoot of Hugo strolling pensively across the lawn, eating a peach in the kitchen, laughing with his son.

"God," I said. "Casey Caruso."

"She's hardly the worst of them. Being interviewed by her is less bad than going to the DMV. Marginally. Her cohost now, what's that moron's name?"

"Richie something."

"Yeah Richie whatever. That guy is so much worse. We did one of those entertain-the-troops things together during the Iraq War. I did stand-up. I don't remember what the hell he did. He's got no actual skills. He's tiny and his suits are tiny. If you looked at the size on the tag it just says T for tiny. Maybe he was the MC. Oh, and he pronounces Iraq with a long I, all folksy. AYE-raq. I mean I'm not that smart, I'm only celebrity smart. But that guy. He's stupid for the record books."

"Celebrity smart," I said. "Like I'm normal person attractive."

He looked down at me. A little tenderly, I thought. "Hey, I'm the one deprecating here."

We had left discussion of Laura behind and I didn't see us returning to it. We were back in the realm of the antic tale. Richie whatever, the Hollywood asshole. He had apologized and it had been weak, but it would have to be enough. It was the best I was going to get.

"They told me it's only a five-minute segment. They'll be in and out."

"All right," I said.

He took my hand and helped me sit up. Maybe he sensed that his apology had been inadequate because he said, "You can be in it if you want." He was still holding my hand. "The segment. Do you want to be in it?"

"Okay," I said.

He laughed. "Actually, I don't know why I said that. You probably can't be in it."

"No, of course not," I said. "Obviously I can't be in it."

He looked at me sadly and I felt sad, too. Why this should make us sad I didn't know. We went downstairs for dinner.

———

Hugo had an idea, he told us, chewing. Ana materialized to bus our plates as we finished with them. We sat in slim-legged burnt-orange chairs at a dining table the size of a landing strip. They tilted us forward slightly, made the conversation feel intent. Hugo was at the head of the table and Spencer and I sat across from each other. Spencer seemed sober now. He wasn't ignoring me and he wasn't making pointed eye contact either. He wasn't trying to nudge me under the table. He seemed so fully recovered from our encounter that I doubted for a moment that it had even happened. He'd taken off his hat to eat dinner. Maybe his dad had a rule.

Hugo held up the flyer the pizza guy handed me the day before.

"Frogger's," he said.

The flyer's slick surface caught the sun and gleamed like a medal. The light in the dining room had a pink quality that seemed impossible. Students of light called it magic hour. Magically, we were all going to ignore the events of the afternoon and press gallantly onward.

"Nooo," said Spencer. "That townie bar?"

He met my eye, too evenly. I had seen this type of pretending before. I'd engaged in it myself. The whole first six months of dating someone tended to go this way. A contest: Who could care the least. Logan and I had been in that phase and possibly we'd never have left it.

I looked back at Spencer and saw a flicker that made his face look young. He glanced away. He wasn't great at it yet, wasn't practiced, but in time he would be. In time he'd be a monster just like everyone else. Just like Logan, just like me.

Ana passed through, setting down a pie in the middle of the table. It was cross-hatched and blueberry, the platonic ideal.

"You almost don't want to eat a pie like that," I said.

Hugo folded his napkin and tossed it onto the table. "Don't you think you deserve to consume something aesthetically perfect?"

"That's literally a pie," said Spencer. He was still acting cool. "That's what they all look like."

"It's what all pies aspire to," I said.

Ana ignored us and cut into it, wedged out a slice. "I've been to Frogger's." She scrunched up her nose. "It's nasty, but ladies drink for free on Tuesdays."

It said something about Frogger's that people kept citing this as its best quality.

"Think of how thrilled that pizza guy will be if I actually show up," said Hugo.

Hugo hadn't interacted with the pizza guy. He hadn't even seen him. How would he know which guy it was? How would he pick him out of the lineup of bad small-town comics? The validation Hugo could possibly get from two minutes of a stranger's excitement seemed insubstantial. A wisp. But what would we do all night otherwise? Sit around in the living room futzing with the remotes? Let the tension build further toward some sort of eruption? Google each other again?

"All right," I said. "Let's do it."

Spencer's mouth was full of pie. "I'm out. There are limits. I can't be seen there."

"By whom?" said Hugo. "Who would be there to see you?"

"Any other person," said Spencer. He had his phone out. He was texting. "Just any other living person."

I was relieved he would not be coming. He would stay behind to smoke more weed and play video games. If he felt lonely, if he felt unmoored by what happened in the bunker, he'd text his friend Scotty a GIF, and Scotty would text back the crying-laughing emoji. Or he'd get Colby to come over, look the other way on the chiropractor issue, smoke her up in the basement rec room even though the Wi-Fi sucked down there. Do whatever it was they did together. Either way, the moment would pass.

"Wear closed-toed shoes," Ana said to me. "It's got a dirt floor."

"What?" I said.

"Frogger's," said Ana. "For summer."

"I think it's supposed to be sand," said Spencer.

I didn't see how the proprietors of Frogger's could aim for sand and miss. It either was sand or it wasn't. But this seemed like a quibble and anyway there was a pie to eat. A pie that was, depending on whom you asked, too good for me, so characteristic it was below discussion, or the exact pie I deserved.

"This will be fun," said Hugo.

I wanted very much to believe him.

———————

Every summer, in advance of Memorial Day weekend, Tommy Frogger's Bar and Grill became, with the help of thirty-six tons of local sand, Tommy Frogger's Beach. The transformation lasted through Labor Day and they brought in another ten tons over the Fourth to replenish. We were lucky to be there while it was still fresh, the bartender told me. People tended to drop things—napkins, drinks, change, straw wrappers, forks, mozzarella sticks, wads of gum—and also to puke.

Ana was right. It looked like dirt.

The bartender smiled at me apologetically. What I had to understand was that the beaches of Long Island Sound were mainly formed by headland erosion, which meant you got a lot of silt. And the sand didn't look like sand per se, not like the sand you'd see on the Cape or somewhere. Those were quartz beaches, those stunning yellow cliffs. Different thing entirely.

"Plus," he said. I got the feeling he gave this explanation a lot. "How much do you know about glaciers?"

"They're giant chunks of ice."

"Well, yeah. The size of apartment buildings. And they move slowly, grinding, grinding, grinding. Grinding the shit out of everything. Picking stuff up and moving it elsewhere as they melt. The Wisconsin glaciation: That's what formed Long Island. So it's sediment in the Sound. And lots of small rocks."

He looked proud of himself. He'd done some research, learned a term. He had a small diamond earring and a goatee. He set my margarita on a cardboard coaster. I licked its salty rim and turned to take in the room. The vibe was confused. An old arcade game sat in the corner, Frogger, the bar's namesake. But even this was muddled by the assertion, right there in the name of the place, that Tommy Frogger was a person.

The rest of the furniture sat on top of the sand—I could tell that they'd taken everything out before putting the sand in, then set it back on top. The spool-shaped tables and varnished wooden chairs listed at random angles. It gave the bar a shipwrecked quality, like it had all washed up there and Tommy Frogger had deemed the arrangement good enough.

Most of the chairs were full. The crowd was in early middle age and largely sunburned. The women wore tank tops, the men cabana shirts. A crop of teens occupied one spool, mall goths drinking sodas out of tall red glasses. I wondered if they were friends of the pizza guy. They seemed around his age. They were trying to rearrange their chairs so they faced the stage in back. Finally one of them, a girl with streaky green hair, emptied her glass into the sand before getting down on her hands and knees and using it to dig around the chair legs.

With difficulty, Hugo picked his way back from the men's room.

I handed him his whiskey. "Was there sand in the bathroom?"

"Yes, but not on purpose. Some had gotten in. In the sink, too, God knows how."

"Should we try for a table?"

"Over here."

He led the way, mounting brown dunes in Italian loafers. He'd staked out a table near the stage, laid his sport coat over the back of a chair.

We sat down and the lights dimmed. The MC was balding. He had a round little belly like a second head. His gray T-shirt held the sweaty imprint of it, a perfect circle. He was doing the one about his girlfriend's tits. How they had gotten so huge since she'd had a baby. It confused him, the bit went. They were great now, but also off-limits. A food source for someone else. How fair was that?

The joke included an impression of the baby nursing. His kid, probably. He smacked his lips and made a high-pitched gurgling sound. People were laughing, even the women in the room. Sand crawled up my ankles and into my shoes. I waited for a twist, for a second level, but none came.

I had been to many terrible open mics. I'd performed at them myself, and watched my friends perform. This was not even the worst I had seen. At least this one had an audience. At least they knew a performance was going on.

Once, when we still lived in the East Village, Audrey dragged me to a comedy night at a coffee shop in the neighborhood.

We would both try out new material, was the idea. Audrey went first and I recognized our error as soon as she stepped onstage. The lights were on and everyone was sober. People sat in front of laptops wearing headphones. Audrey had to shout over the squeal of the milk steamer, the construction outside, the chiming cash register. At one point, a middle-aged woman came in selling individually wrapped roses and porn DVDs out of a black Hefty bag.

When it was my turn, I couldn't do it. I got up and walked outside, watched through the window as they determined that no one named June Bloom was coming up to perform. Audrey found me standing outside the entrance, blowing into my cupped hands. She was furious. She brooded the whole way home, up Second, down Twelfth, up the stairs, down the hall, but didn't speak until we were back in our apartment.

"You don't take risks," she said finally.

"I don't take pointless risks," I corrected her.

I hung my coat on the rickety wooden rack left by the last tenant. It already held six coats, plus hats, scarves, two messenger bags, and a layer of stray mittens strewn across the top like mulch.

"It's too full," she said.

I added my wool beanie. The rack wobbled but held. I felt minorly victorious.

"You're just mad that you went and I didn't," I said.

"We were both supposed to do it. That was the plan."

"But it was so bad." I laughed. "I don't know if you could see, but there was a guy Skyping in the corner. There were no talent scouts there. No bookers. No one was going to sign me. No one was even paying attention. You'd have walked out, too."

"No I wouldn't have," she said. "Not if you went first."

"Don't make this a loyalty thing. The porn lady came in while you were up there. A guy bought a rose from her and gave it to the woman he was with."

"That's exactly why you should have gone. Because that happened."

She added her coat to the rack and we stood waiting for it to fall. It didn't.

"All right," I said. "I'm out for myself. What else?"

"Too easily embarrassed."

The night had been legitimately embarrassing, I told her. Some things just were. Most things. So I had a low threshold for it. That I was willing to concede.

"Big of you," she said.

She hung her bag on the one remaining spoke and backed away slowly toward her bedroom.

"We have to get a new one of those," she said.

I doubted that we'd ever buy a new coat rack. It was so far down my list it was on a second sheet of paper.

"Maybe they have one at the dollar store," I said. "I'll look for one."

"You won't." She said it with sadness, and finality, like that was what we'd been arguing about the whole time. Affordable coat racks and where to find them.

The pizza guy was up right after a Sacred Heart frat boy who talked mostly about parties he'd been to with his brothers. Everything he mentioned was a borderline crime. "*I love to pee off porches,*" he said. "*If I had a choice I would pee off porches for the rest of my life. Or on cars. That time was good, too.*" Outdoors beat indoors for peeing. He moved on to girls he'd hooked up with and I became worried that he was going to incriminate himself.

When the pizza guy walked onstage he was unmistakable. Hugo glanced at me to confirm it was him and I nodded. I don't know what identified him as a delivery boy—he was not wearing his uniform—but it was somehow apparent. He started speaking and it became even more apparent.

"I have a job you might care to hear about," he began. "I deliver pizzas for Paolo's right across the street."

The audience turned around to look.

"You can't see it from here. Why would you guys need to confirm its existence anyway? *Better fact check this one. See if he's telling the truth.* If I was going to make up a job for myself, I'd do better than delivery boy, believe me."

The audience laughed. He wasn't bad. I sipped my drink and felt my shoulders relax. Bombing was as awful for the audience as it was for the comedian. When the scorn ran out that left only empathy. Then you were in the unfortunate position of having to *feel* for the guy, cringe along with him, immerse yourself in his regrets like an oatmeal bath.

"So on paper it's admittedly not the best job. But I'll tell you what's great about it. Other than free pizza, which is never a bad thing. What's great about it is that you get to see the inside of people's homes. People who order pizza from Paolo's have nice shit. Also, weird shit. And there's a third category: nice weird shit. I'll give you an example: antique Ouija board. I'll give you another example: snake tank with three rare snakes. Final example: chair specifically for fucking."

Next to me, Hugo was laughing. He'd always been a generous laugh on the show. Leaning forward and back, slapping his desk in hilarity. Taking a sip of water from his mug and nearly spitting it out. I guess he had to be. He had to put his guests at ease. But there was no reason for him to be laughing now, no reason except genuine amusement. I thought it said something about him that he could still be entertained, that he had not been pickled by so many years in the business. Not fully anyway, not through and through.

"Another good thing about my job," the pizza guy was saying, "is all the great friends I make. Well, not friends per se, but acquaintances. Pizza friends, I like to call them. Some of these people, these pizza friends, have a tendency to expedite the getting-to-know-you process. Do pizza friends respect social boundaries? No. Pizza friends do not. Do pizza friends spend years gradually growing more comfortable with you, slowly and reciprocally peeling back layers of the self, onionlike, until the two of you reach a certain level of intimacy? No. Pizza friends do not have time. Pizza friends need a bunch of old encyclopedias moved and expect you to pitch in. Pizza friends will ask you to help them with their fly because their arm is in a cast, even though you really, really don't want to."

He finished up and everyone applauded. Hugo hollered at him through cupped hands. The pizza guy smiled unguardedly and I remembered what I had told him yesterday about finding some worthier pursuit. I had probably seemed as creepy and overfamiliar as one of his customers.

The MC returned to the stage and I trekked back across the sand to get us another round.

The bartender poured my margarita from a silver shaker. "Are you enjoying the show?"

"Sure," I said. "Parts of it. That last kid was good."

"He's all right. Gets to be a lot of pizza talk after a while. He's in here every week doing his pizza stuff. He should branch out, you know?"

He slid me the glass, frosty and glacier green.

"What would you have him talk about?"

"I don't know," he said. "His family, a bad date, the news, whatever."

I felt offended on behalf of the pizza guy. The bartender had to be there, but no one was making him listen. He was free to retreat to his thoughts at any moment, polish a glass, hum the "Battle Hymn of the Republic." He was free to remember lost loves, their faces and bodies, recount to himself what had gone wrong. Nothing tethered him to the here and now. His mind was his own no matter what.

"Oh shit," said the bartender.

"What?"

He pointed at the stage. The crowd was applauding again. Really cheering. Some of them rose to their feet, then they all did. I understood what was happening immediately. I felt foolish not to have seen it coming. The basement comedy club should have prepared me, if not the years of observing him.

Hugo mounted the stage and accepted a hug from the MC. The audience sat down, though it took awhile. Whenever the applause began to dwindle, someone let out a shout and it started up all over again.

"Hi," said Hugo at last. "Hello."

I had never seen him do stand-up live before. By the time I made it to New York he had mostly stopped. His last big show had been New Years Eve 1999 at Carnegie Hall. Red Hot Chili Peppers had opened. At midnight, balloons fell from the ceiling and ushers passed out champagne in real glass flutes. Bony came out to play "Auld Lang Syne" in a shiny purple tux.

I remembered that night well. I was in seventh grade, at a

party at Andrew O'Hagan's house. It was dull even by middle school standards. Someone had secured a six-pack of Icehouse and we had shared it among ten of us. Warm, bitter, and not enough of it: my first drink. We watched the ball drop and waited for Y2K, whatever that might have entailed. Electronics fizzling off, weak sparks preceding darkness. That was how I began the century, holding my breath in a rec room for a disaster that didn't arrive. And meanwhile Hugo was eight hundred miles uptown in a tuxedo, doing the one about the end of the world.

"I'm so happy to be here tonight at Frogger's," Hugo was saying. "You know, I've played a lot of rooms, but never one"—he paused, looked down at the floor, up at the disco ball unmoving in the center of the ceiling—"quite like this."

I watched the Carnegie Hall performance years later, sitting in a cubicle in my college media center. He looked grainy in the video, greenish, and the audio peaked when people cheered. But it still amazed me, the nerve of it. Claiming a place among the maestros—Leonard Bernstein, Toscanini—to tell jokes. To speak out loud some thoughts he'd had. Notions, he'd called them.

"Hey, that last guy was good, wasn't he?" Hugo addressed the pizza guy directly. "Maybe you can help me get a job over at Paolo's now that I'm out of work."

I could only see the kid's back, but his delight was obvious. His head bobbed up and down on his skinny neck.

"We're not hiring," he said. "But I can take your information to keep on file."

"Oh sure," said Hugo. "I'll just write down my personal email and phone number for you. Would that work? You already have my address."

He didn't have to do much up there. His outsized presence was enough. He could have done the Our Father and gotten laughs. He could have read from the phone book.

"I guess you're wondering what I'm doing here," said Hugo. "I'm here with a friend. That's her at the bar. The mortified one. Wave to everybody, June."

They all turned around and looked at me. I raised a tentative hand.

"June heard about this place," he said. "She's got her ear to the pavement, that June. She heard the open mic night was supposed to be good. Isn't that right?"

I nodded. "Sort of."

Someone was taking video. A few people, actually. I counted three with their phones in the air. It would be on the Internet tomorrow. Millions would hear my muffled "sort of."

"June is visiting from New York City," he said. "Great town. Have you guys ever been?"

Laughter, boos. It was a forty-minute train ride away.

"You haven't, huh? Well, it's one for the bucket list. Let me tell you. Have you guys heard about Brooklyn? Lots happening over there. I haven't been personally, but from what I understand, it's a whole borough devoted to eating breakfast late in the day. Everyone there is something called an influencer. June, am I getting that right?"

The crowd turned and looked at me again.

"More or less."

I sipped my drink.

"Sorry, June. I'm not quite done with you. Tell them where you live."

"Bushwick," I said.

More boos, this time from the table of kids.

He said to me, "You hear that? The kids are booing Bush-wick. Must be time to move again."

He took a couple of steps toward them. "You guys seem smart. While I've got you here, maybe you can help me understand my son. One of us is an asshole and I'm trying to figure out who."

He went on like that for a while. The jokes were unre-markable, but the crowd's enthusiasm made up for it. He grew red from the neck up, and half-moons of sweat formed in each armpit. I began to wonder if he would ever leave the stage. He was more animated than I'd seen him the entire last season of *Stay Up*. It made me wonder why he had spent twenty-five years shackled to a prop desk. He didn't like it, I realized now. He hadn't liked it for a long time.

Afterward, he bought a round of drinks for the whole bar. He made the bartender turn on the disco ball. He took over the music and played "The Weight" and everyone sang along. The windows fogged up. I found myself drinking my third margarita alone near the Frogger console. Hugo'd brought me there to make up with me and show me a good time and already he'd forgotten. I decided to step outside.

We were in a brick strip mall with green roofing. Wal-greens, liquor store, nail salon. It was nice, as strip malls went. We had taken the MG again and it was parked next to a big black Hummer with chrome trim. I thought maybe I could drive home this time if I got my bearings.

I walked into the Walgreens and browsed the aisles. It was cold and dry and smelled like packaging. Any Walgreens in the world would have that smell. I looked around for some-thing to buy. I wanted the tactile experience of handing over bills and getting back coins. I put some things in a basket. A bottle of water, two packs of waxed mint floss.

I watched a young woman shelve cough syrup for a while. She seemed calm, spaced out, like she was on the cough syrup herself. It was the same look I'd seen on the face of the shopgirl the day before. Boredom so total it delivered you to the astral plane. I knew the feeling from my agent's assistant days, my audience page days, my receptionist days. You could function in that zone. Answer the phone or take an inventory of the supply closet. Chat pleasantly with tourists from Michigan. Meanwhile your brain made the connecting sound of the early Internet and played a video of a dog you'd never laid eyes on running through a field.

There were days as a receptionist that I felt sure I'd fall asleep. I worked far from any windows and the artificial light drained me. I used the bowl of Werther's Originals we kept next to the visitor sign-in sheet to devise a reward system. Answer three phone calls, get a Werther's. Make it to eleven o'clock, get a Werther's. One hour left in the day, Werther's. The people who came and went from the office, who stood pressing the down button and checking the time, who were headed out to rehearsal or to lunch or to tape segments, could not have suspected that someone in their midst was so bored or eating so much hard candy. After I was promoted I came to doubt it a little myself.

Hugo found me in the greeting card aisle with a fistful of condolences. All of them skirted the issue. Wishing you deep reserves of courage for the trials ahead. Hold tight to memories for comfort. Lean on your friends and family for strength. Don't forget to care for yourself in times of sadness.

"Who died?" he said. "Your fourth grandparent?"

"I was . . ." I looked down into my basket. I had added a purple desk fan. "Trying to sober up."

"Do you actually want any of that stuff?"

I shook my head. He took the basket from me and set it down at the end of the aisle.

"We'll just leave that here. Are you ready to go or do you want to get a flu shot? Have some photos developed? I think they have a blood pressure machine over here."

His shirt had mostly dried, though it was now very wrinkled. He smelled like whiskey and fried food.

"Did you eat something?" I said.

"I might have had some wings. They were there. It's not like I ordered them. Who are you . . . Laura?"

I followed him back out through the store. The woman who'd been stocking cough syrup had moved on to nail polish. We passed her on our way out and I could hear her humming to herself atonally. I had to stop myself from saying good-bye to her.

Outside, Hugo said, "A bunch of people from the bar are coming back to the house to hang out for a while. Maybe go for a swim. They'll follow us over."

I looked around. The crowd from Frogger's had spilled out into the parking lot. People leaned against the building smoking. The door opened and closed, letting out gasps of music and laughter.

"Oh. Really?"

"Yeah, just the MC, the frat guy, and a handful of teens."

He held the door of the MG open for me.

"I don't think . . ."

"I'm kidding. No one's coming back. I've got limits, believe it or not."

He opened the compartment that held the convertible top and accordioned it into place. Then he got in the front seat to adjust the mirrors. He seemed refreshed, almost manic. With a flourish, he put a piece of gum into his mouth. He snapped on a pair of driving gloves and I started to worry.

"Are you okay to drive?" I said.

"They really liked me in there." He looked away from the road to smile at me. "Maybe I'll get back into doing stand-up. It feels good, doesn't it?"

He was forgetting about all the ways it didn't. The bad lifestyle, uncertain income, self-doubt, hecklers, flat beer, empty clubs, hangers-on. The depressing people you encountered. The puking, fear, dry mouth, limp French fries. The cocaine cut with baby laxatives. The comedown. The deflation that hit ten, twenty, sixty minutes afterward, a day afterward, four days, even if you did well. The way your voice could sound so thin the first time it rang out in a quiet room. The way it made you seem vulnerable, young, old, sad, tired, wounded beyond repair. The way it gave away everything about you.

Or maybe those things never bothered him.

I said, "It can, yeah."

He gunned it through a yellow light. It was 10 p.m. and the road was mostly empty. He took a left turn that swung us wide into the other lane.

"What if you opened for me? We could go on the road. I haven't been on the road for years. Have you ever been on the road?"

"No."

"We've got to do it then. It'll be great. I'll get back to my roots. You'll work on your act. We'll live in hotels and see all the kooky shit they have out in America. Corn palace.

Big blue cow. World's largest frying pan. Do you like that kind of thing?"

"Yeah," I said. "That stuff's all right."

I allowed myself to imagine a road movie starring the two of us. Room service omelets, whiskey late at night. My act would get good. Then it'd get great. By then we'd be close. We'd take a day off and knock around a little town. In a used bookstore I'd find a first edition I wanted, Thurber or something, and he'd surprise me with it later. We'd stop only because I was getting too many offers. Movies, TV shows, a stand-up special. We'd fuck—why not? I pictured myself in a terry cloth bathrobe looking out a window, then I moved on to something else, our farewell show at Madison Square Garden. Hometown crowd, standing ovation, *I'm so happy to be back here in New York, city of my heart and my one true home.*

"Laura warned me not to expect anything from you."

"Fuck Laura. Laura's out of the picture. Laura doesn't get a say anymore."

"Since when?"

"Since today at twelve o'clock. We officially severed our professional relationship."

"The bad news lunch," I said.

"Are you laughing?"

"I'm sorry. It was just that you guys elected to play tennis after that. You chose to keep torturing each other when it would have been easy not to."

"That's me and Laura," he said grimly.

"So she's not your manager anymore?"

"She wants to"—he let go of the wheel to make air quotes—"move on to other projects."

We were in backcountry now, on an unlit road, and I
noticed for the first time that the round little headlights of
the car didn't do much. They gave off maybe four feet of
wobbly blue light.

"She thinks we've reached"—he made air quotes for a
second time—"a natural conclusion."

The car swerved slightly, the lights panning onto the
wooded shoulder.

"Can you maybe not do that? I can understand from your
tone when you're quoting her."

"Talk shows are over anyway. Done for. Any joke you make
on the show, any sexy little monologue joke, by the time it
airs, someone has already done it on Twitter but better. Twelve
somebodies have already done it better. You think you're fast,
clever, sexy. These people on the Internet are faster, cleverer,
sexier. And they're not even using their real names. They're
using some nonsense word and a blurry picture of a duck."

It unnerved me how much he was saying the word *sexy*.

He slammed the brakes: There was something in the road.

I shouted, "Opossum!"

It was the size of a dog. I saw its beady eyes flashing white
in the headlights. I saw its flesh-colored snout and grotesque,
curling tail. Then I was lurching forward. The MG had a few
flaws. The lap belt that had so charmed me earlier pinned my
hips to the seat. My head hit the dash. Next to me, a similar
thing was happening to Hugo. Only he wasn't wearing the
belt at all. His chest was driven into the steering wheel, his
head into the windshield. A crack webbed out from where
he'd hit. Somehow he managed to slide it into park.

We stopped a foot short of the opossum. I couldn't believe
it hadn't fled. Why hadn't it fled? Was it rabid or just stupid?

Was it trying to die? It looked at us for a second longer before slinking away. I watched its tail slide across the ground and out of the range of the headlights. Then I sat up.

I could already feel a bump forming on my forehead and my right hip hurt where the seat belt wrenched me back. Otherwise, I was fine.

"Are you okay?" I said to Hugo.

He didn't respond right away. The steering wheel had knocked the wind out of him. He had a cut somewhere on his head and I couldn't tell how bad it was. Blood dripped over one eye and splattered his shirtfront.

"I swallowed my gum," he said.

He sat up, touched his face with two fingers, looked down at his hand in wonder. He must have forgotten he was wearing gloves.

"My moneymaker," he said. He was joking.

I said, "It's bleeding a lot."

"Faces are really vascular. I remember that from when Spencer was little. He used to run face-first into furniture. It probably looks worse than it is."

"Do you have anything in here? A napkin or something?"

I opened the glove compartment. Pristine. No spill of documents, no owner's manual, no first aid kit. It was for his gloves and nothing more.

"This isn't the type of car you eat a burger in," he said.

I felt around under the seat.

He craned to catch a glimpse of himself in the rearview mirror. Blood ran from the tip of his nose and landed on the upholstery. "There's nothing under there. Let's go home. We're a couple miles away."

"I think you need stitches. Or anyway, a professional to

tell you that you don't. Let me take you to the hospital. Look at you. You're fucking up my car."

He started to smile, then grimaced in pain. "*Your* car."

I unbuckled my seat belt. "Yeah."

"You're driving?"

"Yeah."

"You were afraid yesterday."

"I'm not anymore. Come on. I'm serious."

He held his hands up in surrender. "Okay, okay."

We switched seats. I was still afraid, but it didn't matter. Nothing did. I felt good. I'd imagined a similar emergency in Roman's driveway, but I hadn't anticipated I'd like it. It must have been chemicals, the same chemicals that made scared moms able to lift semis off toddlers. Who were all these toddlers getting trapped under semis? I stomped on the clutch and the car made a horrible sound.

The hospital was easy to find. The soothing British voice of my cell phone GPS directed us to a brick building with windows of greenish glass.

"I'd marry her," Hugo said of the voice. "I'd lose everything for her."

The waiting room was full of potted flowers. A woman holding a toddler slept in one of the chairs. Across the room, an older couple hunched close together, whispering over a brochure. Hugo blinked through the blood. The spots on his shirt had dried brown.

"This is nice," he said. "I've never been here before."

We approached the front desk.

I said, "My friend hurt his moneymaker."

"We'll also be needing a new transmission," said Hugo.

We were enjoying ourselves. The ride had been fraught. I stalled out, ground the gears, soaked the gearshift in palm sweat, soaked my clothes. The engine whinnied like a young horse. By the end I was blowing through red lights just so I wouldn't have to downshift. Now it was over and we had made it. The adrenaline was wild. My pulse throbbed in the bump on my head.

The intake nurse cocked a drawn-on eyebrow. "Did either of you lose consciousness or vomit?"

Hugo winked at me with his good eye. "Not since Friday."

She took us to a back room and gave us paperwork to fill out while we waited. Hugo sat on the examination table and I took the low, spinning stool.

"You're remarkably bad at driving," he said. "It's impressive."

"Thanks."

He tapped his own head where my bump was. "Your horns are coming in."

I touched the bump at its tender center. The skin felt tight and hot. My hip throbbed where the seat belt had wrenched me back. Still, I had fared better than Hugo, who looked, with his bloody face and crazed smile, like a serial killer who'd just finished up for the night.

I said, "Don't you have a doctor of your own you want to do this? A plastic surgeon?"

"I don't give a fuck anymore. They can use a shoelace if they want."

Neither of us made any move to fill out papers. The doctor showed up and we continued our joking. She seemed neither amused nor unamused. She seemed tired and professional. She wore purple scrubs and a clean white coat. I held an ice pack to my head while she checked my eyes with a flashlight. She cleaned Hugo's face, found the cut up near his hairline, shot anesthetic into it, cinched it up with three staples.

She said, "My father's a fan." She held up her phone. "Do you mind?"

"You want me to call him?" said Hugo.

"Just a picture."

Hugo said, "No, let's call him."

She glanced at me to see if he was kidding. I shrugged.

"I'm serious," he said, and motioned for the phone.

The doctor called her father. It was late now, after eleven. I could hear his startled hello on the other end.

She said, "Dad, I'm here with Hugo Best. He just came into the ER. Laceration. Nothing serious. He wants to talk to you."

She handed over the phone.

Hugo said, by way of greeting, "Your girl just stapled me up like a pile of documents."

A nurse came in and asked for insurance cards. Hugo handed me his wallet so he wouldn't have to get off the phone. I fished through until I found it, and his driver's license, too. He was sixty-eight, three years older than he publicly claimed. At some point, a lifetime ago, those three years had made a difference. Now they didn't.

"Are we almost done here?" I said.

Hugo mouthed *sorry*, but made no move to hang up. He was talking about Philadelphia for some reason. I guess the doctor's father lived there.

I put the ice pack back on my forehead. The lump under-

neath it was a wooden knob. This was what it was like to be
with him. His attention was impossible to hold. I could take
my top off and he wouldn't look over. Not until he'd charmed
the random dad he had on the phone. Not until he'd made
the doctor smile.

Hugo hung up and asked her for a lollipop.

"Come on, I've been good, haven't I? You weren't exactly
gentle with that stapler."

He wouldn't change. That much I knew. I knew it from
how he acted at Frogger's. But what about me? I was mal-
leable. I could get used to it. People did it all the time. Just
look at Gypsy, a study in adaptability. She'd had her victories.
The house, the doula. And the rest she was willing to brush
off. I could be like Gypsy, and in time it wouldn't bother me
either. I could succeed where Allison and countless others
had failed.

The doctor shook her head affectionately. "You guys drive
safe."

———————

The diner was silver plated with a rotating neon sign. Just
what you'd want, Hugo said, pulling into the parking lot.
In the bathroom I looked at the bruise on my head. It was
reddish purple and not as tall as it felt. I knew it would turn
yellow and green over the next day, bloom into something
worse. I splashed water on my face and dried it with coarse
paper towels from the dispenser.

Back at the table, Hugo had ordered us coffee and a slice
of pie to share.

"More pie," I said.

"Diner pie," said Hugo. "Different thing entirely. That pie earlier was for impressing other people. All looks, no pesticides. This pie is for oneself."

I touched it with my fork. It had a pale crust of meringue on top, a trembling layer of lemon below. I didn't want it at all. Between the two, I'd take the pie with airs. But I was having coffee late at night with a famous comedian. This is what I had longed for. This is what I had, in my obscurity, been missing.

I took a bite. "It's too sweet."

"We need the sugar. We lost a lot of blood."

I sipped my coffee. We sat at a booth by the window. Every so often a pair of headlights swooped by. The place was empty except for a couple of guys in the corner. The waitress swiveled on a stool at the counter with one shoe off.

"Were you serious before about touring together?"

"Sure," he said. "I've got nothing better to do."

I tried not to let his answer hurt me. "That's not true. There's lots you could do."

"Like what?"

"You talked about traveling. So travel. Go ride camels in Morocco. Climb Kilimanjaro. Get some expensive outerwear. A shell. Some of those boots with a lot of different hooks."

"I've been already."

"Where?"

"Everywhere. Everywhere I'm interested in."

"Change directions, then. Do something totally different. Build houses in Haiti. Open a wine store in town. Run for public office. Write crime fiction. You like art—learn to paint. Go back to college. Be one of those late-in-life degree seekers, in it for all of the right reasons and none of the wrong ones."

He stirred more sugar into his coffee. "I'm not going to do any of that stuff."

"A sitcom, then. A movie. *Cruise Ship III: Even More Cruise Ship.*"

Hugo had starred in *Cruise Ship* in the nineties. He played a con man on the lam posing as a cruise ship director. He wore crisp maritime whites and a big fake mustache. The detectives who were after him also ended up on the cruise ship. It was somehow enough of a success to make a sequel. Kirstie Alley was in it. I could never remember how, in *Cruise Ship II*, they justified being on a cruise ship again.

"What else you got?" said Hugo.

The waitress came over and refilled our cups. Hugo seemed on the verge of getting her to weigh in. It was his favorite kind of thing to do. Especially because she looked twenty-five and wore a tight peach-colored uniform.

I took a breath. "How about this: Take your huge platform and use it to do some good. Promote some voices that don't get heard as much in comedy. Produce shows. Use your influence to get projects funded. Projects by people of color, I mean. And women."

"You mean you," he said.

"No," I said. "Well, yeah. But not just me. People who deserve it and otherwise wouldn't break through."

He sat back against the squeaking red booth with his arms crossed. "That's interesting. I didn't know you were like this."

"Like what?"

"Earnest. A do-gooder. I'm wary of do-gooders. They're holier-than-thou. They have other motives. Even the Red Cross is out there misappropriating funds. Burning up money. Do you know what most of the donated money goes to at these so-called charity organizations? The salaries of the people who run them."

"People would like you for it," I said. "It would help make amends."

"I don't need to make amends. I've made amends."

"All right," I said. "Just a suggestion."

He ran his hands through his hair. It was tousled from the doctor's handiwork. She'd pushed it out of the way and it had stayed half standing up. His staples made a crooked path across his forehead. He looked like rakish Frankenstein.

I didn't understand, he told me. The extent of his commitments. It was easy when you were young to be romantic, have ideals. You didn't have responsibilities. You weren't tired. You didn't have to tithe a certain percentage of your income to Phillips Exeter Academy. You didn't have houses. You didn't have to pay people all over the globe to take care of those houses. To go turn on the water every once in a while so the pipes wouldn't burst. You didn't have employees: The concept was laughable. You didn't have a staff, hundreds relying on you to keep the massive, ludicrous operation afloat so that they, in turn, could take care of their houses and educate their kids.

I had lost the thread. It had become a sprawling complaint about the upkeep of his empire. None of the things he mentioned seemed relatable to me—caretaker salaries, winterizing the chalet. I had mentioned promoting good work, not joining the Peace Corps. Not going into the woods to live deliberately.

The more you had, he was saying, the more people wanted to take it away. Just look at the Kitty Rosenthal thing. Look at how much everyone loved it. The press was gleeful. Beyond gleeful. Salivating. Turned on. And the way they treated him, like he was sick. Like he had planned the whole thing. Like he was some kind of predatory figure, instead of what he really was, which was a dupe. Too open and trusting, maybe even a little stupid, but definitely not the coldhearted villain they made him out to be.

"This," he said. He patted his side, his stab wound. "This is the perfect example of what people will do to you."

"What do you mean?"

"The person who did it was someone I had helped over the years."

"The fan? You'd tried to help the fan?"

"I knew her. We had a relationship, kind of. I'd given her money. Not a ton, but some. She wanted more. They always want more."

"Spencer didn't tell me that you knew each other."

"Spencer doesn't know," said Hugo. "We decided he didn't have to. It's a grisly thing that happened, what, twenty, twenty-five years before he was born? There are some things kids shouldn't know."

"So she was a girlfriend?"

He shook his head. "Just a girl I knew."

"And she went to jail?"

"She's out now. For a long time. She moved to Canada when she got out. Which, why bother? Might as well just stay in." He paused. "I'm over it, if you haven't noticed. It doesn't bother me. I don't walk around afraid of getting stabbed. I don't have dreams about it or any of that. I didn't flinch when you approached me at Birds & the Bees."

I waited for him to smile, but he was serious.

"I approached *you*?" I said. "You approached *me*."

I wasn't crazy. He'd been waiting for me in the hallway, not the other way around. He'd been studying the pictures of comics with his hands in his pockets. He'd been nose to nose with a portrait of Shecky Greene.

"Are you sure?" He sipped his coffee. "Whatever. Whoever. The point is, I didn't think you had a knife. I didn't worry about it."

I almost laughed. As an example of his resilience it made no sense. I'd been onstage. How could I have known he was there? Or did he think I would stab him just because? Did he think I had a knife at the ready in case any opportunities arose? In case any likely victims crossed my path? His idea of who posed bodily menace to whom was upside down and infuriating. It made me want to stab him.

I reached for a butter knife resting on a folded paper napkin.

"How should I hold it?" I said. "Overhand like this? Or underhand, more like this?"

"Whichever feels more natural," he said. "Every assailant has to decide for herself."

"Overhand then."

I took a couple of experimental jabs in his direction.

He said, "You couldn't break the skin with that thing."

"I could."

"You couldn't."

"I could if I got you in the right place. In the throat. In that belly of yours."

"You couldn't. Look at your arms."

He reached forward across the table and squeezed my bicep harder than he had to. I dropped the knife. It clattered against my saucer and the waitress looked over.

"See?" he said, sitting back. He forced a smile. "Weak. Just like I thought."

He got up and paid the check, and we left, stopping near the door so he could spoon pastel mints into my hands. He did too many, intentionally, as a joke, so I had to hold my hands together to carry out the chalky mound. I tried to be charmed by it, to let the gag transport me, but I didn't feel amused. I felt that I was carrying too many mints and nothing more. Outside there was nowhere to put them but the ground. I laid them down near the curb like I would a baby chick. Something deserved to be treated delicately, even if it wasn't me.

———

My head pounded and light sparked at the edges of my vision. Hugo wanted to go for a swim. He was still keyed up, bouncing around the dark kitchen, popping the cap off a bottle of Advil and shaking some out for me. He wouldn't be able to sleep, he told me. Not a chance. He thought the pool might help.

"Look at it," he said. "So cool and green."

I was keyed up, too—I'd had two cups of coffee. But the pool seemed like a bad idea. Hugo had a concussion. He'd lost blood. I didn't want him to die on my watch. I'd become, forever, a witness. The person present when Hugo Best died.

I said, "I don't think you should. I keep picturing you floating facedown, silhouetted by the pool lights. Cops peering over the edge and snapping pictures."

He said, "You're thinking of the opening of *Sunset Boulevard.*"

He started getting undressed, sliding his feet out of his loafers, headed for his belt buckle next. He was going to do it. He was going to get fully nude right there in the kitchen, without permission or preamble.

"I have to go to sleep," I said.

He stopped, belt undone. I got a glimpse of the top of his briefs, the logo there. "Okay. Long, strange day. Maybe tomorrow."

I went upstairs to the guest bedroom, changed into the Exeter T-shirt. Went to the bathroom to brush my teeth. I checked my forehead, unchanged, and the bruise on my hip, a purple and red splotch the size of my fist, chaffed rough by my jeans.

In the hallway I encountered Spencer, leaning against the door to his room. Light seeped out from behind him, like maybe he'd been waiting up. He wore sweats and a T-shirt.

"What happened to your head?" he said.

"We pretty much hit an opossum."

It was less taxing than explaining that we hadn't hit an opossum, the opossum lived on, but that we had gotten hurt anyway. In some ways the opossum bested us, it put us in the hospital just by sitting in the road, and in other ways it brought us together. When I looked at it, I'd seen pure animal evil. I had a feeling I'd be thinking about the opossum for a long time.

"I have one here, too," I said.

I pulled up the shirt so he could see the bruise on my hip. I didn't know what I was doing. Yes, I did. I knew exactly. But I also knew it was stupid.

He reached out and touched it with the tips of three fingers. His touch was hot. He let his hand drift slightly to the lace of my underwear, where it cut across my hip. He let it drift lower, under the waistband. He pulled it out and let it snap back against my bruise.

"Ow," I said, though it hadn't hurt.

"Do you want to come inside?" he said.

He sounded like an adult at the end of a date, someone I'd meet on an app, only he was seventeen and he meant his childhood bedroom. Where his backpack was, his Xbox, his history textbook with its oil-painting cover and warped pages.

"No, thanks," I said.

I wanted to think that this was the moment that marked the real difference between Hugo and me. He had said yes and I had said no, which should have made me superior. But really if the circumstances had been different, if we weren't in Hugo's house, if I wasn't so put off by Spencer's eagerness, by his transient child's bedroom, maybe I would have. I had blundered into the right choice. It still counted, but barely. When Audrey and I had discussed it on Friday, we hadn't considered that the object of my repulsion might be me.

"You bitch," said Spencer.

He said it tiredly, though. Without brio. He sounded like his dad as he said it, delivering some uninspired line on the show. Like he really didn't want to, but there it was on the cue card. Occasionally, Hugo would make an aside after a line like that. *Jesus, who writes this stuff,* or similar, and the audience would laugh. I waited for Spencer to do something like that, something to break the fourth wall. But no, he had really called me a bitch.

I let the shirt fall back down over my hip. "Good night, Spencer."

Back in the guest bedroom, I closed the door. I stood in the dark until I heard a faint splash from the yard and went out onto the balcony. Hugo was naked in the pool. His body slid yellow-green through the water. He had a fluid breaststroke

that had nothing to do with his usual physicality. He ducked
his head under and I thought of the amount of blood on his
neck, face, and forearms, in his hair and ears. Now it was
in the water.

It filled me with anguish, it was so unfair. These rich
people fucked up their pool every single day. I remember
thinking: *If I had a pool I'd treat it so much better.*

Monday

Hugo woke me while there was still mist on the field and we played tennis. I was groggy, he was, too, and we rallied instead of playing for points, breaking often, not really talking.

His head looked fine, except for the Band-Aid covering his staples. Mine was worse, a purple-green knot, off center, that tugged the skin of my forehead taut. I felt the need to hold the whole apparatus still while I played, like I had a stack of books balanced up there. Every time Hugo caught sight of it he winced.

I hadn't slept well. I'd still been awake when Hugo came inside from his swim. I could hear him running the kitchen faucet, switching off lights, coming upstairs. He paused outside my door, just for a second, cleared his throat faintly, and moved on. I lay there wondering about that throat clear until an uneasy sleep took me, the kind of sleep where you keep waking up and trying to reconcile the room you're in with the room you're used to. Where your brain keeps telling you the exit isn't where it should be, that it's been moved on you or deleted altogether.

We played for an hour, maybe more, and then we stopped. The sun coming up over the trees had started baking the moisture out of the grass. It smelled like chlorophyll and the great outdoors. My sweat stung faintly on the surface of my

skin. It was all the alcohol I'd been drinking, squeezing its
way out of me, and I was glad. It made me feel clean.

"You're better than you let on yesterday," said Hugo.

We were walking back across the field.

I told him I could sometimes do things better when I
wasn't trying, was that strange? He said no, not at all. Some
people were that way. I was just probably not terrific at han-
dling pressure, hence the throwing up before performing. I
agreed and told him that's why I'd die instantly in a survival
situation like a natural disaster or a pogrom. He said hmm.
I regretted bringing up pogroms before we had coffee.

He went in and made us omelets. There was food in the
house now. Noam had restocked the essentials plus a bunch of
Noam stuff like pluots and Tuscan kale. I changed into my suit
and went for a swim. I could sense Hugo watching me through
the plate glass. I floated on my back and looked up and tried
to relax into being watched. The sky was still streaked with
pink and the pool was green and the trees were black. Everything was quiet except the lap of the water over my stomach
and bruised hip, and the sound of the grass shushing itself.

I had never really considered the morning anything other
than a crucible. I'd had an hour commute: JMZ to Delancey,
BDFM to Rockefeller Center. Then a street block and an
avenue block to the office. Once a month or more something
would go wrong, a signal problem, an unexplained delay. The
platform would grow fuller and hotter, the people pressing
in against each other, against the stairwell and sticky pillars.
On those days, I clutched my iced coffee or did my deep
breathing, tried not to think of bodies thrown onto tracks
and decapitated, tried not to touch anyone or be touched.
Without fail, someone would be playing an accordion.

Once on the train, the car would be so packed I'd end up in the very middle with nothing to hold on to, straining with my fingertips to steady myself on the ceiling while a businessman breathed deeply into my armpit. Kids would come by selling candy and telling made-up stories about their basketball team, but you absolutely could not buy from them. If you did, you opened the door to considering their lives, why they might be selling candy on the subway in the first place, and your own inability to help kids like them in any meaningful way. At that point, futility would overtake you.

By the time I made it to work I'd have the same frizzy hair and rumpled clothes as everyone else in Manhattan. Only certain elevators went up to our floor, so there was another waiting period as the whole crowded elevator bank watched the LED screen—the brass plate of light-up numbers had been pried up and replaced the first year I worked there—descend from twenty-six to one, sometimes lingering mysteriously on a floor for minutes on end.

Up in the office three discrete crises would already be under way, the clock ticking down to our daily deadline. A broken copier, an obscure prop that needed to be sourced. A bit that Hugo deemed not good enough, not ready yet, that had to be rewritten. I went where they wanted, came when they called me. That was how the morning passed. Not quite in a panic, but panic-adjacent, a cousin of panic with eerie physical similarities.

In the afternoon there was an exhale. The show taped at four, finished at five, and in that hour there was nothing more the writing staff could do. Not for that day's episode. What would happen would happen. We'd work on the next

day's show, the next several days' shows, calm for a couple
of hours at least. In the morning we'd wake up, cold sweat,
mounting fear, to do it all over again.

But drifting in Hugo's pool, I saw it didn't have to be that
way. The morning could be mellow, a time for exercise and
birdsong. You could plant a wall of trees between you and
the world and go for a life-affirming swim. All it took was a
handful of seeds and a plot of land worth millions.

Hugo came out with two plates, set them down on the
table, went back in for silverware. I climbed out of the pool
and he tossed me a big white towel. We sat down to eat. He'd
put goat cheese in the omelets, and toasted rye bread. The
coffee had come out ink black and velvety. He conceded that
Spencer might have been right about the Chemex.

I felt smugly satisfied. Had we done it? Had we hit our
stride? Was this what we'd be like together? Civil, serene,
mutually appreciative of breakfast. It was a nice idea, if
nothing else.

Hugo said. "The Sunday paper's still floating around
somewhere if you want it."

"I'll pass," I said.

The best thing to do with the Sunday paper was throw it
out wholesale if you felt like it, without so much as glancing
at the crossword. That's when you knew you'd arrived at
self-actualization.

Hugo had done a good job with the eggs. The omelet
was fluffy, flecked with herbs. There was no reason for him
to know how to cook eggs well, no reason for him to have
any normal-person skills at all, so it impressed me that he
did. We had our conversation about comedy then, the one
he'd promised me. He asked me to name the ten best living

comedians, present company excluded. I thought a minute, chewed my toast, and told him.

"Wow," he said.

"What?"

"You didn't say Don Rickles."

"You said living."

He paused, breathing in. The pool made its quiet sound. Celebrity deaths: There were so many of them. They buzzed across the screen of your phone and were gone. If you were as big as Don Rickles, as big as Hugo, you got a nice obituary, a couple of tributes from people who knew you. A picture of your face appeared at the Oscars for half a second. Then nothing for the rest of time.

"I forgot he was dead," said Hugo. "Living or dead then."

I thought a minute, drank my coffee, and told him.

"You still didn't say Don Rickles."

"Maybe I don't like him that much. Wasn't he a dick?"

"Publicly, yeah, that was the joke. Privately, not at all. Also, you rank Chappelle too high."

"You would say that."

"What's that supposed to mean? Are you calling me racist?"

I was, a little bit. "No."

"Because, if you remember, Richard Pryor is my favorite comedian ever."

It was possible to like a black comedian and still be racist, but I decided to let it go.

"Forget it. It's probably generational."

"So you're calling me old then."

I laughed. "I guess."

He picked at a piece of crust with his fork. "I notice I didn't make your list."

"You said present company excluded."

"Yeah, but if you felt strongly enough you could have made an argument."

"I think you're funny," I said. "I thought that was obvious."

I looked at him to determine if he was appreciative. I couldn't tell. His need for reinforcement had no bottom. Any compliment would only continue to fall endlessly through space, like a rock thrown into a well that never makes a splash.

"Don Rickles wasn't even that old," he said.

"Are you kidding? He was in his nineties. Is that not old?"

"Was he? I guess he was."

"He was always good when he came on the show," I said. "I liked you two together."

"Don't patronize me."

We sat back and looked at the pool. I had killed the mood by mentioning mortality. The only way back was to get Hugo talking about himself again.

"What about you?" I said. "Who's in your top ten?"

He drank his coffee and told me.

"Lotta white men," I said.

He said, "That's who did comedy until recently. And yes, I know the problem is endemic. And yes, I know the culture rewards women's tits and men's wits. And yes, I know when you look back at a lot of early stand-up it's about how women are nags who withhold sex. I know all that shit, okay? I'm on your side. I still like George Carlin, though. He's really funny. And Robin Williams, and yes, Don Rickles, and the other guys I named. I'm not going to sit here and pretend I don't. I even like Woody Allen. I know I'm not supposed to. I know he's 'problematic.' Right? That's what you guys say? Problematic? But what about that one he does with the moose?"

He did a Woody Allen impression. I guess it was inevitable. He did the one about shooting a moose and driving to a costume party with it strapped to his fender. The moose woke up in the Holland Tunnel, it went. There's a law in New York City about driving with a moose on your fender Tuesday, Thursday, and Saturday. And so on. Hugo was a competent mimic, not a master, but he could do almost anyone and you'd get the picture.

"Well done," I said.

"Do you have a Woody Allen?" he asked.

"No."

"Of course you do. Everyone does."

"I don't," I said.

"Come on," he said. "Try."

"Okay, but you'll regret it."

I tried. I did a line from *Annie Hall*: *Two elderly women are at a Catskill mountain resort, and one of 'em says, "Boy, the food at this place is really terrible." The other one says, "Yeah, I know; and such small portions."*

It sounded like a birdcall, the way I did it, and also managed to be anti-Semitic.

"Jesus, you weren't kidding," said Hugo, laughing. "Never do that again."

"I told you," I said.

He laughed some more. I was happy he was having fun, even if it was at my expense.

"Can't you do any impressions?"

None, I told him. Not Christopher Walken. Not Sean Connery. Not even Borat. I didn't understand how people were able to do them at all. I didn't know how to hear a sound and translate it into a sound I made myself. I was missing

that wiring, the funny voices wiring. It was one of the things
that held me back as a comedian.

"You seem to think you have a lot of things holding you
back," he said.

"I do!"

He paused. "I'm problematic, too, aren't I?"

"Is that rhetorical?"

"No, I really want to know."

"Not to a Woody Allen degree. Not to a Cosby degree.
But kinda."

"Kitty Rosenthal?"

"Yeah."

"I had no idea how young she was. That's the truth. June,
look at me." He made long, meaningful eye contact with
me. "I promise you."

"I believe you," I said, even though I didn't really.

I believed that he believed what he was saying. He had
been high on drugs and power. He probably hadn't thought
to ask Kitty Rosenthal her age or chose not to see through
her lie about Barnard. He had probably laughed about it in
the dark, loud club, and poured her more Grey Goose. It had
been easy, I was sure. I had seen for myself the night before
how easy it could be. But whatever actually happened had
been overwritten by his public story about it, told and retold
to lawyers and reporters, until it felt real, until he bought it
himself.

"Do your Woody Allen again," he said.

"You said not to."

"Come on."

I did it again. It came out completely different but still
catastrophic. High in parts, low in others. Hugo's shoulders

shook as he looked out on the pool. He was problematic, but I'd have done it all day to keep him laughing like that. I'd have done it till my voice went hoarse.

"We should go get dressed," said Hugo at last. "The caterers will be here soon."

He made no move to get up.

"Why don't we bag it?" I said.

"Bag it?"

"Yeah, bag it. Call it off. Call up the caterers and whoever else and eat the deposit. I'll even make the calls if you want."

"I can't."

"Sure you can," I said. "You're rich. You can do whatever you want with impunity. Isn't that what we've learned?"

"You don't understand. We do it every year. People will be disappointed."

He had the most dysfunctional relationship to "people" I'd ever witnessed. He owed them and they owed him. No one could ever pay the other off. Not fully. He had to be the person they expected and they had to keep admiring him. And if either stopped, then what? He'd sink back into obscurity like the rest of us and have to think about the mail and the weather and his relationships and how to be good.

I wanted his fame and hated that I wanted it. I thought I deserved it. Some remote part of me even thought I'd get it. One day, eventually, with zero supporting evidence. I knew fame was dumb and empty. Hugo did, too, probably. He must have. Everyone did. And yet.

I thought if I could convince Hugo that none of it mattered, then I might believe it, too. If I could talk him out of caring, I'd stop, too. If he could be better than it, then I could, too. We could sit there for one afternoon, free as the dolphins, while the sun sparkled down on the water and the clouds passed through so slowly we didn't notice their passing, until we looked up, finally, and found a whole new sky.

I said, "Who cares what people think? Let them be disappointed. Like who, anyway? Paul McCartney?"

"He's not coming this year. He's on tour."

"Well, there you go. The third best Beatle won't even be there, so why bother?"

"And the first best member of Wings. What would we do if I canceled the party? What would we do all day?"

"Whatever people do. Go to Home Depot. Get some shelf brackets, some mums in a pot, a door hinge. Go to the mall; is there a mall around here?"

"There's a mall in Stamford, yeah."

The thought of Hugo walking around a mall made me sad. The all-absorbing din, the smell of soft pretzels. The image of him contemplating a hat in the window of Lids or wandering, bewildered, into a Hollister.

"Or we could stay home and be bored," I said. "Doesn't that sound nice?"

"Does boredom sound nice? Not really."

"We could turn off our phones and just sit here."

"Millennials glamorize boredom because you've never truly experienced it. And because you have a lot of time left. You try growing up in a world with three TV channels and no Internet and see if you ever elect to be bored again."

"Okay," I said. "All thrills, no boredom. We'll play that game where you stab the knife between your fingers risking grave injury."

"Mumblety-peg," he said.

He finished his coffee, thinking. He seemed on the verge

of agreeing to it. He was still sitting like that when two guys in white polos and khakis rounded the house and waved their arms at us. They were from Fairfield Rental Center and they wanted to know where the tent should go.

Hugo's chair scraped the patio as he stood. "Sorry. We'll have to play mumblety-peg another day."

He shook their hands and asked after Kent, the owner of the rental place, a friend of his. They talked about Kent for a minute—he'd just had a pool put in at his place, stay tuned for epic pool parties—and went out to the field to decide where the tent should go. I watched them pace off its dimensions before stacking our plates to carry them inside.

In the kitchen, another rental center guy was hefting a rack of wineglasses.

"How's Kent?" I said.

He just looked at me as I brushed past him.

A small city bloomed on the property. Its industry was party. Its citizens smoked cigarettes and wore the uniforms of the service industry. Everyone knew what to do without being told and operations slid on the smooth casters of money.

After more deliberation, the rental center crew unfurled a big white tent, pounded stakes into the ground, secured the legs in a high-pitched whirring of drills. They set up foldout tables and rickety white rental chairs and a parquet dance floor and risers for a band, and then they left and a second, separate crew came through, snapping open tablecloths and arranging purple and white hydrangeas in square vases of chunky glass. The hydrangeas were meant to resemble the ones in the yard, everything summery and harmonious, and they completely did. They looked great.

The gardener mowed the grass again, eliminating the millimeter that had irritated me the day before, and sheared the bushes by some infinitesimal degree. The pool guy returned. He wore his headphones as he dipped in his gray hose, bobbing his head to the beat. I wondered what he made of cleaning the same pool three days in a row, if he felt like Sisyphus, if he was losing his mind, but I didn't ask.

I watched all this from the guest bedroom. Or anyway, I monitored the progress. In between I flipped cable channels on the giant TV and read the news on my phone. I felt like I was in a hotel room. The news I read, even the bad news, affected me the same way it would in a Hilton DoubleTree in an unfamiliar city. The anonymity and high-thread-count sheets made the headlines too remote to care about.

Spencer popped his head in, hair tousled from sleep. If he was resentful about the night before, he didn't show it. He stuck around and watched a few minutes of a home improvement show—a Dallas couple was renovating their kitchen—before pronouncing it "played." He motioned me onto the balcony as more workers dragged a smoker beyond the tent and started cooking meat. A guy in a chef's jacket and toque prodded the red-brown contents with tongs.

"A whole pig," said Spencer. "They cook it so tender it falls right off the bone. Then you can tear it apart with your fingers."

The weather was undecided again. One minute it was overcast, the next sunny. I wondered what would happen if it rained, if there was a contingency plan, a rain date, or if everyone would just cram into the house, ash cigarettes in the succulents, track mud all over the living room floor, get too drunk and steady themselves on priceless works of art. The wind blew and smoke enclosed the pool.

"I guess I didn't realize it was going to be such a big deal," I said.

"We tried to tell you."

"What are we supposed to do while they're setting up?"

"Is there something you want to do?" He leaned back against the railing of the balcony. It sounded like an offer.

I thought about what people did on Memorial Day. What were the people I knew doing? Hiking, probably. Dipping kayak paddles into cold, clear water. Going to the beach. Audrey would be at a barbecue in Brooklyn, my parents out on the Feldmans' boat. Logan, I didn't know. Maybe he'd be at the same party as Audrey, maybe he didn't celebrate for some esoteric reason he'd love to explain to me. I told Spencer I couldn't think of anything to do in that house that we hadn't already done. He smirked and said that he could.

A moment later we smelled the pig, rich and bitter, carbon and fat. "Let's go get some lunch," he said.

Downstairs we found the kitchen transformed. Caterers wiped down glasses and unpacked phyllo dough, white logs of mozz, Carr's crackers. Sliced citrus and squeezed filling out of pastry bags. They were immoderate with parchment paper, tearing it off in great translucent sheets, saying *excuse me* and *behind you* to Spencer and me, carrying hot pans high above their heads. Someone iced champagne. That was his whole job as far as I could tell. To shovel ice from here to there, uncrate champagne bottles, wipe them down with rags, and put them in the ice. It looked like he'd be there awhile. There was that much champagne.

I attempted to open the refrigerator, but a blond lady in an apron shook her head.

"Something key is chilling in there," she told me, but she wouldn't say what.

I returned to Spencer empty-handed and he went in himself. He came back with a plate of tiny smoked salmon sandwiches, triangular and studded with capers, and a bottle of champagne. They let him have whatever he wanted because he was young and rich, famous for being born, because his abs were visible through the gaping arm holes of his tank top, and because no one had ever said no to him thus far and they weren't going to be the first.

We took our spoils down to the basement rec room and ate on the red vinyl banquette. I put the plate between us—a pungent, smoked fish buffer. We hadn't grabbed glasses and we drank directly from the champagne bottle, passing it back and forth. I'd showered by then, and done my best to cover the bump on my head with makeup. I couldn't hide its elevation, though, or the stretching effect it had on the top half of my face. Spencer squinted at it in the weak light of the rec room.

"That bad?" I said.

"It's not the best," said Spencer.

He lifted the cold bottle of champagne and held it against my head. It was either his way of making amends or just his latest attempt to fuck me. There was a third option, too, that we were friends now, but that seemed unlikely. Condensation dripped down the sides of the bottle and he took it away.

"I'm leaving this afternoon, by the way," he said.

"What? You're not staying for the party? But the pig. The meat so tender you can blah-blah-blah."

"There's a week left of school. I have to get back."

"That's stupid," I said.

"It's whatever."

He passed me the champagne bottle and our fingers touched. I moved back an inch. We were underground again, I noticed, just like we had been the day before. It gave our interactions a feeling of end of the world. Like nothing mattered anymore and we were duty bound to procreate.

"Are we gonna talk about what happened yesterday?" I said.

"Why?"

"I don't know, maybe you feel weird."

He laughed.

"Okay, we won't talk about it."

He took the bottle back, making an elaborate show of not touching me.

"What will you do next week when school ends?" I asked. "Will you come back here?"

He shook his head. He was meeting his mom in Thailand. They were traveling a bit after her movie wrapped. She did work with kids in Cambodia. She'd helped set up a school. And then on to LA for the rest of the summer. He had a bunch of friends out there, people he'd grown up with. The last week of August he'd return to school. I pictured him and his mother in first class. They'd each take an Ambien and pull down matching eye masks. She seemed like the type of woman who applied products to her face throughout the flight to keep it hydrated. I was willing to bet that when Spencer was with her he was that way, too.

"What about your dad?" I said.

"What do you mean?"

"You're not going to spend any time with him this summer?"

"That's kind of not our arrangement."

"Why not?"

"Honestly? He's not that interested. I mean, does he seem interested to you?"

He didn't seem interested. He seemed tired and baffled and overwhelmed. He seemed mainly interested in himself and poor at hiding it. I surprised myself by feeling bad for Spencer. He was a child of privilege and, like Ana had said, needed my compassion like he needed another car. But I felt bad anyway. There were benefits to having parents who cared about you immensely, even if you felt suffocated by their caring.

"You stay with him," said Spencer. "You're having fun here."

I had not been having fun, not consistently, though I knew what he meant. It had been a kind of tourism for me. Now I was at the part of the vacation where I contemplated packing everything up and moving there.

"I can't stay with him," I said.

"Why? What do you have to go back to?"

I thought of my apartment, the spill of mail, the crying baby upstairs, Rocco's rotting feet, iguanas crawling all over each other in the window of Just Pets, Lars at his peephole watching us come and go, okay spring rolls from Okay Thai, the L train shutdown again for repairs, accepting a connection request on LinkedIn, my regular call with my parents on Sunday nights, trudging twelve blocks to a passable grocery store, overdraft fees, changing the font on my résumé, someone's phlegmy cough at Birds & the Bees, and dating again now that Logan was out of the picture.

"I told you that I'm seeing someone," I said.

"Oh yeah. The baloney app guy." He laughed and passed

me the champagne. "Does that mean you're going to keep seeing him?"

I took a sip. The bottom fourth of the bottle had grown warm and flat.

"Probably not."

Saying it out loud made it final. I felt sadness and a fragment of relief. Sadness for the unceremonious way it had ended. Relief at not having to defend the weekend to Logan, or make how I'd treated him fit together with my conception of myself as a mostly decent person. Now whatever I did at least I wouldn't hurt anyone but me.

"I need to look for a job," I said.

"My dad could help you with that. Isn't that why you came here in the first place?"

"That's insulting."

"Is it?" he said.

Was it? I stood up and brushed the crumbs off my lap. There was one mini-sandwich left.

"It's all yours," I said.

He made a face. "You have it."

"What if I don't want it?"

"You do," he said. He picked up the sandwich and thrust it at me. "I know you do."

"I don't. I had too much already."

"Stop being stupid and take it."

It seemed like we were talking about something more than the sandwich. I almost ate it just to end the exchange, but it looked soggy and unappealing. I didn't like the damp, pink way the lox were hanging out over the bread. I especially didn't want it because Spencer wanted me to want it. That made it even more disgusting to me.

"No one has to eat it," I said.

"Someone should!"

I wanted to laugh but he sounded distraught. Or as close as he came to distraught, which was distraught dialed down to 0.001 percent. It would make him good in movies some- day, I thought, his complete understatement of harrowing emotions. That was what they said looked best on the big screen: a super handsome face kept super still.

"No one has to eat it," I said.

Gently, I took the sandwich from him and put it back on the plate. We both looked around for something else to talk about. I studied the framed album on the wall. Hugo's dated sideburns and the joke shop gun.

"What's this room all about anyway?" I said. "It doesn't go with the rest of the house."

"He put it in after the fact, at the height of the show. My mom hates it so much. It's kind of hilarious. She says it's the most Queens thing you could ever possibly do, putting a room like this in a house like this. She wanted a workout room instead." He turned around and knocked on the wall behind us. "It's not even real brick. They used to have parties down here when I was little. There's a working spotlight and everything. My dad's comedian friends would tell jokes." He stood up, stretching. "I'm sure everyone found it embarrassing but him."

I picked up the bottle, empty now, the plate with its lone creepy sandwich. "I'm sorry you're missing the party. It seems like it'll be a good time."

"It'll suck. Bunch of old saddies getting wasted."

A porthole had opened between us, but now it was clos- ing and I was mostly glad. For the next couple of hours we could return to harmless flirtation and shared skepticism of his father. We'd come close to crossing a line, but we hadn't, and I counted that, cautiously, as a win.

"He'll be okay," I said. "Your dad. He's got friends. He's got Bony. I'll check in. I'll come for visits. Before you know it he'll be on to the next project."

"Yeah, like what?" said Spencer.

"Maybe he'll do one of those shows where he plays himself but famous actors play everyone else in his life."

"Do we need more of those shows? Be honest."

"He'll be okay," I said again.

———————

We came up from the basement to Hugo standing in the kitchen. He was all cleaned up with product in his hair, the jacket of his summer suit slung over the back of a bar stool. He smelled like aftershave. He started picking canapés off a tray and dropping them into his mouth one by one. The blond lady was letting him. He wanted to know what we kids had been doing down there in the basement for so long.

"Endlessly fucking," said Spencer, and then, "I have to go pack."

He went upstairs.

I said, "He's kidding."

"I know," said Hugo.

It bothered me how quickly he said it. He was still chewing, looking for the next thing to put into his mouth.

"But we could have been," I said.

"I guess."

He didn't care. He wasn't jealous. I watched him eat in silence. Half the caterers were watching, too.

He swallowed. "Casey Caruso is on her way. Remember? The people from E?"

"Is there something you want me to do while they're here?"

"No, no. Just telling you is all. You can use Jan if you can catch her before she goes."

"Use Jan how? Who's Jan?"

"The hair girl." He touched his hair with his fingertips. It had been trimmed, cleaned up at the temples. His eyebrows had been groomed. He had makeup on, too; the gash on his forehead had disappeared beneath a layer of putty. "Jan. The girl who just did my hair."

I wasn't going to use Jan. I wasn't going to run out into the driveway shouting *Jan, Jan, is one of you Jan?* I wasn't going to drag her back into the house with her shears and bottles of mousse and instruct her to get to work on my head.

"I don't want to hold Jan up," I said.

"It's your call," he said. "But you do know I pay Jan, right? It's not an inconvenience. Jan is compensated for her time."

Every conversation was about money. Even the ones about something else. He could hand me a York Peppermint Pattie with a price tag of fifty cents and this would require hashing out. We'd both pretend we didn't care, that the fifty cents meant nothing. But I'd feel insulted or that I owed him. And he'd feel like a lord dispensing candy from his mount. This was the chasm that yawned between us. My pride, his ego. Jokes could help cross it sometimes, but not always.

"I don't want Jan," I told him again.

He looked at my hair a bit too thoughtfully, nose scrunched. No one likes to have her hair looked at like that.

"Ugh," I said.

I caved and went to go get Jan.

Casey Caruso arrived in a fuchsia sheath dress with a protective sheet of plastic affixed to her head. I watched Hugo lead her and a producer around the grounds. Her improvised head wrap came undone in the wind and one end flapped behind her like a flag.

On the patio, two guys from the crew wrangled cable. Hugo had liberated some sliders from the caterers, and they ate them while regarding the white tent through sunglasses, each with one foot up on an apple box.

Jan did my hair, angrily. At one point I realized she had scissors out and was trimming it without my permission. She had a gender reveal party to go to that afternoon, she told me. Her sister's baby. They were going to pop a balloon, and if pink confetti came out it was a girl, and if blue confetti came out it was a boy. Now she was going to miss the balloon popping.

"I'm really sorry," I said. "Could someone tape it for you?"

She roughed up my head with texturizer, slapping around near my ears. "It won't be the same."

Afterward I went into the guest bathroom and put on the cream-colored dress. It was featherlight, angelic, nicer than anything I owned. I couldn't wear a bra with it, which I hadn't realized, and it made me feel sort of nude. In another context I might have liked feeling that way. I reapplied makeup to the lump on my forehead. The swelling had gone down some, but its 3-D quality was still a problem, as was the way it yanked my right eyebrow up toward my hairline.

By the time I walked downstairs, the interview had started. A PA stopped me in the kitchen and put a finger to his lips. We were on a set now. The caterers had been sent out for a smoke and everything was quiet except for the sound of Casey Caruso, seated in a Danish armchair, asking Hugo what he would do next, now that he was free to do anything he wanted.

"Well," said Hugo. "I haven't really decided. I was thinking a long vacation. Maybe the Côte d'Azur. Or Havana."

"Ooh, Cuba," she said. "Do you know how to salsa, Hugo?"

Hugo said, big smile, laugh from Casey, "You could teach me."

Casey Caruso clasped her hands in front of her and tilted her head to the side. Her hair had held up all right. It was multilayered blond and brown. It looked like a lot of thinking went into each individual piece, and also not that much like real hair. Hugo sat across from her in one of the armchairs. He looked relaxed, handsome, amused, like he had been on vacation for months already. A fresh layer of makeup had been added to the fissure in his forehead. Except for the odd texture, you couldn't see it at all.

"Have you ever considered a role outside of the spotlight?" she said.

"I'm glad you asked, Casey," said Hugo.

He looked up past the camera and caught my eye.

"I've been thinking a lot recently about what I can do to give back. I think established comedians have a responsibility to amplify the kind of voices we don't hear from as much in comedy. Which is to say, not white men. Women, people of color, differently abled people, people from diverse economic backgrounds. You know, comedy favors the wealthy, just like all the arts. Because when you're young and still figuring it out, doing open mics, working some entry-level job, whatever, you can lean on your parents. People raised in lower income households don't have that luxury."

Casey Caruso nodded along to everything he said.

"As you might know, Casey, I come from a working-class background myself. My father was a mechanic and my mother was a housewife. So I had no advantages on that front. None. They couldn't help pay my rent or anything like that. I have experienced firsthand just how difficult things can be for young comedians, and I'm a straight, white man, which makes things how much easier? Forty percent? Would you say forty percent, Casey?"

"I'd say so. Forty percent easier sounds about right," said Casey. "What form might it take, this amplification you're talking about?"

"Well, one thing it would be great to do is promote projects by people who otherwise wouldn't necessarily get a chance. For instance, there's never been a better time for women in comedy."

He named some female comedians on the rise. They were pushing boundaries, he said. They had schooled the world on the question of whether or not women are funny.

"They are," Hugo concluded. He looked at me again, eyes twinkling. "I think we can lay that one to rest. Anyway, it would be great to help break out talent like that. Give some deserving young woman a chance she might not normally get."

Casey Caruso beamed. "It sounds like you're putting your producer hat on."

"You know, Casey, I may be. I very well may be."

The interview ended and I walked outside. The catering staff slouched around drinking soda, crimped bow ties hanging out of their pockets. All of Hugo's answers seemed prepared in advance, especially the one about inclusivity.

He'd mocked it the night before, dismissed it, then stolen it from me to make himself look good. Another way of thinking about it, I guess, was he'd learned it from me.

I sat in the party tent and took off my shoes. The plastic windows and wet green yard outside made me feel submerged. I wanted Hugo to find me like that, alone in the tent, like the last guest left in the dining room of a cruise ship. A cruise ship that was taking on water. But he didn't come out. Maybe they had more to shoot. Maybe they were just chatting, letting fly about Richie what's-his-face. What a fool he was and how scandalously small.

A bartender came in, a woman about my age, and stood at her post. She was wearing a caterer's white shirt and black pants and had her hair in a tidy bun.

She said to me, "Do you need something?"

I did. I needed a job, a ride home, to go put on my real clothes. I needed to pay my student loans. I needed a haircut at a reasonable price from a place that knew what to do with my hair texture. I needed to call my parents and hear a mind-numbing story about something rude that was said in the deli line at Publix supermarket. I needed them to float me two grand, just until just until just until. I needed a stiff drink.

"Surprise me," I said.

———————

By three o'clock the weather had worsened. The backyard, pool, and white tent were suffused in a fine drizzle. A jazz trio arrived in ponchos and started setting up. I carried my cocktail into the house when it got too chilly. Guests would be arriving soon, and I wanted to see Hugo before he was swept up in the jocularity. The backslapping and cigar lighting, the side hugs and cheek kissing.

He wasn't anywhere, though. Not upstairs, not downstairs. I loitered in the kitchen waiting for him to show up until the blond lady shooed me away. When it was clear I wouldn't find him, I went to the front of the house. There was a white Barcelona chair near the door, and I sat watching for the cars of Hugo's friends. The high heels stepping out onto gravel, the madcap sprints around the house to the party.

An Uber let out two young women, girls really, tall, thin, dressed for the discotheque in crop tops and lace-up pants. The first of the deluge, I thought. He shows up and they just materialize. But then they didn't. It was fifteen minutes before another car pulled in, a Land Rover that produced a barrel-chested guy in khakis and a checked shirt. He wore a tan visor with a corporate logo, hedge fund swag it looked like, and vaped manically as he made his way around the house. Hugo didn't come out to meet him, or the girls before him, or the next people that arrived, an elegant older couple who struck me as European and at the wrong party entirely. He couldn't hide forever, though—manners wouldn't allow it—so I waited.

I was a veteran of waiting, a pro. I could have put it on my résumé. Being a page had been all waiting. Waiting to open the house, to seat the audience. Waiting through Gary Scary's routine, Bony's routine, waiting some more through the familiar rhythms of the show.

My work at reception had been mostly waiting, too. Years of it. For the phone to ring, for the mail to arrive, for people to come out from the office and collect their guests. Waiting to be remembered by the staff members, and waiting to establish a rapport with them.

Occasionally, there was a break from the waiting. An errand of some kind, a document to copy and distribute. Then I got to saunter as slowly as I wanted through the hallways peeking into offices. And sometimes Julian stopped by for a chat. He'd talk to me about what was going on in the writers' room. The projects that week, the feuds, who was up and who was down, Gil's mood, Hugo's. He'd pump me for information. He was mainly interested in what people were saying about him, which was usually nothing. Sometimes I made things up to mess with him. *"Gil mentioned you chew too loudly,"* I told him once, and Julian blanched.

I often wondered if the waiting would come to nothing. I feared that I'd turn thirty at the reception desk, that the office manager would remember and arrange a party for me like she had when I turned twenty-seven and twenty-eight and twenty-nine. That everyone would sign a card. I feared that years would pass, even more years than had already passed, and I'd still be wearing a headset and consulting my laminated sheet of extensions. I feared the day would come when I just gave up and moved on to the next job, a job that carried me fractionally closer to a career, but never all the way. I feared I'd creep forward like that, enacting Zeno's paradox deep into my forties. And then what?

It didn't happen. Two writers burned out and quit unexpectedly. Two women. One spot went to an outside hire, Layla, and the other to Julian. Julian put in a word for me and I interviewed for the writers' assistant job. The first time I sat down with Gil, we were interrupted by his phone buzzing a *Times* alert. My own phone was off.

He looked down. "Shit."

A mass shooting at Chicago O'Hare, nineteen dead, six of them children. The monologue would have to be rewritten on the fly with the tone calibrated. They'd have to consult Hugo about how he wanted to handle it. More news would probably break during the taping—the identity of the shooter, his online radicalization and otherwise clean record, his wild-eyed mug shot, and the administration's hollow statement—dating it before it even aired.

A writer named Tony popped his head in the door. "You're needed."

Gil nodded at him. He was already standing up. To me he said, "Are you sure you want this job?"

"Definitely," I said too quickly, and Gil shook his head.

We rescheduled for a couple of days later, and that time Gil was in a buoyant mood, eating a burrito over his laptop. I watched him take a piece of green pepper off the space bar and pop it into his mouth. A megafamous pop star had been on the night before and ratings had rebounded slightly. In a few months we'd get word we were canceled, but that day he felt good. He hired me.

The strangest part of the wait was the moment it ended. By that point it was such a well-worn groove. You couldn't quite believe it, couldn't quite trust it. Thought at any minute you'd be thrust back. But space was made, in the shift between stasis and motion. And into that space seeped hope. You would not always be waiting. Something had to happen eventually.

My phone buzzed on my lap and I fumbled to pick it up. It was Julian. I'd forgotten that I'd told him to come here.

"You sound weird," he said. "I'm outside. There's a guy

with a clipboard. Do I need to be on a list or something? Did you put me on a list?"

I hadn't thought to put Julian on a list. I hadn't thought there'd be a list. In spite of what I'd been told, I'd envisioned a large barbecue. No barbecue I'd ever been to had a list.

"I'll come out," I said.

I went outside and half jogged through the drizzle. My heels sank into the gravel. The gate was open and a security guard stood waiting to check in cars. He had the hood of his windbreaker up. The paper on his clipboard was getting wet. I reached the gate and saw Julian's Volvo parked on the shoulder. Inside, he sat perfectly still.

"You can let him in," I said to the guy.

A long conversation followed about who I was. He looked around in disbelief. I could hear music playing from Julian's car, a Talking Heads song. The day before I wanted him there, but now I could see that inviting him was a mistake. He already seemed out of place. The Volvo had a missing hubcap and a battered side mirror. Someone had tried to peel the Harvard sticker off the back window and left a streaky mess.

A black sedan pulled up behind Julian's car. The driver tapped the horn.

"You know what?" said the guard. "I don't really care."

"Thank you," I said.

He waved Julian through. The Volvo's tires kicked up gravel. I got into the front seat and said hi and he said hi and we both laughed.

Julian said, "What are you wearing?"

"A dress," I said.

He himself was wearing the blazer he'd had on the one

time I'd gone to his apartment. He'd had the foresight to take the hammer and sickle pin off the lapel.

Julian said, almost happily, "I regret coming here so much."

"I know. I'm sorry. It's my fault."

We had done something stupid and were now being forced to ride out the consequences. The dread was exhilarating. A second guy dressed in all black pointed out where to park. The caterer's van was there, and only a few other cars. Even the MG had been stowed back in the hangar to await repairs.

"I fucking brought something," Julian said.

"What?"

"I brought cookies."

He pulled out a white bakery bag splotched in places with grease and showed me the contents. It was those dusty sandwich cookies with red jelly inside from an Italian bakery.

"Definitely don't bring that in," I said.

It was good manners to bring a food item, he told me. It was de rigueur. Plus, he'd made a special trip to Little Italy. He'd gotten up early to do it. It had been a mob scene down there, tourists everywhere. He thought it might have been San Gennaro.

"San Gennaro's in the fall," I said.

"No one knows exactly when it is." He unbuckled his seat belt. "I'm bringing them."

He located an umbrella under the backseat—a five-dollar bodega umbrella with two broken spokes—and attempted to hold it over us as we made our way to the backyard.

Out on the patio, the rain was melting the ice in the huge chrome champagne bucket and a caterer was looking around for someone to help him move it. Julian grabbed one side and they heaved it into the tent. We paused for a minute, waiting for our eyes to adjust. Julian set his crumpled bag of cookies next to a multitiered cupcake stand on the buffet table. It looked like trash.

"There's something on your head," he said. "What is it?"

"A bruise."

"He didn't . . . He didn't hit you, did he?"

"Nothing like that. Wildlife mishap. Possum in the road."

He was quiet, maybe trying to determine whether he should press harder. I could sense him deciding, feeling around for where the boundaries were. We were far outside the code we'd established. I'd ridden in his car; he'd seen me in a party dress. We'd talked on the phone twice now. Then he seemed to give up.

"This is neither the time nor the place," he said. "But it's opossum."

"I'm aware."

He turned and took stock of the tent, the parquet dance floor, the fairy lights shimmering around the perimeter, the white linen tablecloths lifting and lowering in the wind. The musicians were drinking pilsners, laughing softly among themselves. There were a handful of guests, the ones I'd seen arrive and five or six others. The girls who'd come in the Uber were standing with the hedge fund guy, who continued to vape. The end of his pen glowed blue. One table was occupied by scattered guests who'd left buffer seats between them. The older couple I'd seen before took turns righting a vase that kept falling over, until the woman said, "Enough," and set it on the ground.

Over at the bar, a man in a yellow raincoat and fishing hat was asking a lot of questions. I heard the bartender repeat, "I don't know," several times. The man held his palms up and motioned around the tent.

"Now what?" said Julian.

Julian and I had gotten drunk together before, mostly during our page year, mostly at TGI Fridays. On particularly hard days, Julian could be persuaded to open a tab with his father's credit card. His dad only ever mentioned it to Julian if the bill was truly obscene. It was easy to spend Julian's dad's money, easier still to rack up a tab at Fridays, which had bad food at bad prices—a Midtown hallmark.

We'd drink our sloshing drinks, eat the fruit garnishes, order appetizers, and commiserate about whatever it was that day that had been so awful. A guy who'd gotten handsy, a pigeon in the atrium. The kind of thing that never rose above the level of workplace anecdote. And when we'd had enough to drink, when the guardrails of inhibition were down, we'd move on to our real topic: ourselves. Our opinions, our takes. What we wanted to do and how we wanted to do it. Which comedians were good, which were bad, whose career we'd take, given the chance, whose we'd leave. It was at Fridays that I first heard about *Mates*. Maybe it was at Fridays that Julian had come up with it.

The tent shimmied in the wind and we got drinks. The man in the raincoat was still at the bar, sipping an Old Fashioned garnished with a curlicue of orange rind.

"You two," he said. "Where is everyone? Where is Hugo? What exactly is going on here?"

It was obvious what was going on. The rain pounding the tent made it obvious. The wind gusting in to knock over the chunky glass vases. The tablecloths, wet now, and covered in a spill of purple flowers.

Julian said, "Maybe a miscommunication about the date?"

"I don't think so," said the man. "It's been held on the same day, Memorial Day, every year for twenty years. I should know. I live right across the street. Maybe you saw the place on the way in? Looks like an old villa?" He held out his hand. "Edward McGuire," he said. "Ted."

Handshakes and introductions, and then Ted went on. "I don't get it. I can remember other years that it rained. A certain percentage of Memorial Days it's gonna rain, right? It rained three years ago and everyone just came in the tent until it stopped. No big deal. It was even kind of fun. Cozy. Like camping with two hundred of your closest friends. So if it's not the weather, then what is it?"

He paused like we might actually think of an answer.

"An off year," I said finally.

Ted McGuire sipped his Old Fashioned and watched the storm through the door of the tent. A table on the patio blew over, bringing a chair with it, and none of us made a move to do anything about it. "Who did you kids say you were again?"

It was a fair question, but I didn't want to mention the show to Ted McGuire. I didn't want to hear his condolences about it ending, or his theories as to why. He seemed full of theories. Ted McGuire must have been good at something to secure a giant fake villa in Greenwich, Connecticut, but I doubted his talents extended to media criticism. At some point he'd taken off the fishing hat and his hair was squashed down evenly on all sides of his head. He looked like one of the Three Stooges.

"I'm Hugo's German tutor," I said.

"And I'm *her* German tutor," said Julian, pointing at me.

Ted didn't know what to do with that. "That's . . . huh.

Hugo's learning German? But if you're a German tutor," he said to me, "why do you need . . ." He patted the pockets of his raincoat, searching for his phone. "You know what? I should really call Linda and tell her not to bother coming by. She won't be happy if she treks all the way over here for nothing. Will you excuse me?"

He put on his hat, pulled his hood up over it, drained his drink, and walked out into the rain to make the call. We turned back to the bartender. To thank us for getting rid of Ted McGuire, she opened the nice scotch. Julian told her he'd only ever had it once, at his cousin's wedding at the Rainbow Room.

She said, "Mazel tov."

He said, "It was six years ago."

She said, "Could you legally drink then?"

He said, "Maybe. What are you, a cop?"

I couldn't believe it: Julian was flirting. I'd never seen it before. I knew he dated. He was on the apps like everyone and sometimes he mentioned his girlfriend from college, who worked at a nonprofit and was engaged to a tech bro. But I'd never witnessed any evidence of sexual interest in another person. I didn't think his laser focus allowed for it.

I left him to it and went to the mouth of the tent to watch for Hugo. Rain lashed the house and I pictured it gone, underwater, blown away. The same images sometimes came to me in the city. I'd be walking to the subway after work and see the streets empty and crumbling. Whitecaps on Broadway, trees bent to ninety degrees. Barnacles climbing the buildings like vines. New York will always be there, was something people said to justify leaving it. But it wouldn't be, not always. Maybe it would in my lifetime, but one day it would cease to stand.

It would sink into the rising ocean or it'd go another way. Fire, ice, locusts, class warfare, the bomb. Or excess; that's what brought down Rome. Like picturing my parents dead when I was little, the thought left me bereft.

Spencer opened the sliding glass door. He stood on the threshold, the strap of a duffel bag slung diagonally across his chest. We looked at each other through the rain that came down in loud splashing sheets. It was like seeing him through a fish tank. A whole universe swam between us, creatures adrift on strange, shifting currents.

As a good-bye, I didn't mind it. It was better than a lingering full-body hug or any words we might have exchanged. We'd said what we had to say, about his father anyway. Another conversation would just be a reprisal. It was unlikely we'd see each other again, but we would probably follow each other on social media. The idea depressed me and I resolved not to do it even as I acknowledged that I probably would. In the abstract, I'd have rather lost touch with Spencer, the better to forget all the weekend's worst details, but in the concrete, I was curious about his vacations.

Spencer cupped his hands around his mouth and shouted something I couldn't hear. I shook my head. He shouted it again, but it was just formless boy sound, a sonic blur that didn't resolve into anything like words. I shook my head and waved. His face was a smudge on the other side of the weather. He turned around—navy jacket, stuffed maroon duffel, ubiquitous black Yankees cap—and waving absently over his shoulder, walked into the house.

Julian appeared next to me. "Who are you waving to? Was that Spencer?"

"Yeah."

"Where's he going?"

"The wilds of boarding school," I said. "From whence he came."

"Is he a little shitheel, Spencer?"

Julian already seemed tipsy. His top button was undone and his hair had fallen partway over one eye. I didn't feel like launching into a long description of Spencer's character. I didn't feel like I could explain it anyway, not so Julian would understand.

"Kinda. You know the type."

"We'll see him in a writers' room in four or five years."

"Nah," I said. "We'll see him on TV."

"I want a tour of the house," said Julian.

"What about your girlfriend?" I said.

I motioned back behind us toward the bartender.

"She doesn't get off until the end of this thing. If this thing is a thing."

I looked around the tent. The European couple rose to leave. Ted McGuire was still stomping around the yard. His yellow form streaked past a window. The jazz trio struck up Miles Davis's "So What?" and even I could hear their sarcasm.

"It might not be a thing."

"Let's go," said Julian.

He handed me the busted umbrella, gave the bartender a sheepish smile, and took off across the yard. He held his glass in one hand and used the other as a lid for his whiskey. I opened the umbrella, arranged the fabric over the broken spokes as best I could, and made a run for the kitchen doors.

Inside, the catering staff lounged against the appliances, ignoring us. Trays of hors d'oeuvres sat on the island, daubed and skewered, artfully arranged, ready to be passed. I ate a doll-sized potato pancake, looking the blond lady right in the eyes. She opened her mouth to say something, but then she didn't.

Julian was panting. "Do I take off my shoes?"

"I don't know," I said. "It doesn't really matter."

He looked at me, pained, and bent to untie them. "They're wet. And a little muddy."

I took a certain comfort in Julian's social unease. It reminded me of my parents, their desire to comport themselves perfectly in all social situations and the immense strain this caused them, effectively preventing it. I was like that, too. I had pulled off downward mobility, but the stifling sense of decorum remained. You could live paycheck to paycheck, no assets, no cushion, cover your bills with a kind of credit line three-card monte, and still you beat your brains out over whether or not to take your shoes off in a well-appointed living room.

I took mine off. We lined them up by the door, his brown suede desert boots, my low heels. Julian had also taken his socks off, arguing that they were just as wet. We both gazed down at our bare toes on Hugo's hardwood floor, something I never expected to see.

Ana came in and handed me the cordless phone.

"For you," she said, and walked away.

Julian said, "Someone called you here? On a landline?"

"I have no idea," I said, and into the phone, "Hello?"

It was Roman. "June," he said. "Listen. I called to talk about what happened in the hot tub the other day. You were right that we shouldn't have had Heaven in there."

"Well that's . . . Really?" I said.

"Hell no, I'm kidding. I called because I can't make it tonight and I want you to tell Hugo."

Julian mouthed to me, *Who is it?*

I covered the receiver. "Roman Doyle."

His lips parted slowly and stuck like that. Julian had been one of Roman's favorite targets. Roman called him an Ivy League snowflake, a Jewish American princess. Asked him to recite his Torah portion. Found out his father worked on Wall Street and terrorized him with it. And when people complained to HR, which Julian did, which a lot of us did, Roman issued a semiapology and Hugo stepped in to smooth the whole thing over. We didn't want to become one of those PC writers' rooms, did we? One of those trigger warning rooms? Where you couldn't even joke about something as anodyne as rosacea or obesity or having a limp without someone running out in tears?

I said to Roman, "Why not tell Hugo yourself?"

A long silence. I could hear in the background the bark of a sports announcer narrating a game. Julian was shaking his head slowly.

"I just can't," said Roman. "It's a bummer."

"A bummer?"

"Yeah, it sucks too bad. Dealing with him right now."

"Why aren't you coming anyway?"

"Go to the window," he said.

I turned around to face the yard. The light outside was yellow-brown. Chunks of hail pelted the tent and pinged the kitchen door. The swimming pool frothed like a hot spring.

"Biblical business," said Roman. "End times. Ellen feels weird about it. Superstitious. She wants to stay home and read the tarot."

"Ellen?"

"Sorry, I meant Gypsy. Ellen was her name before. Back in Texas. She never felt like it had anything in particular to do with her. The name Ellen. Unlike Gypsy, which fits her perfectly. It wasn't until she started calling herself Gypsy that she really came into her own."

"But the word *gypsy* . . ." I started to say.

"Can you not this one time?"

"Fine."

"There are a lot of people there, though, right? So he probably won't even notice that I'm not there."

"Not a lot, no," I said. "Not very many at all."

He was quiet again. "How bad? Fifty not a lot, or zero not a lot?"

"Closer to zero than fifty."

"No Laura? No Bony? No finance dudes wearing, like, vests? No neighbors? That guy Ed or Ted isn't there who lives across the street in that horrible Italianate place? He's always showing up at Hugo's parties."

"Ted is here," I said. "Ted and basically no one else. Hugo had a fight with Laura yesterday. I don't know where Bony is. He chose today not to be a sidekick."

"Shit. Should I come? I have to come, don't I?"

It was probably useless, unless he was going to phone tree all of Hugo's other friends. All the famous comedians and hedge fund guys and golf buddies and hot women half his age. The whole dusty Rolodex, because you knew he had one, with a cloudy black lid and heavy off-white card stock, purchased for him by an assistant in the eighties and still kicking around the house somewhere.

"Don't come," I said. "It won't help."

It would only make the problem more pronounced, I told him. Underline it. Roman should call him tomorrow and make amends, take him out to lunch or to the strip club or to the sketchy massage parlor. Tell him Ellen/Gypsy distrusted hail.

"We don't go to strip clubs together," said Roman.

"Sure," I said. "Maybe you can ask him yourself if he's okay, while the two of you eat your crab salads or get your happy endings."

"You're being gross," said Roman.

I felt a rush of anger. He was the gross one. A big, seeping blemish on the face of the show. I was tempted to tell him how much the staff hated him, but I knew he'd only laugh. We weren't even a staff anymore, just a loose association of people bound by a failed cause. Plus, he hated us right back. The way we voted and the things we read, our educations and the causes we cared about. It would please Roman to know that I'd once seen Gil spit into the gutter on Forty-eighth Street after saying his name. I could see him repeating that one to his hot tub friends. I could see them laughing about it under the brims of their hats.

What's more, he was a shoddy guardian of Hugo's well-being. They all were: him, Laura, and Bony, too. They were falling away now that they didn't need him anymore. Now that he wasn't in a position to do anything for them. I couldn't believe how obvious it was.

"I think we're done here," I said.

"Will you tell him I called?" said Roman.

"If you want."

"Tell him Heaven got sick. That's a valid excuse."

"I'm not saying that."

"Oh right, your integrity."

We hung up and I put the phone down on an end table.

"Should I even ask?" said Julian.

"There's not that much to tell," I said.

Only that I'd gone to his house, drunk his booze, smoked his weed, saw where his daughter was born. Only that I'd tried to understand his wife and failed. Tried to understand *him* and failed.

"Roman can't come."

"Good," said Julian.

I gave him the tour I had given myself on Saturday morning. The furniture, the art, the wine cellar and basement comedy club. He walked onto the stage and said something into the mic, but it wasn't on. His voice sounded quiet and without resonance. What he said was: *This place gives me the creeps.*

I took him down another level and into the bunker, flipped on the light. He thought it was impressive. He'd hated the comedy club—it felt like a mausoleum, he said—but this room he got. He walked the rows, studying the stickers and pointing out his favorite shows. He liked the ones from the early days that experimented with form. He liked that they risked total failure from the ground up. His favorite episode, maybe ever, was one from the nineties where they'd found another guy named Hugo Best living in the Keys and gone down and shot the show in his living room. Hugo wasn't even in that episode; the other guy had hosted. His best friend, Graham, had done Bony's job, playing the show in and out of commercial with Jimmy Buffett covers. He'd done a good job, the other Hugo. Such a good job that it made you wonder why any schmo off the street couldn't be a talk show host. Which had been the point.

"Then Hugo quit making shows like that," said Julian.

He stopped in front of a row of tapes, stretched his arms to their full length. "For instance, this whole section could go right in the trash."

It was the last shelf chronologically, the most recent run of shows going back a year. Last week's tapes had not made it there yet, by whatever means they'd arrive, and there was room left for them. There was room, too, for more tapes. The previous week's would slot in and there'd still be a foot of bare shelving. The whole shelf below it sat empty, and the whole shelf below that. They'd be empty forever unless Hugo took up taxidermy and filled them up with bug-eyed squirrels and geese in flight.

"What was the date of our first show?" asked Julian. "As pages?"

We found the relevant month and year and tried to puzzle it out. We narrowed it down to one or two days. Neither of us could remember which day of the week it had been.

"Who was even on?" I said.

"It was that grande dame. The one who's still got nice breasts."

"That's right."

I remembered it only dimly. Much more real to me was the physical memory of standing up for so many hours. Tingling pain pulsed up and down my hamstrings. My feet felt huge and archless, two bags of blood jammed into sneakers. The fatigue was mixed with a crazy adrenaline, the adrenaline fueled by marrow-level certainty that I would make a mistake. So I missed the actress, her prepared witticism, her youthful cleavage, her story about her tomato plants or grandchildren or the movie she'd done as a girl with Alfred Hitchcock. Or

I'd seen it and not seen it. Which is what happened with the
show more or less permanently and faster than I expected.
It became the backdrop to my more immediate concerns.
Which was to say, a job.

I reached for the shelf and pulled out the video in the
range of our first day and handed it to Julian. It left a con-
spicuous gap, which I covered by spreading the tapes out
more loosely.

"Take it," I said.

"Are you nuts?" said Julian. "He'll notice."

"He won't. But if he does, they're digitized. His assistant
will make another copy."

"I think you've gotten too comfortable in this house."

"It means more to you than it does to him, so the moral
thing to do is actually to take it."

"You've lost it," he said. "You're Robin Hooding."

"Take it. You came all the way out here."

He held it in front of him, running his thumb over the
label. Then he tucked it under his arm. "Fuck it. What the
hell."

We left the bunker and went back upstairs. I kept expecting
to run into Hugo. I wondered how I'd explain Julian's presence. I had invited him on impulse and promptly forgotten
about it, and now he was here in the house, barefoot and
dripping, committing a theft I had goaded him into. The
main hazards of this life were one's own impulses: rogue,
slippery, and plainly demonic.

Hugo wasn't on the second floor either. Spencer's room
looked different. The mound of clothes had been loaded
into his duffel and spirited away to New Hampshire. The
bed had been made, probably by Ana, and the room smelled

like cleaning product. The guest room had been cleaned up, too, my presence mostly erased. My tote bag had been tidied and tucked in a corner, my glasses on the nightstand returned to their case.

At the end of the hall Hugo's door was open. I had a momentary premonition we'd go in and find him dead. Inert on his bed or blue faced and swinging, finished off by a belt of premium leather. But the room was empty and unhaunted, except for the Stella, looming like the great and powerful Oz, made spookier by the shadows of raindrops streaming down the window and the odd quality of light.

I paused on the threshold—I had a nervous feeling about being in there, like we were about to get caught—but Julian went to the window. Tentatively, I followed.

Outside, the tops of the pines bent toward the house and then away. The wind on the roof of the tent made a muffled rustling. Something metal had torn loose and rung at intervals against a tent pole.

With a glance at the door, Julian went into the walk-in closet in the corner of the room. I followed him, asked him what he was doing, and he told me he was looking for pinstripes. I think he expected a row of identical suits, lined up like superhero costumes. But there weren't any. Just shirts and pants, shoes stowed in cubbies, a stack of cashmere sweaters on an upper shelf, and the smell of cedar. The pinstriped suits had been kept in the wardrobe department in the city on a series of flimsy wheeled racks, and now they would go I didn't know where. One to the Smithsonian, one to a charity auction, a couple to Hugo, and several more to the Dumpster.

"Let's go," I said. "We're overstepping."

"Overstepping? You made me steal something earlier."

He rattled his videotape.

"I was younger then," I said.

"We all were. Just let me look for a minute."

He opened a shallow drawer and started rifling through socks. It hadn't taken much to embolden Julian. One scotch and a petty theft. I didn't know what he thought he was going to find. Maybe he wanted a talisman, something charged with Hugo's success that he could carry around for luck. Cuff links, a coin, a money clip. I remembered what Hugo had said at the diner. The more you had, the more people wanted to take from you.

He held up a silk tie, flipped it over to study the label. "Classy guy."

"Do you want to hear a secret about Hugo?" I said.

Julian said, "Always."

"He was stabbed, back in the seventies. It's a big, mysterious thing. A semisecret. Spencer told me about it. It happened at a comedy club, apparently, outside of one, and Laura saved his life. I asked Hugo, but he was cagey with the details. It happened, though. He was definitely stabbed."

Julian shook a cigar box, opened it up, and smelled the inside. "Oh yeah, by his sister, right?"

"What?"

"His sister, Vivian. Do you think he'd notice if I took one of these?" He held up a cigar. "Or is stealing more than one thing overkill?"

I stared at him.

He said, "You're right. Probably overkill. Just one thing makes narrative sense. Two is too much. Weakens the symbolism."

He put it back into the box, put the box back into the

drawer, moved on to shoes, studying brands, knocking shoe trees together.

"What do you mean his sister did it? How do you know about it?"

"I don't know. It's out there. I read about it in one of the books, I think. Not sure which one. The unauthorized biography, probably. It's one of those open secret things. Everyone knows about it and talks about it. So not a secret at all is what I'm getting at."

"It wasn't in his memoir."

"Of course not. He hates talking about it."

"But it's not on the Internet either."

"You sure about that? Did you look?"

He brought out his phone. It hadn't occurred to me to look. An episode like that I thought I'd know about. And if it was on the Internet, why wouldn't Spencer know about it, too? Did he blindly trust what his father told him, or did he, like me, assume he already knew everything there was to know about Hugo Best? I waited, overwhelmed by the cedar smell, by the wool and leather smell, by the closeness of the space.

Julian said, "Yeah, right here. You just didn't look, did you?"

"I didn't look."

"'In 1978, Hugo Best was stabbed by his sister, aspiring actress Vivian Bechkowiak, outside the Comedy Store on Sunset Boulevard. He was treated at Good Samaritan Hospital on Wilshire Boulevard for multiple stab wounds and penetrating abdominal trauma, and held for observation for six days.' See?"

He held up his phone to show me the article he was reading. "Granted this site is called celebrityinjuries.com, so grain of salt. But those are pretty much the facts, I think."

I sat down on the floor. The closet was carpeted, beige, thick pile. I ran my hand over it. Julian sat down across from me, still holding a dress shoe. Hugo could tell me whatever he wanted, conceal whatever he wanted. That was his right. So why did I feel blindsided by the omission?

"Why wouldn't he tell me?" I said. "He told me other things."

Julian perked up. "Like what?"

"I don't know."

Now that I thought about it, he hadn't really told me that much. Facts about wine. His preferences in comedians. A story about Studio 54 that seemed untrue. Some broad strokes about his history with Laura.

"You're withholding," said Julian. "Don't withhold."

"I'm not withholding."

"Have you hooked up with him?"

"Don't say hooked up. You sound like an eighth-grader."

"I'm just curious if his—"

"Julian."

"But he's good at fucking, right? You can tell he's good. Actually, I could see it going either way." He paused. "At least tell me what you're getting in return."

"Getting?"

"It's a quid pro quo thing, is it not? I mean, no offense."

I thought about it. I hadn't wanted to admit it, but it kind of was. Hugo hadn't spelled it out; he didn't have to. It was obvious, inherent. Like the foundation of a house. You didn't ever see or think about it, but it propped the whole thing up. Though I had pretended otherwise, the two of us spending even one minute together outside of work could never be anything but transactional. And I had known that. I'd known it all along and even enjoyed it, enjoyed the feeling of transgression, the illicit thrill. The yeasty buzz it gave me to be using my young-womanness at last shrewdly, at last toward some quantifiable gain, at last with a modicum of control.

"I guess it is," I said.

"Right. So what are you getting?"

"I don't know. It's not like we signed a contract. Are these things usually explicit?"

Julian said, "You didn't pin him down on anything concrete? You're not going to end up with anything. I would have pinned him down. I would have made him say what I was getting."

I laughed, imagining Julian bartering with Hugo in advance of some sex act. Cutting a deal, getting him to throw in extras. What was sex worth anyway, in the favor economy? Mentorship? A useful introduction? A job? And how did it break down? Did full penetration earn you more? Could you save up a bunch of credits from smaller stuff, hand jobs, light groping, and bank them toward a bigger payoff? Or were you supposed to hold out on the sex, dangle it, until you got what you wanted? I voiced a few of these aloud.

Julian said, "You don't make a very good opportunist."

I shook my head. It didn't come naturally to me. I lacked the grit. Maybe it was why I hadn't succeeded in my career. I didn't have what it took to go out and take what I wanted through manipulation or force. I wasn't cold-blooded.

I thought again of Hugo's sister.

"What if she had a good reason?" I said. "Vivian. She must have had a reason. People don't stab without a reason."

"Sure they do," said Julian. "Things happen for no reason all the time. They canceled the show for no reason."

"They had a reason. You know they did. Don't connect this to the show. It's completely unrelated."

He said, "I'm sorry, but I can't really think about anything else."

His face collapsed and he started to cry. I was startled. The first time we had ever hung out together one-on-one and he was showing me the whole range. Earlier he'd flirted, now he sobbed. I reached out and patted his arm, the one still cradling Hugo's patent leather shoe. He cried harder.

"Come on," I said. "You're gonna be great."

He was Harvard educated, medium rich, brilliant, if you could stand him. He would get another job so fast it had basically already happened. But he wasn't crying about his job prospects, I realized. He was crying for the loss of an idea. The idea of the show and working for the show. The show as temple, the show as religion. He hadn't been jaded before and now he was. He'd believed before and now he didn't. He was new before and now he was scarred. And what a loss. Seriously, if I thought about it, what a loss. A boy who had dreamed of opening monologues and canned laughter under a triptych of Wayne Gretzky action shots was now just another wounded adult weeping in a stranger's closet.

I pried the shoe out of his hands and put it back where it belonged.

"But I'm not done looking," said Julian.

"We're done," I said.

We turned off the light in Hugo's room and went back downstairs. Everyone who'd been in the tent was now in the kitchen. The musicians had their feet up on their hard black cases. Ted McGuire had taken his coat off and cornered Ana near the fridge. The two young girls were sitting on the island: one was braiding the other's hair. The place had the feel of a doomsday party. The air of cheer that accompanied worst fears confirmed. The bartender made gin and tonics and handed one to each of us. I still didn't like gin, but I drank it anyway.

She asked who we were and Julian said a couple of nobodies. Everyone laughed. He seemed better. He was using his pillaged videotape as a coaster. I guess he'd cried it out. I was jealous. He'd shown up, had some good booze, gotten closure. Now he could go back to the city and find a way forward. Let the years condense what had happened into a hard, bright story to be told at dinner parties. But where was my catharsis?

The clock over the stove read six, two hours after the party's appointed start time. Ana stretched plastic wrap over the hors d'oeuvres and cheeses. She told us that a few other people had called with their regrets. Hugo's lawyer and his assistant. The director Brett Ratner. It was the weather, they said. Such a weird, grim night.

We drank our gin and watched the wind undo a lot of expensive landscaping. At one point a car pulled into the driveway, headlights shining dully in the rain. Ana jumped up to greet whoever it was, but by that time the car had already pulled back out.

"Not enough cars," she explained solemnly.

The guy in the chef's jacket cleared his throat. "So what should we do with the pig?"

I pictured them taking it outside the gate and rolling it onto the curb. Discarding it the way you did an old futon in the city. I pictured it lying there with an apple in its mouth. I pictured its eyes, like the opossum's, dead and reflective.

"Where's Hugo?" I asked Ana.

She motioned outside. He sat alone in the tent. Through the plate glass, I could see him there in his summer suit, legs stretched out in front of him, frowning into a drink.

"How long has he been out there?"

"I don't know. Forty minutes, an hour."

"He's the one that sent us in here," said the bartender.

Ana handed me a striped golf umbrella and said, "You go rescue him now."

I made a run for it from the kitchen's sliding doors. Under my bare feet, the pool deck was gritty and unexpectedly warm. I crossed the stretch of wet grass and Hugo rose to greet me.

"No one came," he said.

"Look at the weather."

"Not even Bony Suarez. I made that fuck's career."

I lowered the golf umbrella. "I came," I said. "Is that worth anything?"

I actually wanted to know. Hugo looked at me for the first time.

"You look nice," he said.

"Thanks, Jan does good work. She trimmed it a little."

"That's her secret. She always trims it a little. That's the Jan magic." He rubbed the shoulder of my dress with his thumb. "This is pretty."

His attention still did things to me. I suspected it would even if my jumbled feelings resolved into hatred. My crush on him had been cultivated over a lifetime, and only grown more complex. He was a person to me now, and a person who could help me if he chose to. If he liked me enough. The setting only made it more pronounced. The lush backyard that went on forever, the house, not a museum but almost, which I could see lit up like a lantern through the flapping entrance of the tent.

"We can't stay out here," I said. "We'll get killed by lightning bolts. I'm holding an umbrella. That's a textbook don't."

"Did I see Julian in there?"

"Yeah."

"I'll take my chances out here."

"I invited him," I said. "It was a bad idea. I'm sorry. I did it yesterday after we played tennis. I was feeling vulnerable or something. I don't know. He's under strict orders not to mention *Mates*, if that helps at all."

"You don't have to apologize for inviting your friend. You thought it was a party." There was a bottle on the table next to him and he refilled his glass. "They cooked a whole pig. An animal died."

"Forget the pig," I said. "The pig won't go to waste. Everyone will take some home. Their families will be grateful. Ted McGuire will take some to Linda."

"I don't want to go in there," he said. "The idea of sending all those kids home."

I understood. He'd have to offer an explanation, be dry about it. Pretend he didn't care. He'd have to make a joke.

"Then let's not," I said. "Let's go somewhere else."

He finished his drink and poured two more fingers.

"*Duck Soup*," he said.

I opened the umbrella, blue and white, wide as a second tent.

"*Duck Soup*," I agreed. As if I knew what that meant, as if that's what I had been saying all along.

———

Duck Soup was a yacht docked in Greenwich harbor, named for the Marx Brothers classic. I had seen the movie a long time ago. I didn't remember much about it except that Groucho becomes the improbable leader of a small, failing country, and possibly it's racist. And of course, the famous mirror scene, where one character pretends to be another's reflection, perfectly imitating every move. The illusion is so effective that eventually the viewer loses track of who is reflecting whom.

Hugo texted Cal to take us to the marina, and he pulled the hulking black SUV around front. We hunched under the big umbrella, skirting the house to meet him. The lawn was drenched now, warm and muddy, and my bare feet sank in. I didn't bother to grab my shoes or say good-bye to Julian. I caught a flash of him as we passed and he looked fine. He was laughing anyway, and drinking, which is about as much as a person can ask for. I knew I would see him again. One way or another, and likely sooner than I expected.

It was cold in the car, so Hugo turned on the seat warmers. My back and legs became hot, right on the threshold of unbearable and pleasant. Hugo sulked with one foot up on the seat in front of him, unwrapping a stick of gum from a pack in the ashtray. I remembered our ride out here. It hit me like a long-repressed memory, though it had only been on Friday.

Cal parked in the marina and pulled out a newspaper. He was confident we wouldn't be long. This was no kind of night to be on a boat, even one that was docked. He wanted to know what kind of sick crackers go on a boat on a night like this.

The hail had given way to rain and the dock was waterlogged, slick. White hulls rose on either side, creaking as they pitched in the rough water. Hugo walked swiftly down this corridor, yanking me along with an arm looped through mine. We had forgotten the umbrella in the car, and the rain made translucent dots on my dress.

Duck Soup was indistinguishable from the others. It sat between *Bernadette* and *My Way*, all three of them Alpine white and sheer as cliffs rising out of the water. Hugo helped me aboard and led me to the cabin, reciting pertinent features. The boat was long, I gathered. The boat could move fast. The boat had various amenities. He kept calling it "her." He named some of the famous people who had ridden on her and the places they'd gone. This mogul to the Hamptons, this rap collective to Miami, this now-disgraced politician right through the eye of a tropical storm and all the way to Turks and Caicos.

Belowdecks the churn of the bay felt less pronounced. In a central salon he turned on the lights and stood back to watch my reaction. The room had dark wood paneling and modern maroon couches. It was cozy and luxurious, in perfect taste like all his possessions.

"Wow," I said, though I was getting tired of being impressed.

"I'll make us some drinks. Choose an album."

He ducked into the galley. Naturally the boat would be stocked for the eventuality of a last-minute pleasure cruise. Everything he wanted was anticipated and planned for, there already like built-in shelving. If he wanted a change of scene, his boat awaited. If he wanted a cocktail, he had only to reach out his arm.

A long shelf held hundreds of CDs. I went looking for something moody, maybe some Coltrane for a rainy night, and found that they were all comedy albums. Hundreds of them in jewel cases, alphabetized.

"Of course," I said aloud.

In the Bs I found Hugo's own albums, four of them from his early career. I pulled out *Second Best*, the one that had gone gold and hung on the rec room wall. There was Hugo with his gag gun. He looked young, my age maybe, on the brink of thirty.

I popped the disc out of its case and put it on. Hugo's early work had been political, angry. I could hear in his cadence and intensity the influence of Lenny Bruce. *You dig, man?* and that sort of thing.

Hugo returned with our drinks and set them down on the coffee table. I sat cross-legged on the floor. The maroon couches rose and fell, and through the salon windows I could see *Bernadette* doing the same.

On the stereo, young Hugo was doing the bit about baby Richard Nixon. Richard Nixon had been orchestrating cover-ups since infancy, it went. Baby Richard Nixon had his guys bug the delivery room where he was born. Baby Richard Nixon had transcripts of very telling conversations between the OB-GYN and the RN on duty. And so on.

"Turn this off. It's embarrassing."

"No it's not," I said. "It's good."

"Turn it off," he repeated, more firmly. The boat yawed and the drinks slid off the table and spilled on the rug. He knelt to right the glasses.

"June." He softened. "Please."

The audience was laughing and applauding. I reached up and turned it off.

He'd sunk to the floor, with his back against a sofa. The

boat was large, but the inside had a compact feel, a feel of the world in miniature. Sitting there on the floor we could have been two kids in a fort.

"I can't stand to listen to that stuff anymore," he said. "It makes me feel like an old cliché. It makes me too conscious of my mistakes."

"Which cliché?" I asked. "Which mistakes?"

"Oh, just all of them."

Women for one, he said. Young women. The same thing you always heard: a string of infidelities unspooling toward infinity in both directions. Kitty Rosenthal, but not just her. She was the one people knew about. A stand-in for all the Kitty Rosenthals. She just showed how reckless he'd gotten, how brazen. How desperate he was to explode his marriage.

Allison had known. Of course she had. She knew who he was when she married him. And besides that there was plenty to tip her off. He'd been discreet at first, and then less discreet when it became clear that she was just going to ignore it. If she asked him where he'd been he'd tell her the dentist. Every time, no matter what time of day it was, ad absurdum. It became a joke between them. A dark, cruel in-joke, sexually charged, and not exactly funny.

They didn't see that much of each other anyway. She spent half the year in LA shooting her sitcom. She preferred it to New York, the sameness of the weather and low-carb options, the infinity pools that linked up seamlessly to the horizon. Spencer had been born in the city, but mostly raised in Malibu. Hugo would visit them a few times a year, or they would visit him, or they would all meet up on vacation in Aspen. Toward the end, the stretches between visits got longer, the visits themselves shorter. The Kitty Rosenthal situation—the public humiliation, the reporters waiting for Allison near school pickup, outside of yoga, in the parking lot of Whole Foods—was a good excuse to kill what was already dying on its own.

"I think she enjoyed playing the scorned woman when the time finally came," he said. "She enjoyed the dark sunglasses."

She gave an hour-long primetime interview, dabbing at her eyelashes with a tissue, invoking God and her fans and her stellar costars, her TV family who also happened to be her best friends. She hammed it up. But she deserved her moment and more for what she'd endured. He only wishes they'd both done better by Spencer. He was seven at the time and took it badly. Even though they were an unconventional family to begin with, even though they spent most of their time apart. Spencer blamed Hugo, still did. His resentment had grown, acquiring depth and nuance, and would continue to grow as he became an adult.

And it wasn't just Spencer. Hugo had other kids, too. He had two daughters from his first marriage who wouldn't speak to him, who hadn't for years. Smart girls older than me who'd done all kinds of things. Racked up academic achievements, become professionals, had babies, refused his money. That they'd become whole people was a miracle that had nothing to do with him. Their upbringing had been in the 1980s, a decade he'd spent systematically alienating their mother, shredding his nasal passages with high-quality cocaine, and flying out west for meetings about *Airplane* knockoffs that ultimately never made it to preproduction.

And all of this would have been fine. All of this would have been permissible if the work had been worth it. Performers, artists, were given leeway for a certain amount of personal weakness, a certain amount of ego. The idea was that their genius justified their bad behavior, that on the cosmic balance sheet their contributions came out ahead of their indiscretions.

"Problem is," said Hugo, "that mine haven't."

He looked down into the glass he was holding, as if he could wish it full again.

"That jackass in the dress shop was right, you know. They pushed me out. They wanted to bring in fresh blood, someone young, and Laura agreed with them. She could have fought, for me, with me. But she didn't. She talked me into ending it. She was right, too. They probably should have done it years ago. Now she's going to produce *Stay Up* with this new kid. *Stay Up with Eric Marshall.* Does it sound right to you? It doesn't sound right to me."

He pointed to the cover of *Second Best*, still lying out near the CD player.

"That guy would hate me. He'd think I was a panderer and a sellout. A prick."

I was silent. Hugo looked at my face. "This is the part where you're supposed to disagree."

I couldn't disagree. But I could inch toward him across the space that rose and fell like someone breathing. I could rest my hand on his still-firm bicep. I could give myself over to whatever compromise lay ahead.

———

In the master bedroom, we stripped to our underwear without touching each other. Out the cabin's portholes: rain-slashed darkness.

Hugo smiled at me apologetically and turned his back as he yanked off his pants. He hung his suit carefully on the back of a chair, pants folded into a tidy column.

I pretended to look at the floor. Under his clothes, Hugo wore a kind of support garment, a black Lycra leotard for men that held in his pecs and stomach and did God knows what to his dick. He hadn't been wearing it the night before when he'd gotten undressed in the kitchen. At least I didn't think so. That meant he put it on for special occasions only — the party or his TV interview. When he peeled it off, his flesh found its natural sag.

I undid the three buttons on the back of my dress and let it fall to the floor. I assumed a half-reclining pose on the red and gold bedspread. Hugo was still struggling with his shapewear. The crotch had snagged on the finely wrought toe of his wingtip — why had he left his shoes on? — and he was stumbling around near the bed in slack white briefs. He had a big man's lack of grace, and the list of *Duck Soup* wasn't helping.

At last he yanked the garment free and tossed it across the room. He watched its trajectory with slumped shoulders, absolutely miserable. But we were here now, beyond the reveal of his girdle, no reason not to press on.

He stood by the bed, fingered the fabric of my underwear. "Lovely," he said.

This close I could see a dusky flesh-brown line along his jaw. He was still made up from his E! News interview. His staples were showing through at his hairline and the cakey foundation made his face poreless and plasticine. Between the shapewear and the makeup it was going to be like fucking my maiden aunt. All at once I was flushed with misgiving.

Misgiving and also pity. Fame had destroyed him, bred in him pathetic, masculine vanity. He had chosen it, sure. But a long time ago and without knowing it would lead to this: to be turned into a hack, a rouged-up joke, and finally cast out.

His briefs were graying at the waistband and I looked away as I slid them down. I took his dick in my mouth and felt an absurd stab of pride when he started to get hard. There were things I didn't want to be thinking about. I didn't want to be having a montage of my time at the show play in my head. I didn't want to see myself sandbagging the theater, shaking Hugo's hand, standing outside with Julian during the first snow of the year. I didn't want to see myself answering phones, playing Thursday Bingo. I certainly didn't want to see myself collating scripts for the writers. That's what I was thinking about while I sucked Hugo Best's dick: collating.

His eyes were closed and he kept a hand on my head the whole time, kneading lightly with his fingers. When he came he made a small choking noise and gripped the back of my neck with a violence that surprised me.

After it was over he moved to cover himself up with a sheet.

He said without malice, "Was it everything you dreamed of?"

He lay against the headboard now, depleted. It was one of those moments that almost couldn't be endured. I felt like jumping up to pace the room, picking something up and putting it down, making a joke, or being mean just to get a reaction. Anything so I wouldn't have to be pinned there feeling it. But I was pinned—I had climbed on the bed, too, and he'd thrown an arm across my chest.

So I stared at the ceiling of the boat, maybe the first boat ceiling I'd ever really stared at, and felt terrible and said, "Not really."

Rolling over to look at him, I noticed the raised scars on his sternum and rib cage. The light was dim, emanating from bulbs hidden in the walls. The scars were the only gritty things in this perfectly nice room. I'd left South Carolina because it was too slick and easy there, its manners covering a multitude of sins. I left because I longed for something authentic, to be poor, to experience life without a syrup coating. And now that I had gotten it, now that I'd been broke in New York for more than a decade, I could see that it was also untenable. It ground you down. You couldn't live well and you couldn't live badly. Since they both meant nothing, I concluded, you might as well be rich. You might as well take the good life, leave your principles on the table, do whatever you had to do.

I ran my finger along the scar on his sternum. "Why did Vivian do it?"

"You figured it out," he said. "How'd you know?"

"The way you talked about it. Something was off. And then Julian thought to Google it. It's on the Internet, you know."

He sat up on one elbow to look at me.

"I know. I'm shocked Spencer has never looked for it. You didn't tell Spencer, did you?"

"I didn't tell him. But maybe he trusts you, is why. Maybe he likes you more than you think."

"I wouldn't go that far. Anyway, the facts he has are all true. The blood, the cab, all of it. It just wasn't a stranger. It was his aunt who did it. Put a kitchen knife in her car. Drove to the Comedy Store to hurt me. I didn't want him to know that."

I revised my picture of what happened. I imagined his sister, jittery in her car, replaying years of grievances in her mind. The kitchen knife, her resolve. The sound it must have made: a wet crunch. Had she planned where to hit him so he'd survive? Or had she meant to kill him and failed? And why did I need to know anyway, right now, at this moment? Why did I want him to be human again, the victim?

"So why'd she do it?"

"I guess she was mad."

"You guess?"

"Okay, she was mad."

"But why?"

It was about money. His family saw him on TV. He'd been on Carson and was touring, but he wasn't actually that famous. They thought he was more successful than he was. They thought he owed them something. He helped out when he could. His mom had cancer and he paid for the treatment. He bought her wigs. Different colors and styles so she could experiment.

"The wigs weren't a big deal," he said. "I don't know why I'm bringing them up."

When they fell behind in the rent, he paid it off. He took them on small vacations. Nothing fancy, but places he could manage. Fort Lauderdale, the Finger Lakes. They got bolder and asked for more. They wanted a house. They got mad when he couldn't swing it or didn't want to. They got mad when he ignored their calls.

Vivian especially felt slighted. When he left for California she still had three years of high school. His parents had been adamant that Hugo go to college, but with Vivian, they didn't push it. After graduation she lived at home and worked as a waitress. She wanted to act. She was smart and pretty. She had red hair like their mother. Maybe she was talented. Hugo didn't really know. Anyway, she couldn't get a foothold. She couldn't understand why he didn't help her more. He did help her, some. He put her in touch with people he knew in New York. But he was preoccupied with his career, and anyway he couldn't make someone hire his sister. Or he could later—later he could force almost anything through—but not early on.

He resolved to cut them off. Actually he tried a couple of times. He had a soft spot for his mother, who was magnetic and funny. His dad had accrued some debt and she convinced Hugo to bail him out. The second time, Laura helped him stay firm. Make no mistake, she said. They will ruin you. They would loot your house if they could. They would strip it for copper wire. She was right, as she was about most things, but it wasn't easy to hear.

The next time Vivian asked for something, Hugo said no. She was moving to Los Angeles and she wanted him to rent her an apartment. Only until she got on her feet, she said. Then she'd take over the payments. As an isolated request it would have been reasonable. But he'd already paid for acting classes, headshots, teeth whitening, audition clothes, a voice coach, a professional reel. He'd paid to have her low hairline redrawn farther up her skull. Who knew what that procedure entailed? It cost twelve hundred bucks.

He told her no. She'd have to get the money some other way. She'd have to save up until she had enough, just like everyone else. He reminded her that he moved out there on a Greyhound bus with a single duffel bag. He stayed at a crappy motel until he figured things out. The kind of motel where people brought a prostitute or killed themselves.

He was harsh, he admitted, maybe too harsh. He didn't hear from her for a while, didn't hear from any of them, so he figured she got the message. He thought she was embarrassed and needed some time to get over it. He was on the road eight months of the year anyway. The next time he saw her was in LA.

"You know the end of the story," he said. "She'd been calling again. Or someone had. Calling and hanging up. Laura answered once and told her to cut it out. But I didn't think she was going to show up with a knife. That still blows me away. It was so surreal I have trouble believing my memories of it."

When he first saw her out there on the sidewalk he was happy. She wore jeans and sneakers, a yellow T-shirt, a ponytail. She looked younger than she was, like a high school kid. He forgot, in that moment, to be wary of her. He forgot to find her presence strange. He said something to her. He said her name. She came toward him across the sidewalk. She was walking awkwardly, holding something. The rest was vague. His brain was protecting itself from the rest. He'd laughed for some reason, he could remember that. Laughed and felt insulted. The pain he could not remember.

"I was in the hospital for a week. She just missed my lung."

"She went to jail," I said.

"Only for a year. My lawyer leaned on the DA to get it knocked down to a misdemeanor. Battery causing serious bodily injury. I didn't want to testify. I wanted it to be over. My career was on the rise. I didn't want to be best known for getting stabbed by my crazy sister."

He looked pained, describing her that way.

I said, "Where is she now?"

"She lives in Calgary. I don't know what she does for a living. Every couple years she messages me on social media and my assistant blocks her. I hope she's made a bearable life for herself. It was tragic, but I can't see the point in thinking too hard about it anymore."

"And your parents?"

"I bought them a house eventually. In Florida. They won on that front, I guess. They're both dead now. My dad passed six years ago, my mom a year after that."

The boat creaked against the dock. He had a faraway look on his face. I was sorry I'd brought it up.

"You mentioned you have a brother," he said. "What does he do?"

"Russell, yeah. He's a musician in Austin. He plays the guitar."

"Is he any good?"

"If you like that kind of thing."

"What kind of thing would that be?"

"Bad music."

He chuckled. "Different industry. You're probably safe."

Even if Russell was a comedian, even if I was someday successful enough to snub him, it was hard to imagine him exacting his bloody revenge. He was in a jam band. He rode his bike everywhere. When I visited him the year before he took me out to the desert at night to look at stars through his telescope. He hung out at a vegan burrito place and knew every single person who came in. I worried that he would adopt too many stray dogs and let them ruin his house. Not that he would stab me.

"I don't want to talk about Russell," I said.

We had sex then and we didn't use a condom. He hated condoms, he told me, never used them, and didn't have one on him anyway. I'd been off the pill for a while. With Logan I was waiting to go back on it, using condoms, being careful, until I determined it would last. Hugo entered me, skin-on-skin, and I felt horrified and a little excited. What if I had his baby? I thought, and a fully realized life sprang up in front of me like turning the page of a pop-up book. A house to my specifications complete with a child's nursery, a little laser-cut lawn out front waving in the breeze. We could get the windshield fixed on the MG and it could be my car. Really mine. The baby couldn't ride in it, of course, so I'd need another one, too. We'd need to go visit the hangar again for something safe. We'd get Cal to install a rear-facing car seat. Even if we divorced I'd be okay. I'd have the best insurance ever—ten fingers, ten toes, with blue eyes that looked just like Hugo's. And whatever I chose to do with my life, I could do it at my own pace.

I don't know how he got it up twice. That was more impressive to me than any of the features of the boat. Maybe he'd taken something. If he had, I hadn't seen him. It would have been when he ducked into the galley to get us drinks. It would have been working its way through his bloodstream as we listened to his record.

I've often gone over it since, trying to determine whether the sex was good or bad. It was neither, I think. It was fleshy and tender and I did most of the work. I didn't have an orgasm, which I attributed to the Art Garfunkel factor, the inability to relax in the presence of a celebrity. The closest I got was a feeling of bleak triumph at having so successfully collapsed the distance between Hugo and myself that he was actually *in* my body. I couldn't have gotten any closer without eating him.

When it was over, something had changed between us. There wasn't another lounging period. He got up and started dressing. I had only been wearing two articles of clothing. I found these and put them on and was dressed instantly. I located the bathroom, peed self-consciously, aware that he could hear it. My hair was tangled, from the moisture and the mattress, and my face stricken. We had fucked and it wasn't enough. It had been fun only if fun meant no one had gotten injured. It hadn't solved the problem of what I was going to do next. And certainly it hadn't told me anything about who I was or what my life meant now that Hugo would not be at the center of it. I felt stupid for thinking it would.

"Cal can take you back to the house," Hugo said when I came out. "And later, whenever you want, to the train station."

"What about you?" I said.

He wanted to spend the night alone on the boat. He needed to commune with Poseidon, he said, and looked at me in surprise, as if he just remembered that jokes existed.

He showed me to the deck of *Duck Soup*, hugged me briskly without getting too close. I hopped off myself, unassisted. The temperature had dropped and the rain had ended. I wanted not to look back, I wanted not to be that type of person, but I did and I was. He was still standing there in his summer suit. He'd put his jacket on and everything. He had his hands in his pockets and he shrugged at me, the shrug he did on TV. I shrugged back, same shrug, and then turned around and walked to the parking lot, barefoot, trying not to get a splinter.

———————

Cal kept glancing at me in the rearview mirror as he drove me back. He offered to stop for fries if I was hungry. I told him my problem was amorphous and existential. You couldn't just throw fries at it.

"I doubt that," he said. "But okay."

He had on an R & B station and he turned it up. After a weekend of too much talk, the corny hooks and autotuned voices were a revelation. He explained that the singer we were listening to had just come out as polyamorous. He'd held a press conference and declared that he saw romantic potential in all people. He felt ready to embrace a loving relationship with everyone on the planet, he said, everyone at once. Haters, of course, excluded.

"Isn't that a beautiful thought?" Cal demanded.

"Beautiful," I agreed. "If ridiculous."

At the house, he idled while I ran in for my bag. There was no reason to prolong the inevitable. There was no reason to look around for Ana or take a pensive moment out by the pool. I told myself I'd be back without really believing it. A thought to get me through while I checked under the bed, walked back down the hall, collected my shoes where I'd left them by the sliding glass door. The kitchen was quiet. The staff had packed up and departed, returned the rented glasses to their crates. The liquor bottles clumped together on the island looked like the city skyline and offered the same fickle comfort. I was tempted to pour a drink for the train just to be picturesque, but I decided not to. I still had the whole ride in front of me, plus all I'd have to confront when I surfaced—the cupcake stands and luxury watch stores, the four-dollar bottled water at Hudson News. Sober I could soldier through it, drunk it seemed insurmountable.

I got my chance to take the train home late Monday evening. It was the 10:12, not even the last train. We were too early, but I told Cal to go, there were probably things he wanted to do with his night besides sit around in downtown Greenwich staring into a darkened lacrosse store.

I waited on the platform instead, found a jacket in my bag. The wait wasn't even that bad. It was a matter of believing that the train would come for me, holding out hope, however misguidedly. When it did come, I was relieved. That, at least, had worked out.

There weren't many passengers on the train and the few I saw were drinking. A man in a suit sitting by himself sipped from a flask. Two kids holed up near the bathroom had forties of malt liquor duct taped to both their hands. All four of their hands, I guess. I remembered that nauseating game, Edward Fortyhands. Playing it on a train was a variation I'd never seen before. It inevitably made you puke, and I couldn't imagine wanting to puke like that—in motion, far from home, and powerless to help yourself. The idea of it made me lonely.

I found a seat in a car that was totally empty. Alone in my cream party dress I felt like a spurned bride, or maybe, more accurately, a bride who'd fled. I don't know what happened to the dress I'd come in. I hadn't been able to find it in my bag or the guest bedroom. I had lost it over the course of the weekend. It was gone forever.

———

I never saw Hugo again, though part of me wanted to. I never heard from him either, not by phone, not by email. I didn't give him my number, but there were ways. People on staff had it. A contact sheet existed somewhere with everyone's phone number and email address. I knew because I'd made it. I'd spent hours out of body with boredom filling in those white boxes.

I could have called him myself. At first I was waiting to see if I was pregnant. But then I didn't even after I knew I wasn't. I also could have contacted him through Spencer, at least to see how he was doing. Spencer and I connected online like I knew we would. He had six hundred thousand followers on Instagram for his pictures of prep school and ski trips and Scotty and his abs. I had 119 for my pictures of misspelled signage. Sometimes Spencer would throw me a like or leave a comment, and I hated how much it delighted me. It was inappropriate, but that wasn't why I didn't ask him to put me in touch with his dad.

I didn't do it because Audrey said not to. Audrey said wait, he'll come to you, think about the power imbalance. She said don't you think he owes you an apology? But what it actually came down to was manners. I couldn't impose more than I already had. I couldn't stand up and demand a role in his complicated life. He didn't belong to me; he wasn't mine. I had no more right than the pizza guy.

A calendar year passed and it was spring again, almost summer, right on the line between the two. And that's when Hugo died. He'd let his health slip, put on some weight. He hadn't gotten a sitcom deal or traveled to Oaxaca or Cape Town. He hadn't ridden the ridgelike dunes of the Sahara on the back of a camel. He hadn't climbed mountains or started a foundation for sick kids or helped break talent from under-represented communities. He hadn't found another woman to marry, get him into yoga, make him lay off the scotch, the wine, the gum, the pie. He spent most of his time alone.

Ana found him in his basement comedy club having a heart attack. He'd moved an elliptical trainer down there, set up a little gym. Hand weights, some foam rollers. He'd been trying to get back into shape, newly trying, like that day was the first time. He'd fallen off the elliptical and onto the floor. He made it to the hospital, the one we went to together, but died shortly after. He had smoked for all those years before the gum, done drugs. Lived broadly, not cleanly.

The funeral was open to the public, and I went. I rode with Julian in his dented Volvo. Gil was there, too, Laura, the other writers. Spencer and I successfully ignored each other, or I ignored him and he had too much going on to notice me. Otherwise it was a minireunion. Everyone was sad, but happy to see each other, find out what people were up to, or in my case, not up to. Gil was the show runner for a new sitcom on a streaming site and he'd brought Julian and some of the others on as writers. Laura had successfully revived the show. In its first year, *Stay Up with Eric Marshall* was second in the ratings, the cool alternative, a hit with eighteen to thirty-fours. They all vowed to help me, especially Laura, who smacked her forehead and called herself terrible and said she owed me an email back.

We went out for coffee afterward at a diner on the highway. Not the same diner Hugo and I went to after the hospital, but it might as well have been. It had the same acidic coffee, the same glass case of stale pies. I was tempted to stay on the fringes like I always did, keep to the end of the table, whisper my observations to myself or one other person. But I didn't. I sat in the middle, next to Gil and across from Julian. When everyone started telling Hugo stories I told one, too. I told them about how he did stand-up at Frogger's and then led a forty-person scream-along to "The Weight." How he signed autographs until it couldn't have been fun anymore. How the pizza guy cried he was so touched. That part was an exaggeration, but it could have been true. It was true in spirit.

Everyone laughed at the funny parts, looked sad at the sad parts, and then the focus shifted to Laura's story about a road trip they'd taken in their twenties to one of Hugo's gigs. It was nothing to them, what had happened that weekend. It was a three-minute anecdote recounted at a diner, while a waitress went around and refilled our water glasses.

I couldn't really bring it into focus. Not for a long time. Up too close, things went soft at the edges or multiplied. But later I'd tell it to myself as a joke. Have you heard the one about the dead comedian, I'd begin. His funeral was held on the first unequivocal day of summer. The green of the trees was not to be believed. His kid, drowning in his father's famous pinstripes, was so high he almost fell into the hole, and his longtime sidekick looked on, face shattered like a windshield hit with a baseball bat. Meanwhile, the priest did the bit about the ashes and dust. Thou art dust, it went, and unto dust thou shalt return. And so on.

———————

When my train from Greenwich reached Grand Central that night, I gathered my bag and wove through the crowd to catch the subway home. In the main terminal, I stopped to look up at the ceiling, a staggering shade of blue, dotted with constellations. I had read that this was an inverted view of the night sky, that it was supposed to reflect the perspective of God looking down from above. I stood there searching for a while until I found Orion and Pegasus and the others. It wasn't hard. The stars were connected with gold lines, so that anyone could tell what they were supposed to be, so that even an idiot could figure it out.

Acknowledgments

Thanks first of all to Esther Newberg and Zoe Sandler, my brilliant agents at ICM, for their guidance and continual reassurance. Thanks to everyone at Scribner, especially my editor, Daniel Loedel, who understood the book immediately and made it so much better.

I'm grateful to the Millay Colony and the NYC Center for Fiction for the space and resources to write.

Thank you, Lee Ellenberg, for answering my questions about working in late night.

Thanks to my mother, Shelley Somers, and my sisters, Bailey, Molly, and Taylor Somers, who are also my best friends. Thanks to the Liebermans.

Thanks to my husband, Josh Lieberman, for his love and support, for taking care of our young daughter so I could write, and for reading the book at every stage and making suggestions, occasionally good ones. Thanks to Josh, too, for the use of *Mates*, a riff we've been doing together for ten years that I'm somehow still laughing at. I can't believe it made it into print.

Finally, I want to thank my father, Bill Somers, who died just a few months shy of the publication of this book. I only ever cultivated a sense of humor to try to amuse him, so if I am at all funny, he's why. He taught me that humor has a lot of functions, not least of which is sticking it to people, but it also makes a good bulwark against despair. Thanks, Dad.

BOOK
CLUB
FAVORITES

READER'S
GUIDE

Stay Up
with
Hugo Best

This reading group guide for Stay Up with Hugo Best *includes
an introduction, discussion questions, and ideas for enhancing
your book club. The suggested questions are intended to help
your reading group find new and interesting angles and topics
for your discussion. We hope that these ideas will enrich your
conversation and increase your enjoyment of the book.*

Topics and Questions
for Discussion

1. June doesn't give her roommate, Audrey, a serious answer as to why she accepts Hugo's spontaneous weekend invitation (for "fun" and because there's a pool at the house), but her thoughts in the moment about Hugo's smile give us a clue. Why do you think June goes to Connecticut? If you were in June's shoes, would you have accepted Hugo's invitation?

2. Over the course of the weekend, June tells a number of lies: how she and her boyfriend met, what her major was in college, that she doesn't care if people find her funny, etc. In some cases, we know from her inner thoughts that these lies are intended to subvert the preconceived notions that June, in her cynical way, suspects that other people have about her. In other cases, June is lying to herself as much as to others. Identify an instance where June isn't being totally honest with herself. Why do you think she is avoiding this truth in particular?

3. On Saturday Hugo cracks a joke to June after overhearing a tense phone conversation she has with her boyfriend in the car. Relieved, June thinks, "Banter I could do. It was [Hugo's] sympathy I didn't think I could face, the thought that I had come here and

made him feel bad for me" (page 64). Why is June so loathe to accept Hugo's sympathy? What does this scene reveal to us about the role banter, and more generally humor and comedy, play in her life?

4. Spencer and June are closer in age than June and Hugo. Compare their respective roles within their own families, based on June's memories of her parents' visit to New York (page 124) and Spencer's interactions with Hugo over the course of the weekend. Which family would you rather be a member of?

5. "I wanted [Hugo's] fame and hated that I wanted it," admits June (page 201). How do June, Hugo, Spencer, and Julian see fame differently? Is fame more than a fickle friend for anyone in the novel?

6. During his interview with Casey Caruso, Hugo emphasizes the importance of supporting female comics despite dismissing June's points about inclusivity the night before. June wonders if he has stolen her ideas simply to make himself look good or if he has genuinely learned something from her. Which do you think is true?

7. Discuss your reactions to the revelation about the fan who stabbed Hugo. In what ways, if any, did this change your perception of him? Why do you think Hugo keeps the details a secret from Spencer?

8. There is a lot of comedy in *Stay Up with Hugo Best*. For June's father, comedy is "for making people laugh"; for June, comedy is meant to "challenge the culture" (page 128). Which did this novel as a whole do more of for you?

9. From Kitty Rosenthal to the events aboard *Duck Soup*, discuss how Hugo and June's relationship comments on the #MeToo movement and the questions raised about power dynamics and sexual assault. Did Hugo have "funny business" on his mind the whole weekend?

10. June is twenty-nine years old and well past her teenage years. Nevertheless, *Stay Up with Hugo Best* can be thought of as a coming-of-age story. How has June changed in the three days she spends in Connecticut?

11. We learn Hugo's fate at the end of the novel. Where do you imagine June will be in five years? What will she be doing with her life?

Enhance Your Book Club

1. With your book club, check out recordings of some of the comics June and Hugo idolize, including Don Rickles, George Carlin, Bob Hope, Richard Pryor, Lenny Bruce, and Andy Kaufman, and discuss your reactions to their various styles of comedy.

2. Read *Labor Day* by Joyce Maynard or *Independence Day* by Richard Ford, two other novels set over holiday weekends. Compare the techniques used by the authors to tell a complete story over a short timeline.